MURDER makes an entrance

BOOKS BY CLARENCE BUDINGTON KELLAND

Dance Magic
Rhoda Fair
Miracle
The Steadfast Heart
Conflict
Contraband
Scattergood Baines
Scattergood Baines Pulls the Strings
Youth Challenges
Efficiency Edgar
The Hidden Spring
The High Flyers
The Little Moment of Happiness
The Source
Sudden Jim
Gold
Speak Easily
The Cat's Paw
Dreamland
Roxana
Spotlight
Star Rising
Skin Deep
Arizona
Valley of the Sun
Silver Spoon
Sugarfoot
Archibald the Great
Heart on Her Sleeve
Alias Jane Smith
Land of the Torreones
Double Treasure
Merchant of Valor
This Is My Son
Stolen Goods
The Great Mail Robbery
The Key Man
Tombstone
Dangerous Angel

MURDER
makes an entrance

by Clarence Budington Kelland

Harper & Brothers, Publishers
New York

Library of Congress catalog card number: 55-6584

This book was published serially under the title of Hollywood Calling!

MURDER makes an entrance

chapter ONE

"So," said the young man in the fantastic Hawaiian shirt and the incredible sports coat, "so you got this idea. So you want to make a pilot film. So you want to muscle into this television racket."

"That," said the other young man, who was dressed conservatively in a neat gray suit and wore a carefully selected necktie, "is the general idea."

"Then," continued the first speaker, "you got to make the conservative, efficient, businesslike approach."

"Such as how?"

"There's your name. Two strikes on you. John Miller! Look at any film. Look at the credits. Do you see any John Millers or William Smiths or Henry Joneses? With names like that every time you swing you whiff. You come from Atchison, Kansas. Not only is it impossible, it's a bottleneck."

"But your name is George Brown and you come from Topeka."

"Don't say it out loud. So I'm a greenhorn when I come here and my square name's George Brown. Do I move? Does a head-waiter bow to me? Does Darryl Zanuck wave hello when I walk past his table? So I go conservative and my name's now Zagic Quiros, and I sprout these sideburns and I'm a genius from Czechoslovakia. So I'm a genius MGM brings over here." He spread his hands. "MGM brings over so many of these foreign

1

geniuses it can't remember if I'm one of them or not. So I get by."

"But you have no accent, George."

"Soft pedal that George. Zagic's the name. You should hear my accent. Why, when I'm working and my temperament gets going nobody can understand a word I say. I got to use sign language. So I got standing." He waved in a lackadaisical manner at a passing gentleman. The gentleman waved back. "See. See what I mean. Cecil de Mille."

"Does he know you?"

"Sure he don't, but now he thinks he does. See? I wave at him careless, like he's just another fellow. Two, three times I wave at him that way. So he takes it for granted he knows me. That's conservative business. Other important men see De Mille and me wave back and forth, so I'm in. Get the idea?"

"About this television series of mine—" John Miller said.

"We ain't come to that yet. We're working up. Now I lunch here or Romanoff's or like that every day. Sure I can't afford it. So I have a cup coffee and a sinker for breakfast and pie 'n' ice cream for dinner. Lunchtime is when to be seen the right places. It's a conservative investment. Now take your biography."

"What about my biography?"

"You write two-three stories for magazines. So you get hired to come out here to write scenarios. What happens? You get an office and sit in it. Everybody forgets you been hired. Your salary check comes regular but nobody knows you're alive. So after six months you get sore and quit. Nobody cares. There's your biography."

"I was alive twenty-five years before I was hired to come out here."

"That don't count. Your biography starts when you come to Hollywood. Now you're on your own, sleeping with an idea and panting to get in on this television oil strike. Hot and bothered to make a pilot film and get to be another *Lucy*. There's a hundred saps around with the notion they could run *I Love Lucy* off the screen if they can rent a ten-by-twenty garage and

2

whittle out a pilot film for peanuts. . . . How much dough you got?"

"Not much," John Miller said.

"So you hear these fables about somebody made a film in his attic for three thousand bucks and sold it to one of the networks or a sponsor for gold like they got in Fort Knox. What you got to get is a shot of disillusion."

"You haven't even listened to my idea yet," protested John Miller.

"What's an idea?" demanded Mr. Zagic Quiros. "An idea's an egg that ain't any good till you get a hen to set on it and hatch it. Anybody can have an idea. The tough proposition is getting you a hen." He stood up and waved vigorously. A tall, slender young man with a harried look approached their table.

"Monk," said Zagic, "here's the feller I want you to meet. John Miller, a scribbler at Warner's. Monk Savage. Monk's a producer or something at MCA."

Miller and Savage shook hands and Savage seated himself. He refused a drink. "I've half an hour," he said.

"I want you should take John on your lap and tell him the facts of life," said Zagic. "Like how much it costs to make a pilot film. I bet he don't even know what a pilot film is."

"A pilot film," Savage said wearily, "is the first film you make of a proposed television series of plays. It's your bag of samples. It's what you use to sell your series to a network or a sponsor."

"How much does it cost to make one?"

"A thousand dollars an hour," Savage said promptly. "Say a total cost of thirty thousand dollars."

Zagic whistled, and raised his thick brows at Miller. "That," he said, "gives you an inkling. Thirty thousand smackers!"

"Why so much?" John asked.

Savage was wearily patient. "You've got to have a cast," he said. "You've got to have a script."

"I have the script," John said.

"You've got to have your crew, and equipment and studio."

"How much crew?"

Savage counted on his fingers. "Production supervisor, director,

3

assistant director, camera man and assistant, gaffer, boom man, prop man, set decorator, art director, construction foreman, script girl. Petrillo takes five per cent of the gross for canned music."

"We're not making *The Birth of a Nation*," John objected.

"You," said Savage, "are making a show to run twenty-nine and a half minutes with commercials. Twenty-six and a half minutes without commercials. You can't waste a minute. Minutes cost money. You've got to have a finished product in three days at the outside, two days if possible. That means either two or one days for rehearsal. One day for actual taking. You're not making a motion picture that takes months. There is no time for retakes. You've got to be right the first time. You're using up ninety-five feet of thirty-five millimeter film a minute. You've got to operate a separate sound track. Three kinds of sounds registered—dialogue, music, incidental sounds like doors slamming, motors starting, birds singing. Handled by the mixing box. It's speed, speed and speed. Every minute lost or wasted is important money. It's a new technique. Compared to motion pictures it's a hundred-yard dash against a marathon." He sighed in a discouraged sort of way. "So, if you haven't got at least twenty-five thousand dollars—forget it." He unjointed himself slowly and stood up. "And," he said in parting, "if you get your pilot film made the chances are about fifty to one you won't be able to peddle it. . . . Nice to have met you, Mr. Miller. So long, Quiros. See you around."

"There," Zagic said with the air of one who had clinched an argument, "you have it in a peanut shell."

"Savage," said John, "works for a big corporation with millions to spend. He can see no other way of doing than the big way. Maybe his is the best way of producing. Probably it is. But I don't believe it's the only way."

"Still got that dream about making a film in a barn! You're nuts, John. Look, if you got a script you better get you an agent and try to sell it to one of the networks, or MCA."

John's face was grave, set, determined. "I'm going to make

a film," he said grimly. "And it isn't going to cost any thirty thousand dollars."

"When I was a kid," Zagic said, "I hiked out to run down the end of a rainbow and scoop in the pot of gold. What I come home with was an empty stomach and a blister on my heel. Since then I been practical."

"Nevertheless and notwithstanding," John said grimly.

Zagic shrugged. "Who am I? I'm a pal. I give out first-class advice. You make with a shrug. So what do I do with sorrow in my heart? I string along." He searched out a folding checkbook in an inside pocket and regarded his bank balance ruefully. "So I save up for my old age. What good's old age? I amass me a fortune of seventeen hundred and sixty-two dollars and eleven cents. With a careless gesture I blow it on a pipe dream. I kick in with fifteen hundred leaves of cabbage. I don't buy a piece of the show. I'm not that dumb. It's a personal loan."

"Sheathe the fountain pen," John said with a grin. "I'm not ready for financing yet."

"When you want it," Zagie said. "And take a gander at who approaches!"

John took the gander. He saw, making her way between tables, a woman who rolled along rather than walked. She was definitely fat. Her figure consisted of billows and rolls of flesh, and her body was topped by a head adorned with golden ringlets of the sort made adorable by Mary Miles Minter many years ago. The face beneath the ringlets was a vapid, baby's face with enormous blue eyes and the sort of make-up favored by mechanical dolls. She came to a halt beside the table very much like an ocean liner docking at its pier and beamed upon John Miller.

"Shove over," she said in a twittering, piping voice. "Make room for America's Darling—and plenty of room. What you doing in this platinum-coated beanery? Who's the character with you? What's he made up to represent? Where's my boarder? Did I mislay my boarder?" She craned her neck and numerous chins jostled each other; then she waved frantically and uttered a falsetto yoo-hoo. A slender young woman in a severely tailored dress flushed with embarrassment at being made conspicuous, but made the best of the situation.

"Johnnie Miller—my boarder," she said and frowned at Zagic. "Also a character, name unknown. Shove over, Character. Lucky you boys are here. We wouldn't have got a table. What's everybody eating?"

"Does the boarder have a name?" John asked.

The fat woman wrinkled her brows. "I call her Toots," she said. "I can't remember names. What is your name, Honey?"

"Quality Piper," said the girl.

"You thought up a good one," Zagic said. "It'll do. It rolls. You'll go places. Just for laughs, what's your square name—Schwartz?"

"Quality Piper," the girl repeated.

"If that's your story, stick to it," Zagic said.

"Shut up, Character," the fat woman piped. "To coin a phrase, what's in a name? I'm born and christened Maggie Toohey, but Mamma brings me to Hollywood and I get renamed Dolly Dove. Want the story of my life?"

"I've heard it," John said with a smile.

"Then hear it again. I like to tell it. I weigh a hundred and twelve pounds and I got these curls. It don't matter that I bleat like a sheep, because it's in the silent days. Thumbnail biography. I get more popular than the Keystone Cops. America's Darling, that's me. But I look into the past and I peer into the future. The past is Mamma that weighs two hundred flat, and Aunt Minnie that weighs ten pounds more. The future is that I got three-four years and then the adipose sneaks up. You don't keep on being America's Darling if it takes a derrick to lift you. So when it rolls in, the cash, do I build a bastard Italian villa with two swimming pools? Or do I sink it in annuities? What happens is the latter. So now I sit cozy and eat three times a day with a couple snacks in between. There's a lot more to it but I'm too hungry to relate."

That was, indeed, the biography of Dolly Dove, whom all America cuddled in its arms for a few brief years—and who then vanished in billows of adipose tissue.

"Look," said Zagic, "don't you miss being famous?"

"Sure," said Miss Dove gaily. "I pined away to a skeleton of a hundred and ninety-eight pounds—and more to come. If you got common sense you don't need fame. . . . Hey, waiter, I want a dozen oysters, a steak about so big, mashed potatoes, green beans, a tossed salad, three cups coffee and some of that chocolate cream pie. What's for you, Toots?"

"Chicken sandwich. Tea," said Miss Piper.

"Sententious, ain't she?" asked Miss Dove admiringly. "I got a spare room in my apartment, so why shouldn't I take a boarder?"

"Not to talk to," Zagic said. "She don't gust conversation. What's matter with her? Lame tonsils?"

Quality Piper remained mute. Zagic peered at her disgustedly. John Miller regarded the girl with interest. She was not demure. That wasn't the word. She was not suffering from embarrassment. She was quite self-possessed. Still! That expressed her. She was just still.

"You in the movies?" Zagic asked her. She had aroused his curiosity.

"Yes," she said. That was all.

"Must be the silent movies," Zagic commented, and gave her up.

"She," said Miss Dove, "is a script girl."

"Look, Miss Dove," Zagic said. "Johnnie is all haunted with the idea of making a pilot film. You been around. Tell him it can't be done. In particular it can't be done without mazuma."

A shrewd look settled upon Miss Dove's doll-face. "If you got any notions," she said, "it can't be done with any of mine. I'm tighter than a girdle. . . . Wants to make a pilot film, does he? Been listening to fairy tales. Television! . . . Toots is script girl on some television shows. Tell him it can't be done, Toots."

Toots remained mute. Miss Dove frowned. "Come on, baby. You're hep to television. Can he do it?"

Miss Piper was regarding John Miller with a sort of intense gravity, as if she were studying him under a microscope. It made him uncomfortable. He never had been looked at that

7

way before. By sheer effort of will he stared back, but her eyes did not waver. She was a strange young woman.

"Well," demanded Miss Dove impatiently, "can he do it?"

Miss Piper continued to scrutinize John Miller. Her lips parted. She was going to speak. "Yes," she said.

She had contributed a monosyllable to the conversation, but it was a definite, emphatic monosyllable.

"Dog my cats!" exclaimed Miss Dove.

Miss Piper addressed herself to her chicken sandwich as if nothing else existed in the world.

Zagic Quiros rested his elbows on the table and glared at Miss Piper. "Could you," he asked, "contrive to excavate a couple more words? Could you kind of propound, or argue, or fetch out facts in favor of this cockeyed opinion of yours? Could you bolster up?"

Miss Piper arrested her sandwich on its way to her mouth. She let her eyes rest briefly upon Zagic. "No," she said.

"Lemme out of here," Zagic said. "I ain't allergic to folklore, but she's a zombie." He struggled to his feet. "You coming, Johnnie?"

"You might as well," twittered Miss Dove. "Toots has used up her quota for today."

chapter TWO

John Miller lifted the telephone in his McCadden Place apartment. It was not a luxurious abode. The bed folded into the wall and a tiny kitchenette sufficed to get his breakfasts. The voice that came over the telephone was not to be mistaken. The twittering tones of Dolly Dove, America's ex-Darling asked if he were John Miller. When he admitted it she extended an invitation.

"I'm the best cook in Hollywood," she announced. "How about sampling it tonight? Bring along the Character. Bring along the script for this television thing you're wasting time on."

"Why?" John asked.

"I got curiosity. It flatters what vanity I got left to have somebody read a script to me. Seven o'clock."

"Will the boarder be there?"

"What do you care?" she demanded.

"I like to hear her say nothing," John answered. "Seven o'clock. I'll capture the Character."

At seven o'clock John and Zagic Quiros walked up one flight to the apartment of America's ex-Darling. There was a large living room furnished in the style of twenty years ago. It abounded in vases and brass jardinieres and was embellished by a life-sized crayon enlargement of the photograph of a stout gentleman with whiskers.

"Papa," Miss Dove said proudly. "Owned the best saloon in Brooklyn. Seventy-foot bar."

"He looks," said Zagic, "like he was his own bouncer."

Miss Dove was flattered. "He could handle any three men in Flatbush with one hand tied behind him. Him and Mamma together could quell a riot."

Quality Piper came into the room, walked its length to a sofa and seated herself, hands in lap. John Miller frowned. Her progress across the room had been surprisingly graceful, without embarrassment, with a curiously certain carriage. Not until she had seated herself did she take notice of either John or Zagic. Then she nodded, uttering no word.

"Anyhow she could smile," Zagic said.

Miss Piper did not smile. She merely sat at ease, lips slightly parted and looked from one to the other of the three people in the room.

"First," said Miss Dove, "we eat. I can't think on an empty stomach." She led the way ponderously into the dining room and seated her guests. "Corned beef and cabbage," she announced. Zagic looked disappointed. "But *what* corned beef and cabbage!" said Miss Dove.

It was indeed corned beef and cabbage with proper side dishes, but it was more than a mere delicacy. As Miss Dove had prepared it the most exacting gourmet would have bowed in reverence. Zagic took his first reluctant mouthful, then he stared at Miss Dove and devoted himself wholeheartedly to his plate. Miss Piper ate daintily, but with appetite. Miss Dove consumed an amazing quantity. There was no conversation. There followed a pumpkin pie and coffee. At the end Miss Dove sighed an enormous sigh of repletion and burped in a ladylike manner. Zagic raised both arms above his head and shook hands with himself. "The winner and new champion," he said. "I don't care which: will you marry me or take another boarder?"

Miss Dove and Miss Piper cleared the table. They placed a can of beer before each individual.

"Now," directed Miss Dove, "you read your piece, Johnnie." John Miller, somewhat embarrassed, brought his brief case, opened it and produced his manuscript. He read it well. It was a simple episode but it had a beginning and a middle and a climax. It rode close to the edge of farce but it was not farce. There were sly humor, broad humor, situations, suspense, but even the most absurd complications were somehow credible.

Zagic pounded on the table. "Colossal! Stupendous! . . . Better than that—it's good!"

"Dry up, Character," Miss Dove said severely. "Let's get a verdict that is a verdict. How about it, Toots?"

Miss Piper hesitated a moment, her eyes upon John Miller. "Yes," she said.

" 'Yes,' what d'ye mean 'yes'?" demanded Zagic.

"Sure?" asked Miss Dove.

"Yes," said Quality Piper.

"What I call a searchin' and analytical criticism," said Zagic bitterly. "You ought to write for the papers."

"Covers the water front, don't it?" Miss Dove demanded. "In one word—yes. Anyplace it can be improved, Toots?"

"Yes."

"Where?" asked Miss Dove.

"Housekeeper," said Quality Piper.

"You think the housekeeper needs doctoring?"

"Yes," said Miss Piper.

"How?" asked Miss Dove.

"Other things first," said Miss Piper.

"My gawd! Three words," marveled Zagic.

"Sure," Miss Dove said. "Other things first. We had to find out if it was any good?"

"Why?" asked Johnnie. "What's it to you?"

"I'm smart," Miss Dove said smugly. "I been around. I've coped. You've got no money to speak of, Johnnie. You got no thirty thousand dollars to make a pilot film. You got to do it cheap."

"Right."

"Before you can make a film you got to have a troupe. Actors cost money."

"Right again."

"Don't pay 'em," said Miss Dove.

Johnnie grinned. "There's Equity and Screen Actors Guild and other little knickknacks like that."

"Circumvent 'em," said Miss Dove.

"I wouldn't care to do that," Johnnie said. "Ever hear of a conscience?"

"I got one," Miss Dove said. "Had to hear this script. Had to find out what kind of actors you'll need. Your script fits. This idea is a co-operative."

"What?"

"A stock company, like, with all actors owning a piece. Working for themselves. Look. Television's a kind of Pulmotor for actors on their deathbed. Some have even been dug up out of their graves. Names that were once famous. And then faded out of sight for one reason or another. There's one thing about the public. It can neglect, but it don't forget. Not if the public gets nudged and reminded. This town's full of famous has-beens. Television's resurrecting some of 'em. Now in this script of yours you got two spots for resurrections. Look, Mary Pickford hasn't acted for years, but announce a picture by her and see what happens. Even sponsors remember names. I can name you twenty old timers that would throw conniptions to get a chance for a comeback. D'ye think they wouldn't yelp with joy to be offered a co-operative chance?"

"How about the necessary younger actors?" Johnnie asked.

"Get a couple of promising never-was folks. If this show of yours goes, it depends most on the two old ones. The father and the housekeeper. Dig up a pair of dead ones that once had big names. Offer an opportunity to a couple of young ones that never been heard of."

"It might work," Johnnie said.

"It would," said Miss Piper.

"But you can't get the technicians to come in on a co-operative. The unions."

"That's a cost you can't cut," Miss Dove said. "Not wages. But you can eliminate."

"They say I must have a production supervisor and a director and an assistant director and an art director. They wouldn't come in on such an arrangement."

"No," said Quality Piper.

"No, what?" demanded Zagic.

"One," said Miss Piper.

"Who would do it, and who could do it?" Johnnie asked.

"I," said Quality Piper.

"Hot damn!" exclaimed Zagic. He sneered. "A producer's got to talk. So's a director. Actors don't go for telepathy. Got to have words, syllables, phrases 'n' even whole sentences."

"Dry up, Character," snapped Miss Dove. "First thing's to find a father and a housekeeper. Build around them. Whole thing's a partnership. Everybody shares. Proportion of shares to be worked out. The troupe owns the show."

"Call it what?" asked Zagic. "Names mean a heap. Publicity value. Maybe even numerology."

"Famous Names Group," said Quality Piper.

"Got it all worked out, have you?" snapped Zagic.

"Yes," said Quality Piper.

"I s'pose you got the cast picked, too."

"Housekeeper," said Quality.

"And who would that be?"

"Dolly Dove," said Miss Piper.

"This," snarled Zagic, "is a bloody, blasted, two-timing conspiracy."

"Possibly," said Quality.

Miss Dove was gasping like a porpoise out of water. "It ain't," she piped. "This I never heard of. Me! Lousy nonsense. I got a nice, easy life. I'm too dead to skin. You put this over on me, Toots. Honest Injun, Johnnie, I never even thought of it till Toots unwrapped it."

Johnnie was leaning forward. There was excitement in his eyes. "Famous Names!" he said. "Dolly Dove, America's Darling!"

"America's Dumpling," snorted Miss Dove. "Look, it was half my fat and half my voice that bombed me out of pictures."

"Comedy voice," said Quality Piper.

"Right," said Johnnie.

"Publicity," squeaked Zagic. "Resurrection of Dolly Dove. Gone but not forgotten. Oh, let me loose on it."

"Miss Dove," Johnnie said, "don't tell me you're bogged down in contentment. Don't tell me you don't yearn for the limelight."

"Johnnie," said Miss Dove, "it's a dratted pose. You know it's a dratted pose. I'm a danged old fire engine horse. Every time the alarm rings I make a rush for the harness." Tears streamed down her enormous cheeks. "Johnnie, if you want me in—if you don't think I'll gum the game—I'll plumb pray the saints to shower you with blessings. Oh, man! Oh, man! Ain't it going to be glorious to scramble up out of the tomb."

"Now listen, folks," Zagic said dubiously. "This is shapin' up like a mob scene. Co-operative. Too much democracy. Too many spoons in the stew. Everybody stickin' in his oar. I'm tellin' you nuts that in this business there's got to be a boss."

"True," said Quality Piper.

"So. . . . And who's going to be this boss?"

"I am," said Miss Piper promptly.

"Over my dead body," yelped Zagic. "No zombie's goin' to be my boss."

"Dry up, Character," said Miss Dove mildly.

"We'll decide that point later," Johnnie said. "After all, it's my show."

"Now," said Quality Piper.

"You're a writer, Johnnie," said Miss Dove. "No practical experience. Probably no executive ability. Toots has been a script girl, and she knows the game from soup to nuts. She knows how to boss and how to produce. I been livin' with her and watching her. She's got what it takes."

"In sign language," growled Zagic.

"Yes or no?" asked Quality.

"An ultimatum?" asked Johnnie.

"Yes," said Miss Piper.

John Miller studied her face grimly. For a full minute he scrutinized her. To his surprise he saw there not only intelligence and shrewdness and determination, but something else he had not expected to find. It astonished him. It was a curious, arresting, elfin sort of beauty. He had not looked at her as a woman but only as a creature uttering monosyllables.

"Stand up, please," he requested.

Quality arose and stood calmly while he scrutinized her. She was of middle height, possibly five feet six inches tall. She was slender and severely tailored. But now that he looked at her as a human being and an interesting human being, he saw that even her severe tailoring could not conceal a graciously made body, a figure to make one gasp.

"But—but you're beautiful!" he exclaimed.

"Is that," she asked, "a defect?"

"Four words," snorted Zagic.

She seated herself primly and waited in silence.

"You win, Miss Piper," Johnnie said. "You're the boss until you prove you can't handle it."

"Don't worry," Quality answered.

"Any orders?" Johnnie asked ironically.

"Leave the script," she said. "Meet tomorrow night."

"Skedaddle," ordered Miss Dove.

They said good night. Miss Dove enfolded Johnnie and emplanted a moist kiss. Miss Piper contented herself with a grave nod. Johnnie and Zagic descended to the street where Zagic stopped and confronted his friend.

"Why'd you do it, Johnnie? . . . Why'd you do it?" he asked almost tearfully. "Givin' in to that zombie?"

"A lovely zombie," John Miller said.

"Fallin' for a map and a set of legs!" Zagic expostulated.

"No," John said, and shook his head in some bewilderment. "It was something else. Some quality. You can't define it. But it's there. . . . What that girl's got, Zagic, is the right to command. By divine right, I guess. I don't quite understand it, but wherever Quality Piper sits is the head of the table."

chapter THREE

John worked over his script, modifying the part of the house-keeper to fit the proportions and character of Dolly Dove. Dolly was effusive about it; Quality Piper gave terse approval. John found that when technical matters were involved Quality was well able to express herself. She did not waste words but those she used expressed her meaning and conveyed information. But in ordinary social conversation she took no part, especially if the talk turned upon herself. It was not exactly that she was secretive, but she certainly showed marked reserve. After half a dozen meetings John's admiration for her efficiency and execu-tive ability increased, but his personal acquaintance with her did not increase. So far as he was concerned she had no past. He did not learn her age. He did not learn where she had been educated, or where she had been born. He had no idea what her history might have been before she came to Hollywood or what had brought her to the fantastic city. He could not accuse her of being secretive, but definitely she did not disclose.

She laid the script on Dolly Dove's dining-room table, which had become a part of their office equipment.

"I'll put it on the board," she said.

"Meaning what?" asked John.

She went to her bedroom and returned with a slotted board and a handful of long, narrow celluloid strips.

"One for each sequence," she said. "Code letters in these squares indicate day or night, what set, weather, special music, sound effects, props."

"Yes."

"Which actors," she went on, "number of pages of script, estimate of minutes necessary to play the sequence."

"Sort of a map of production," John said.

Quality did not find it necessary to respond to this. She sat back, hands folded in her lap, and waited for what was to come next.

There was silence, but it was not an uncomfortable silence. Quality was serene, apparently contented that there should be no conversation. She had retired into herself. John, to whom she was becoming more and more an enigma, studied her openly. Quality seemed unaware of it. No girl ever had puzzled John as Quality puzzled him. He never had encountered a woman who seemed so completely without self-consciousness. She dressed always with taste but with restraint. She seemed to make no effort to enhance her beauty; but on the other hand she did not try to conceal it. Undoubtedly she was lovely, but one had to scrutinize and appraise her to become aware of it.

"Quality," he said, and it was the first time he had addressed her by her given name, "would you like to go to dinner with me tonight? Possibly dancing afterward."

"Is it wise?" she asked.

"Why not?" he wanted to know.

"Better remain impersonal," she said.

"Why? We're associates and partners. Why not friends?"

"It might," she said, "be dangerous."

"To whom?" he asked.

"To you," she responded.

"Why to me?"

"Am I beautiful?" She put the question as impersonally as if she had been wanting to know about the beauty of some third person casually seen.

"I've noticed it," he answered.

"Am I desirable?" she asked in the same tone and with the same manner.

"Physically—yes."

"You," she said with perfect composure, "might come to want me."

"What's against that? If it happened. It's always a chance when boy meets girl. Not that I anticipate it. But we're both free, white and twenty-one. I see no dreadful impediments."

"Bad for the partnership. Bad for you."

"Why for me?"

"Because," she said incisively, "you couldn't have me."

It was not a challenge; it was a cold statement of fact.

"Why couldn't I have you?" he demanded rather boyishly.

"No man can," she answered.

Quite evidently she meant it. She intended that answer to be final—complete and final. But for all her intention it was a challenge. That she declared herself to be unobtainable added to her allure. It awakened a desire that really had not been present before. It raised an obstacle which his stubbornness demanded that he surmount. Not that he suddenly had fallen in love with Quality, but when she made of herself a fruit just out of reach, it was only natural that he should try to reach it.

He spread his hands and laughed. "To go back to the beginning," he said, "will you dine with me tonight?"

There was a brief silence and then she nodded. "Yes," she said.

"Seven o'clock," he suggested, and she nodded. "Romanoff's O.K.?"

"Expensive," she said.

"Once a year," he grinned, "I can splurge."

Miller returned to his McCadden Place apartment, where, as the afternoon merged into evening, he shaved, bathed, dressed. Shortly after seven o'clock a taxicab carried him to Dolly Dove's home. He directed the driver to wait, rang the bell and was invited to ascend. It was Dolly who opened the door. She surveyed him in his dinner coat and nodded approval. "I like a man with a coat that fits," she said. "Come in. Toots'll be ready when, as and if she gets ready. Sit."

He sat, not unmindful of the clicking of the meter on the waiting taxicab.

"Look," she said. "You're a writer. You got no practical savvy. Got a legal department?"

"No. For what?"

"Mainly to check. Keep you out of trouble. Like names. If you got a character in the script by the name of Beelzebub Dinklespiel you got to make sure there's no living man of that name. He might get mad and sue you. Suppose you mention a breakfast food by the name of Dipsy Doodle, and there is such a thing, you can get in a mess. Then there's libel and plagiarism. And censorship and a dozen things you can trip over. You got to be sure before you start."

"Is this your idea?" he asked.

"Toots brought it up."

"Then," he said, "let Toots worry about it."

"She will," said Quality from the doorway of her bedroom. She stepped into the living room and John gaped at her. She was not severely tailored now. She wore a thing that John guessed would be classified as a creation. It made her seem younger, more feminine, more touchable. There was no reluctance on its part to admit the loveliness of Quality's figure. John pursed his lips but restrained the whistle.

"Romanoff's," he said, "will bug its eyes."

He might as well have remained silent. There was no reaction from Quality. It was mildly discouraging.

"She is *not* a zombie," he said to Dolly Dove.

"Just locked up like a safe," Dolly said. "You got to know the combination."

"Shall we go?" Quality asked. "Good night, Dolly."

"Good night, children," said America's ex-Darling, beaming on them as they went out of the door.

John did his conversational best on the way to Romanoff's, but monosyllables were his only reward. Before the cab stopped before the marquee a single word from her seemed like loquacity.

"Is there," he asked, "a topic that interests you?"

"I don't chatter," she said.

"Or," he asked, "are you trying to discourage me?"

"Yes," she said flatly.

He helped her out, and as she stood for an instant arranging her skirt he noticed a man whose broadness of shoulder made him seem shorter than his actual stature. He paused, lighting a cigarette, and John saw his profile. It was the face of a man in his early forties. The hair was brick red and cut *en brosse*. There was a heavy chin and a flattened nose. Manner and bearing were of arrogant authority. He was somebody, but John did not recognize him. He heard a tiny sound from Quality which was the ghost of a gasp.

A second figure appeared—that of an elderly man in an evening coat of an earlier era. It was a very well-made coat but definitely not new, carefully brushed to conceal its age, and worn with an air which, somehow, managed to combine dignity with a curious shyness. He was a handsome old gentleman who had seen better days, and his face was vaguely familiar to John.

He addressed the first comer with stately courtesy. "Good evening, Mr. Salmon," he said. When he spoke you thought of dignified drawing rooms and the courtly ways of an older day.

"Hello, Farraday," the broad-shouldered one said, much as one would reply to a troublesome beggar.

The names Salmon and Farraday identified the two men to John. Salmon's fame was as a horseman, an owner and breeder. Reputed to be wealthy, he was spoken of as a backer of enterprises. Farraday's name brought recollections. Kent Farraday, one of the great names of the screen of twenty years ago. In his time, in the day of the silent pictures he had stood upon the pinnacle. He had been America's ideal of the suave, cultured gentleman, a star of the first magnitude. Then he had vanished from the firmament. It was with a sort of painful shock that John recognized him in this scrupulously neat but rather threadbare figure. Remnants of the old charm and courtliness remained, but obscured by a shyness and humility imposed upon him by years of evil days.

"May I have a word with you, Mr. Salmon?" he asked.

"Get away from me, you cadging old bum," Salmon said roughly.

Kent Farraday did not cringe. He drew himself up and spoke with courage. "Mr. Salmon," he said, "I have earned the right to a courteous response. There was a day, sir, when you would have considered it a distinction if I spoke to you. It is not a worthy thing for a young man such as you to insult an older man such as I. Sir, it is important to me that I have a few words with you."

"Get away from me, you damned old nuisance," Salmon said, and shoved the old gentleman away from him so violently that Farraday almost fell to the sidewalk.

John felt an upsurge of outrage. He took a step toward Salmon and confronted the man. "That," he said in a controlled voice, "was not nice."

"So what?" demanded Salmon.

"There was a day, sir," John answered, "when a bounder like yourself could not have gotten an introduction to Kent Farraday."

"Want to make something of it?" Salmon demanded belligerently.

"Why, yes," John said slowly. "I think I do. I think I owe this to a man who has been an honored American."

He was as tall as Salmon, but less bulky. If there were any disparity in weight John did not consider it. He burned with resentment and resentment flamed into action. He moved his left fist, but did not use it. Instead he struck straight from the shoulder with his right. It impacted flush against Salmon's square jaw, and the man went down as if he had been smitten with a club.

"Good," said Quality Piper, whose presence John had forgotten.

He stood over Salmon, waiting for the man to arise. Salmon lifted himself to his elbow, shook his head, bewildered, half conscious. Gradually he hoisted himself to his feet and stood swaying.

"Well?" asked John.

"I," said Salmon shakily, "do not engage in street brawls."

"You just engaged in one," said John.

"Which," said Salmon viciously, "I shall not forget."

He did not enter Romanoff's but walked a bit unsteadily up the street.

John turned to Quality. "Did I seem to hear you say 'good'?" he asked.

"Yes," she answered.

"Then," he said grinning, "I needn't apologize."

Kent Farraday stood dignified, but with face working with emotion.

"May I ask your name, young sir?" he asked. "My name, it seems, is familiar to you."

"Familiar and honored, Mr. Farraday. My name is John Miller."

"In these decadent days," Farraday said with a touch of the grand manner slightly theatrical, "it is rare and wonderful to encounter chivalry—to realize that the tradition of Sir Galahad has not vanished from the earth."

"I just got sore," John said uncomfortably.

"A praiseworthy soreness. . . . May I beg to be presented to your lovely companion?"

"Miss Piper," said John, "Mr. Kent Farraday. A great name."

"A famous name," she said with significance.

John caught the undertone of her words and his glance was a question.

"Father," she said.

"By Jove! The father! . . . Mr. Farraday, will you do us the honor to dine with us?"

He cast a glance down upon his meticulously pressed clothing as if to satisfy himself of its fitness. Then he smiled and there was something eager and pitiful in his smile.

"It is long," he said, "since I have been accustomed to dine in places of this quality."

"Then it's time," John said. "Also Miss Piper and I may have a matter to lay before you."

"I shall be happy to join you," Mr. Farraday said, and they entered the restaurant. Once at their table and their order given, John addressed Kent Farraday.

"Sir," he said, "this may be a fortunate meeting for Miss Piper and me." Rapidly, succinctly, John put into words the plans of the Famous Names Group. He described its co-operative features, admitted the lack of money. "It will be a small company," he said. "And then, Dolly Dove has agreed to accept the role of the housekeeper."

"And you—you want me for the role of the father!" said Farraday in a voice so faint it was all but inaudible.

"More," said Quality, "than any other actor in the world."

The old gentleman's face worked, tears dimmed his eyes and he brushed them away with the backs of his hands.

"For me," he said tremulously, "this is a night of splendor—to realize that I am wanted."

"The people of this country," John said, "do not forget. Millions remember you in *Clouds and Stars,* your great performance in *Vagabond Gentleman,* in *Mr. Secretary,* in a dozen other pictures. If your obligations permit you to join with us we will indeed deserve the title of Famous Names."

"Mr. Miller," said Farraday, "you know it has been long since I have enjoyed professional obligations." His old-fashioned theatricalism was far from offensive either to Quality or to John. "Like the phoenix, to arise from the ashes," he said with shining eyes. "My children, you have made an old man, a discouraged and thwarted old man—a frightened old man, dare again to face his future. I only pray I shall contribute to the success of your courageous effort."

He leaned to face John, grave, troubled. "Mr. Miller," he said, "you did a splendid thing tonight when you came to the succor of an old man. But, my boy, you have made an enemy of a man of power, of a ruthless, vicious, vindictive man. Be vigilant, my boy. He will not forget."

"An evil man," said Quality.

"Let's not," said John with a shrug, "get in a dither about a

23

one-punch fracas." He frowned. "What do you know about this Humphrey Salmon? How do you know he is an evil man?"

"No one," Quality said, speaking one of her longer sentences, "has better reason to know than I."

"Suppose we forget it," John said a trifle impatiently. Then he smiled and when he smiled his face lighted and suddenly you became aware of a certain boyish charmingness. "Let's be glad. Let's celebrate our good luck." He lifted his glass. "To the latest addition to the Famous Names Group."

"I thank you, Mr. Miller," Farraday said. He was a new man, a happy man. From that moment the dinner was his. The old spark glowed again and he was the urbane, gracious, witty man of twenty years ago. He talked. Anecdotes of the past, of illustrious men and women, came entertainingly from his lips. By turns he was serious and humorous and he enthralled his young companions as much by manner as by the matter of his conversation.

They lingered at the table until, at last, Quality signified it was time to go home.

"We'll drive you to your place, Mr. Farraday," John offered.

"No. Tonight I want to walk. I want to think and to realize." Again he was playing a part. He was the hero in his own drama, and he parted from them with a curtain speech. ". . . want to walk alone and listen again to the playing of violins."

John handed Quality into a cab. "A good night's work," he said.

"Or a bad," she answered.

"Don't," he laughed, "be a gloomy lady of mystery. Haunted by a lurid past. A *femme fatale* pursued by the villain Humphrey Salmon. . . . I'll abolish him for you. I'll exorcise him."

"Better men than you," she said, "have tried."

The remainder of the drive was silence. Quality was mute. He could not reach her. She had retired into herself and he could not induce her to emerge. At the door of Dolly Dove's apartment he said good night. It was not strange that he should be a bit sulky. If she noticed it she gave no sign of awareness.

24

"Good night. Thank you," she said tersely, and climbed the stairs.

John was driven to his little McCadden Place apartment. He walked up to his door and opened it. The room was lighted. He had an instant's time to wonder if he had gone out without extinguishing the light. That was all. He returned to consciousness on the floor sick and dizzy with a throbbing, painful head. He struggled to his feet and stood swaying. There was no one in the room. He staggered to a chair and sat holding his head. There was blood on his fingers. He went dizzily to the bathroom and applied cold water. His thoughts became more coherent. When he returned to his living room he peered about to determine if the intruder had any other object than mayhem. His eyes came to rest upon his work table. His brief case was gone. With it was gone his script of the play. Every paper having to do with the play had vanished.

He sat holding his throbbing head, sick and miserable. The ringing of the telephone seemed a thunderous crash of sound. He dragged himself to the table and lifted the receiver.

"Mr. John Miller?" asked a voice. It was a distinctive voice, contralto, with an edge of humor as if the speaker were enjoying a joke.

"This is John Miller," he said. "Who is speaking?"

"Just a merry voice in the night wishing you well," she said.

"I like to identify well-wishers," John said.

"I'm shy and demure," she told him. "You aren't feeling too well at the moment, I hear. I just called to offer sympathy."

"How would you know I'm in feeble health?"

"You're an important person. How about your travels?" she laughed.

"Did you recently call on me with a blunt instrument?"

"Goodness-gracious no. But I was so sorry to hear about it. I do so hope it will never happen again. That is why I called. To tell you I hope it will never happen again in—say—aggravated form."

"Why should it happen again?" he wanted to know.

"Well," she said hesitantly, but still with that pleasant note of amusement in her voice, "because I heard it rumored that you cultivate the wrong people and seem to be impulsive. I do hope you will be more careful in selecting your friends. And that you will be very, very discreet and not become involved in things."

"What things?" he demanded.

"Things," she said, "that might result in something more grievous than a bumped head. Writing people," she went on, "should stick to their typewriters. Good night, Mr. Miller. So nice to have talked to you."

The line went dead.

chapter FOUR

John Miller awakened to a throbbing headache and to a state of bewilderment. That an intruder should have rifled his room might have indicated a petty sneak thief if anything of value to an individual of that ilk had been stolen. It was also possible that a thief, surprised by John's return, might have struck and run. But no casual criminal would have stolen John's brief case containing his script and notes. He would have been far less intelligent than he was had he not pondered the name of Humphrey Salmon. In all the world Salmon was the only man he could conceive of having a serious grudge against him. Salmon might well have hired a thug to slug him, to beat him up in reprisal for that blow in front of Romanoff's. But he had not been beaten up, as the underworld understands that term. He had been hit but once. It did not make sense that the man would know of the existence of his television script, or, if he did know of it, would have any reason for seeking to possess himself of it.

Certainly he would not have commissioned its stealing out of pure spite. The loss of it could be no more than an annoyance to John Miller. There were at least three other copies of the script. And there seemed no purpose it could serve to injure John, to have abstracted the papers. The whole episode, considered logically, did not add up.

The doorbell rang and John admitted Zagic Quiros who stared at him with head on one side.

"You turned Mohammedan, or is it a hangover?" he asked. "Wherefore the turban?"

"Blunt instrument," John answered wryly.

"Reacts quick, don't he?" Zagic said. "If you was picking the wrong man to slough you guessed good. So you earn a bruised noggin. Of all the men in this town you got to select this Humphrey Salmon to slug!"

"How do you know about it?" John asked.

Zagic was disgusted. "This," he said, "is a place where you can hear a pin drop. D'ye think the tin ears miss it when you unload a ton of bricks? The best odds you can get this morning is three to one your time limit is thirty days."

"What makes this Salmon such a peril?" John asked.

"Coincidences," said Zagic.

"Such as?"

"People he don't like have quick bad luck."

"Tell me about him. What's his line?" John asked.

"On the door of his office it says LAWYER," Zagic replied. "But you name me a client. These rumors say he owns a string of gee-gees, but you won't find his name listed in the book. It's hissed around he's the Say-so in this advertising agency, but his name ain't on the stationery. It's mooted he's strong in the flesh-peddling racket and the literary-agency game, but he don't sign any contracts or autograph any checks. Kind of a professional silent partner. He gets invited to all the big parties, but not to the select small ones. But he's got a lever and he uses it to pry with."

"What you call enigmatic," John said.

"He's a one-man fifth column," Zagic answered. "Now about the conk on the *cabeza?*"

John described the events of last night and Zagic pondered them.

"So they cabbaged onto the script," he said. "That could require precautions seasoned with foresight. We rush off a copy to the copyright office, just in case. Also we register the title of our co-op—the Famous Names Group. Elementary."

"We signed up Kent Farraday for the father," John told him.

"Diggity!" exclaimed Zagic. "Now we got to rope the boy and girl."

"I want a girl," John said, "who thinks she is sophisticated and tries to live up to it, but who actually hasn't outgrown the belief that babies are found under cabbage leaves. I mean a girl who can give that impression. Pretty. With a surface precocity, but really just a kid inside. Then the boy to play opposite her— we don't want a straight lead like a million others."

"Yah," agreed Zagic. "A comic?"

"Verging on it," John said. "Homely and gangling, but a sympathetic character who blunders his way in and out."

"If you want blunders," Zagic said, "just throw a handful of shot into a crowd, and take the first boy it hits."

The telephone rang and John answered. "America's ex-Darling speaking," said Dolly Dove's falsetto voice. "You up?"

"And facing the day with a high heart," John answered.

"One vice I have left," came the voice over the wire, "and only one. I make two-dollar bets on the gee-gees."

"Leading up to what?"

"Santa Anita," Dolly chirruped. "I got a car that I hate to drive in traffic. Also I got four tickets to the club house. Where's the Character?"

"His feet are on my table."

"Have you two knights got chivalry left to take me and Toots to the races?"

John turned to Zagic. "The Darling wants us to go to the track. How about it?"

"Sure. I got a thing in the third race."

"What time shall we kneel before the throne?" John asked.

"We'll have lunch there. Get around when you've cleaned your teeth and got your pants out from under the mattress."

"To hear," said John, "is to obey."

They lounged for an hour and then took a taxi to Dolly Dove's apartment. America's old Darling was arrayed. Her gown was a billowing creation in pastel colors which gave her the general appearance of a cumulus cloud at sunset. Quality Piper was severe in a tailored suit. They were ready for the long drive through vexatious traffic to the race track, and Dolly's car was waiting at the door.

"You look kind of peaked," Dolly said in her piping tones to John.

"He passed the skull test," Zagic said. "Got high marks."

"Talk American, Character," ordered Dolly.

"A tap with a sap," Zagic explained. "Scientific experiment. Which is the hardest—his head or a bludgeon? The head won."

John grinned wryly and felt the spot behind his ear gingerly. "Thick bones are more to be desired than great riches," he said, and told the story briefly. His eyes studied Quality as he spoke. She sat erect, almost stiff, on the davenport, and her face betrayed no emotion. She merely listened. At the end she made no comment. Dolly bustled to him, drew down his head and examined the bump with solicitous fingers.

"I've seen worse," she said in a matter-of-fact way. "Let's shove off."

"You've almost broke their hearts," Zagic said ironically.

" 'There was lack of women's nursing. There was dearth of women's tears,' " John quoted and grinned. "My grandmother used to read Owen Meredith."

"Me," Dolly said, "I prefer Ella Wheeler Wilcox."

She shooed them out of the door and into the waiting car. Zagic took the wheel. After a tiresome drive they parked the car in the vast space behind Santa Anita's grandstand and mounted to the club house where they seated themselves at the reserved table diagonally across from the tote board. It was a gracious day. In the distance the mountains reared; millions of flowers flamed in the great oval inside the track. On all sides of them chatted beautifully dressed women and men resplendent in eye-filling sports jackets. Wherever one looked were faces made familiar to millions by the silver screen. Form sheets rustled, friends exchanged information. There was suppressed excitement and gaiety. To look at that scene made one doubt that anywhere in the world could there be warfare, or misery, or want, or fear. John's face was saturnine.

"While Rome burns," he said to Quality.

"Waters of Lethe," she answered and he glanced at her with surprise. She was not one from whom he would have expected classical allusion. She was too modern, too practical.

Dolly's shrewd eyes darted here and there, missing nothing. They came to rest at a table next but one on their left.

"Look," she said. "The type."

Eight eyes turned to peer at the girl who sat there with an elderly gentleman with a small, pointed beard.

"Aristocratic," said Dolly.

"Snob," Zagic snapped.

"No," Quality said to him.

"If she ain't a snob—what?" he demanded.

"Young," said Quality sententiously. "Skin-deep sophistication."

"That," John gave his opinion, "is what we want. Who is she?"

No one knew who she was. Not one of them ever had seen her before.

"Leave it to Mamma," Dolly said, and surged up from her chair. She waddled between tables and stood looking down upon the young stranger.

"I'm Dolly Dove," she said. "Remember? Who are you?"

The girl raised brows in surprise at being thus accosted, but the elderly bearded gentleman got to his feet.

"Dolly Dove! I remember. How I remember. . . . My dear, you are looking at your mother's only rival. . . . Dolly Dove!"

"In the flesh," Dolly grinned, "in wholesale lots."

"Miss Dove, my daughter. I am Dr. Scruggs. Martha is too young to remember. It is an honor. Will you sit down? Those grand old days!"

"Look, Doc," Dolly said, "what's she doing here? Debutante on a Hollywood spree, or a hopeful?"

"Ambitious," said Dr. Scruggs. "They call it stage struck. Her mother and I protested and surrendered. Summer stock—and then she must come here. . . . Modern young people! I know about removing ailing gall bladders, but this generation of young baffles me."

"Are you *that* Doc Scruggs? The one operated on Ronnie Blake?"

"I am that one," he smiled.

"Take me," Dolly said, "I'm bloody respectable."

"It meets the eye," said Dr. Scruggs smilingly.

"Got some friends I want you to meet. Might come to something. Let's go inside where we can palaver." She turned to her own table. "Inside," she ordered. "Conference coming up."

They trooped into the flower-decked room adjoining the bar and, after introductions, found grouped seats.

"We're television," said Dolly as an opening remark. "We're the Famous Names Group. We've got a script. Calls for a girl your daughter fits like a cork in a bottle. If she can act." Dolly, with unexpected succinctness, explained their co-operative plan. "Could be big; could be a flop." She turned to her partners. "What you think?"

"She's made for it—physically," John said.

Quality only nodded.

"What's her name?" Zagic demanded.

"Martha Scruggs," said Dolly.

"Oh, my gawd!" Zagic exclaimed. "Famous names. There's one for you. There's one for the billboards." Suddenly he beamed. "Famous names, eh? Well, famous names is what we'll peddle. If they ain't got 'em, we'll rechristen. Look, Cutie," he said to the girl, "Scruggs is a three-time loser. Now take Marie Antoinette!"

"You may call me Zenobia if it will get my toe in the door," said the girl.

"Miss Scruggs," asked John, "does the idea interest you?"

"Very much," said Miss Scruggs.

"Would you care to read the part for us?"

"Very much," Miss Scruggs said.

"Thursday evening," suggested John. "Miss Dove's apartment. Eight o'clock." He gave the address. "Is that agreeable?"

Miss Scruggs looked at her father inquiringly. "If I may accompany Martha," he said.

Dolly Dove sighed gustily. "That's that," she said. "I'm darn near famished. You got to feed a body like mine. See you folks Thursday night, then."

They went back to their tables. Food was served to which Dolly devoted her unmixed attention. The horses reached the gate for the first race and Dolly, replete, sailed down like a galleon under full canvas to make her two-dollar bet. Zagic saved his resources to plunge on his sure thing in the third race. He nudged John.

"Here's your soulmate," he whispered.

Humphrey Salmon stood on the step above them looking over the crowd. His eyes fastened upon John and he frowned, then smiled. John watched him approach, beret, immaculately tailored and flamboyantly checked sports coat. John readied himself for come what might. Salmon halted at the table.

"Mr. Miller," he said pleasantly, "I want you to know that I harbor no resentment for what happened last night. I fancy I had it coming to me. I fear I had one over the seven and my disposition was scratchy. I offer my hand."

John, bewildered by this approach, was rising to his feet. Automatically his hand was reaching out for Salmon's.

"Don't," said Quality.

"Eh? . . . What?" John asked.

"Don't," she said.

"Ah," said Salmon easily. "The gracious Miss Piper!" He smiled with amusement. "The monosyllabic Miss Piper. And why shouldn't Mr. Miller shake hands with me?"

"Filthy," she said.

Salmon peered at his palm humorously. "I've washed with scented soap. I've had a manicure," he said.

"No soap nor manicure," she said, "can remove the dirt."

His face was bland; there was no trace of resentment. There was only toleration as at some antic of a willful child. He shrugged carelessly and spread his hands.

"I seem," he said to John, "not to be popular with Miss Piper. I withdraw in disorder. To our future meetings, Mr. Miller. Miss Piper's attitude will change when she knows me better. As she will. Good luck to all of you. Bet on Mayflower in the fifth."

He turned and walked away with something of jauntiness in the set of his shoulders. There was momentary silence at the table.

Then Zagic spoke. "You ain't satisfied to ask for it," he said to Quality. "You got to send an engraved invitation begging for it."

"Quite," said Quality sharply.

"I hope I win on this gee in the third," Zagic said. "I can afford to send a bigger blanket of flowers."

chapter FIVE

"To me," said Zagic Quiros, "it looks like we not only got the cart before the horse, but we ain't got a horse."

"Figures of speech," John Miller replied, "are pretty in poems, but confusing in real life."

"What I mean," Zagic explained, "is we got a script; we got practically a troupe of actors—but cash! We got everything else but." He distorted his homely face with a grimace. "It's like we're fixing to cross the ocean and we got a cargo and a crew, but we got no ship."

"I'm a writer," John said, "not a financier."

"That I noticed," Zagic said. "Too bad your mother wasn't scared by J. P. Morgan." He mutilated the flapjacks on his plate with his fork—the picture of a disgruntled and frustrated man. His small eyes moved about the room gloomily as if seeking for assistance which he knew would not be present. Without interest he waggled a finger at a party sitting at a nearby table. A very emaciated man who wore a muffler instead of a necktie responded. He pushed back his chair and approached Zagic and John Miller. "Move over," he said to Zagic.

"Why?" Zagic asked inhospitably.

"Maybe," said the man, "I got a proposition."

"Not interested in any bank robberies," Zagic said.

"But," said the man, "you could use a bank." He glanced at John Miller. "Who's your chaperone?" he asked.

"He don't want to know you," Zagic said. "Take it somewhere else." Zagic snorted. "Anyhow you know who he is. You know who everybody is."

"All right. I know who he is. He don't know who I am. I'm Sligo McNulty, Mr. Miller."

"He puts buzzers under horses' saddles," Zagic said.

Sligo McNulty ignored this insult. He leaned his sharp elbows on the table and bent earnestly toward John Miller. "Ignore this comedian," he said. "In a nutshell here's what I got to say: You need cabbage and I got lots of leaves." He raised his brows and widened his eyes. "Do I interest you?" he asked.

"How," John asked, "do you know I need money?"

"I'm told by a little dicky bird," Sligo answered.

"What else did he tell you?" John asked.

"He told me you got a scribble for a television show. He told me you got an idea also. He's a critic. He deems this scribble could be a thing. Maybe not so good as *Lucy*, but crowding it. He judges the idea has got merit. He advises me to invest."

"What's my script about?" John asked.

"Father, son, daughter, housekeeper," answered Sligo. "Children thwarting the old man when he gets lured into marriage by assorted sirens. This son, he's always getting stuck on flypaper. Housekeeper's the comedy element, but a wise guy." Sligo was proud of this exhibition of inside information.

"So?" John said. And then, "What's the idea with merit?"

"Digging up has-beens with famous names," answered Sligo.

"You own quite a bird," John said.

"When he flies," Sligo said, "he keeps his eyes open. You look like a fair long-chance gamble to me. So I go up to the window and buy a ticket on you across the board. Win, place and show. I finance the caper."

"You," said Zagic, "couldn't finance a bag of peanuts for a squirrel."

"To make a pilot film I finance you," Sligo said, ignoring Zagic. "Up to and including twenty grand."

John turned to Zagic. "I always knew money was easy to get," he said. And then to Sligo McNulty. "And for this twenty thousand, what do you get?"

"Sixty per cent," said Sligo.

"Leaving," John said mildly, "forty per cent for my script and to divide among the troupe. Very generous, I'd say."

"When I deal I deal fair," Sligo said.

"Mr. McNulty," John said, "there's just one way your little bird could have learned about my script and about the Famous Names idea. Does your little bird carry a sap? Does he lurk behind doors and crack skulls and loot apartments? He is a very naughty little bird, McNulty. Would you like to take off your coat so I can see if you have wings?"

"If he's got wings," Zagic said, "they're like a bat's, covered with lice."

John did not speak for a moment, but regarded Sligo with head tilted to one side and a faint, not pleasant, smile on his lips. "If I were you, Mr. McNulty," he said, "I'd unfold my pinions and take flight. Very abrupt flight. Back to whoever let you out of your cage. My head still aches and I'm peevish. If you're not outside this aviary in ten seconds, I aim to pluck your wings off one by one and use them as a poultice."

"You and what regiment?" Sligo asked belligerently.

"It'll be a solo performance," John said softly. With one lithe movement he stood in the aisle. With another he twisted Sligo and applied that hold known as a hammerlock. Sligo found himself goose-stepping toward the street. John propelled him through the door, loosed him and applied his foot to that portion of Sligo's anatomy provided by bountiful nature to receive such attentions. Then he walked back to his seat and grinned at Zagic.

"The day seems brighter," he said.

"You got rhythm," Zagic said gloomily. "But you haven't studied about how to make friends and influence people."

"Finish your flapjacks," John told him, "and we'll call a meeting." He emptied his coffee cup. "Your friend Sligo was a stupid emissary."

"Maybe not so dumb," Zagic said.

"Enlarge on that."

"It could be this Sligo was delegated to run off at the mouth. Sort of storm signal. To plant the thought that you might be reaching for a live wire loaded with high voltage. Sligo handles no money for anybody. He wangles no deals. He's strictly from under a wet rock."

John was thoughtful. "I'm a writing man. I don't know any sleight of hand. When people pull rabbits out of hats I'm astonished and applaud. I don't know how to cope with legerdemain. I'm a simple soul, and a straight line is the shortest distance."

"So," said Zagic, "when you don't know what to do next you haul off and bob somebody. For a lad who earns his money with his brains you're awful physical. What you need is a vice-president in charge of funny business."

"Who, for instance? Another job for Quality Piper?"

Zagic shook his head vigorously. "She's not a slick chick," he said. "She levels. Not me. I just make noises. When you need somebody who can track an eel through a swamp the one to call in is Dolly Dove."

"Dolly. Nonsense."

"She," said Zagic, "looks like a feather bed with a henna rinse; and she burbles like a half-witted sparrow. But she can out-squirm an angleworm. That fat lady can see around corners. Turn her loose after a fox and she'll come home with its tail. Every con man in Hollywood has had a try at her and she's got a bureau drawer full of their eye teeth. She's tight as Mae West's girdle. She's got the first dime her dad ever gave her, and a convention of swindlers couldn't get it away from her with the help of the snake that tricked Eve in the Garden of Eden."

"Let us then," said John Miller, "go sit at her feet."

A taxicab carried them to Dolly Dove's apartment. Dolly received them in a billowing robe and flapping slippers. She had breakfasted on oatmeal, flapjacks and sausages and was genial. "The Character looks worried," she piped. "What's griping him?"

"First, money," John answered. "Second, skulduggery."

Dolly raised her voice shrilly. "Hi, Toots," she screamed.

"Come out. The boys woke up with problems. . . . Money! Women have two worries—money and fat. Men have two worries—money and women. So we take money worries for granted and go on to other topics. . . . What did you boys think of Dr. Scruggs' daughter?"

"She'll do," John said.

"Toots and I agree," Dolly said. "Now all we need is a boy."

"And cash money," said Zagic. "And brains like a lady fox with a litter of kittens to protect. We got to have a department of counter-skulduggery."

"Why?" asked Quality Piper from her bedroom door.

Zagic repeated the conversation with Sligo McNulty. Quality sat still on the davenport and listened without comment. America's ex-Darling gripped her gown about her ample middle and shut one eye and narrowed the other and nodded from time to time.

"This Sligo McNulty," she said, "cleans cesspools for Humphrey Salmon. A half-witted three-toed sloth knows he couldn't raise twenty thousand cents, let alone dollars. So his proposition was bosh and nonsense. And he knew you knew it was simple pure mallarkey. All right. You've told me. Now we talk of other things while I pay it some mind."

"Right," John said. "You, Dolly, are now promoted to vice-president in charge of chicanery and stealth."

"Toots," said Dolly, "has been snooping. She's unearthed a studio over in Culver City. Complete staff and equipment. It's making a couple of television shows now. A detective thing, for one. The boss of this factory claims he can make a pilot film for fifteen thousand dollars. Reliable. Right, Toots?"

Quality nodded her head in the affirmative. Even so early in the morning, and taken by surprise by unexpected visitors, she was neat and trim as if she had spent hours over her toilet.

"She claims that network television is on the skids," Dolly said.

"Why," demanded Zagic, "don't she say so herself?"

"Why should I?" Quality asked.

"Do you got always to have a mouthpiece?" Zagic asked testily.

"Yes," Quality answered.

"She says," went on Dolly Dove, "that there are three ways to market a television show. You can let one of the networks take it over; you can peddle it to an advertising agency, or better yet you can syndicate."

"First," John said grimly, "you have to have a film to sell."

"We'll have it," said Quality.

"So we got to explore," Dolly said. "How to get the most money out of it? Now, suppose we do business with a network. They take their cut, don't they? And they take plenty. With television it isn't like the old radio days when every station had to hook up with NBC or Columbia or one of the big ones. In radio a station has to use what its network gives. An NBC station can't use a Columbia program and like that. But television's different. The station can pick and choose. It can put a Columbia show at seven o'clock and an NBC show at eight o'clock and so on. The networks can't dictate."

"But they have organization," John said.

"Advertising agencies are better," Dolly said. "But an agency has to get a sponsor. It'll buy your show for a price. The sponsor has to buy time and get an hour assigned to it. Probably it'll deal with a network. Maybe you can get a sliding-scale deal depending on the number of stations that buy your show. You have a sponsor who thinks he knows more about show business than you do, and it meddles. An agency, today, is pretty much forced to do business with a network. An agency takes fifteen per cent of whatever the sponsor spends."

"How is this thing you call syndicating better?" John asked.

"Because," Dolly said, "the backbone of the business done by a little station, say in Phoenix, or Dallas or whatever, is the local advertiser. It's the second-hand car dealer and the department store and the bank and like that. The local station is independent as a hog on ice. It doesn't have to take any show it doesn't want. It can pick and choose. There are around two hundred stations today. New ones are coming in as fast as the

Communications Commission grants licenses. By the time we get this show on the road there may be two hundred and fifty. That means two hundred and fifty possible local sponsors, instead of one sponsor on a network."

"What's the advantage of that?" John asked.

"It means a show will have a possible two hundred and fifty places to sell, and when you sell to one local sponsor you don't have to split with a network. Suppose you sell our show to Phoenix, Arizona. Say for two hundred and fifty dollars. You get it all."

"Less the expense of selling," John said.

"One, or possibly two salesmen," Dolly answered. She was so businesslike it rather startled John. "Your salesman goes into a town with his samples—that's a film, of course. He shows it to the station. The station is trying to sell time to a local advertiser. You've got a good show. Both you and the station try to sell it to, say, the department store. If he likes it the station is ahead because it doesn't have to pay the network rake-off. So it co-operates. Now, with a swell show, you could sell to maybe a hundred stations. With a smash hit like *Lucy* you could sell to more. You have personal acquaintance and contact with each station. Set an average price of two hundred fifty dollars for a hundred stations, and you get a gross of twenty-five thousand a week."

"Sounds noble," John said.

"Deduct," piped Dolly, "a nut of fifteen thousand dollars for your pilot film and a few hundred for your sales expense and what you got? You got plenty and don't have to divide it with anybody. You make more money; the local station makes more money; and the local sponsor pays less for his show. That," she said, "is why Toots believes the network is a dying bird on television."

"Listen, Miss Dove," asked Zagic, "did Miss Piper open her mouth and say all those words to you?"

Dolly giggled shrilly. Again she seemed to be a fatuous, over-weight and silly woman. "We kind of collaborated," she answered.

"I bet what she uttered was the periods and commas," Zagic said.

John shrugged and spread his hands. "We are still short fifteen thousand," he said.

"No," said Quality positively. "Maybe ten."

"How come?"

"No actors' salaries," she said.

"Right."

"Rehearse here," she said.

"That," said Dolly, "will lop a day off studio cost. We'll rehearse the pants off the troupe right here. So we go to the studio letter perfect."

"If we ever get to the studio," John said.

"We will," Quality replied tersely. It was said with a determination that was impressive. The girl willed that their project should be a success. She had uttered the words quietly, with her usual repression, but that, somehow, made her more convincing.

"She's got a whim of iron," Zagic said, "like that fellow said about his wife."

She stood up with lithe, sure movement and disappeared into her bedroom. In a moment she returned with hat on and handbag dangling and walked to the outer door. "Good morning," she said.

"Shall I escort you?" John asked ironically. Quality shook her head firmly and closed the door behind her.

"Well!" John exclaimed.

"Let's talk about a boy for the part," Miss Dove suggested.

"Let's," said John, "talk about Quality Piper."

"In her," Zagic said, "we got an enigma. A simon-pure, three-ply, enigmatic enigma."

"Toots," replied Miss Dove, "is just a nice, straightforward, open-faced girl."

"Says you," retorted Zagic. "She's as open-faced as a bank vault with a time lock on it."

"I think," John said, "it is high time we got a better bird's-eye view of her. She's a hypnotist. With two words she put us in a trance. She notified us she was the boss, and we took it and liked it."

"Regret it?" asked Dolly Dove.

"No," John said promptly.

"You," Dolly said, "are an impractical coot, and the Character is worse. You need somebody to grab the steering wheel."

"Granted," John agreed. "But we're entitled to know something about the driver."

"Such as?" asked Dolly.

"Where she comes from," John said.

"East of here," Dolly said.

"You also," said Zagic, "got a touch of enigma."

"Is her name Quality Piper? It sounds improbable."

"That's her story, and she sticks to it."

"Where and how did you meet her?"

"I put an ad in the paper for a boarder and she answered," Dolly said blandly.

"Of course that isn't true," John said.

"Certainly not," Dolly agreed amiably.

"Will you tell me anything about her?" John asked with exasperation.

"Sure thing. She's sound in wind and limb—and very nice limbs indeed. She's free, white and more than twenty-one. No fillings in her teeth and she can ride a bicycle. If there's anything she wants to keep to herself, you can't pry it out of her, nor likewise also out of me. Her brain ain't just a muscle and the curl in her hair is natural."

"That tells it all," John said, "except does she like dogs and what's her favorite color?" He bent his brows and leaned forward to fix Dolly with level eyes. "What," he demanded, "is between her and Humphrey Salmon?"

"That's the real question, isn't it?" Dolly asked.

"The jackpot question," John said. "They know each other. There's a look in his eye when he sees her."

"What kind of a sort of a look?" Dolly asked.

John shook his head uncertainly. "It could," he said, "be the kind of a look a cat uses when it's planning to leap on a bird.

It could be the kind of a look a man wears when he has a yen for a woman. It could be the kind of a look a man wears when he's a reason to be afraid. Whichever it is, it's a bad look and I don't like it."

"Do tell!" Dolly exclaimed. "And how does she look at him?"

"She just looks," John said.

"Enigmatic," Zagic said. "Like this Sphinx."

"There's something between them. Either she hates him or she pretends to hate him," John said in a troubled voice.

Dolly wriggled her bulk and her chair creaked its protest. Her dumpling face was vacuous, but her eyes were wise and shrewd. Her voice was high, shrill, comical, but for all that she was in earnest.

"I tell you," she said, "and a guarantee goes with every bottle. There's one thing this Toots hasn't any of, and that's pretending. She ain't equipped for it. She couldn't act in a home-made charade. She blurts. If she looks hate then she hates."

John grinned and was frustrated. "If she looks love—what?" he asked.

"I never saw her look it," Dolly answered. "But when the time comes that she does the man had better hold his hat. There'll be a high wind. . . . Now skedaddle, boys. I got housework to do. I cogitate better with a dishrag in my paddy."

chapter SIX

It was on Tuesday morning that John Miller first saw the furtive gnome. He had prepared his own breakfast and gone out for a paper. As he stepped out of the apartment house he noticed across the street a tiny, seedy individual in a cap too large for him. The man, if stretched to full height, would have been no more than two inches over five feet in height, but he was bent like an old man and seemed even shorter. At first glance John took him to be a boy, but the face under the cap was that of a man of forty. The instant John's eyes rested upon him the little man scuttled away.

John turned to the left at the next corner and walked a couple of blocks to a newsstand. He selected his paper, stood for a moment glancing at the headlines and then moved on through the morning crowd. He stopped for traffic at the next corner and glanced about him. Thirty feet behind the same dwarf-like man stood looking in a store window. John thought nothing of it except that he felt a faint stirring of pity for such evident forlornness. The wrinkled face with a jutting big nose in the middle of it was not a pleasant face. It would have been hard had not the eyes been so hopeless. The creature's eyes met John's and turned quickly away. A wino, John said to himself, just emerged from some filthy flop house.

The traffic light changed and John sauntered on with no particular destination in mind. The morning crowd became more dense and John was about to turn off upon a side street to make his way back to the apartment when a hoarse voice speaking in a whisper at his elbow said guardedly.

"Don't turn around, Mister. Just listen."

Without turning to identify the voice John knew it was the gnome. He realized that the small creature had been following him and wondered what new approach this could be by a beggar. Odd conduct by human beings always stirred his interest. He was interested in people and their gyrations and eccentricities. Grist for his mill. He smiled faintly and humored the cadger.

"What's the pitch?" he asked tolerantly.

"Mister," whispered the rasping voice, "I got to talk to you. I got to talk to you today. Private I got to talk to you."

"This," John said, "is a new one. I'm good for a quarter without all the rigmarole."

There was a pause. The little man had not gone away. John was conscious of his continued presence a pace behind him.

"Your name," said the voice, "is John Miller. . . . No. Don't turn around. Don't notice me."

"What," asked John, keeping his eyes to the front, "are you afraid of?"

"Plenty," replied the little man. "I tell you," he said urgently, "I got to see you private."

"Go ahead and see me," John said impatiently.

The voice was pleading, despairing. "I got to scram," it said. "I'm taking a big chance. Mr. Miller, you're a friend of hers."

"A friend of whom?" John asked.

"Miss Quality," was the answer. "On account of her you got to see me."

"Come to my apartment then," John said, suddenly impressed. "Not there."

"Listen," John said impatiently, "I'm bored by this mumbo jumbo. If you want to see me come to my apartment. There or nowhere."

"Mr. Miller, the name is Shiner. I didn't want her to know yet

I'm alive. But you tell her you saw Shiner. You tell her Shiner
wants to sing. I got to scram, Mr. Miller. This isn't safe. . . .
There's a place just beyond Malibu. Ben's Den the sign says.
You drive there tonight, see? Nine o'clock. . . . Tell her Shiner."

Silence followed. John walked along a dozen paces. Then he
turned his head to look behind him. The gnome had disappeared.

"This," John said to himself, "is out of a Class B motion picture."

Nevertheless, the episode was startling. The terror of the little
man had been genuine. There was no mistake about that:
Shiner was afraid. Shiner believed he was taking a chance to
approach John, and he would not have accepted the risk had
it not been an urgent thing. Whatever it was had to do with
Quality Piper—something out of the years that had gone before;
those years about which Quality was so reticent.

If this business continued to copy the standards of a B picture
it would be a trap. It would be a device to lure John to a spot
where malignant characters would dispose of him. But that,
John thought, was silly. There would have to be a reason for
such a business, and there was no reason why anyone should
lure him to destruction. No. Somehow he felt that Shiner was
genuine, and that Shiner's need to see him secretly was urgent.

The thing to do, he determined, was to go to Quality Piper
and lay the matter before her. If Shiner meant anything to her,
if Shiner had been important in her past and could be important
in her future, then John would keep the rendezvous at Ben's
Den. If the name Shiner meant nothing to her then he would
shrug off the whole matter and forget it. Or remember it as only
an odd and senseless occurrence from which it were better he
remain aloof.

On the next corner he signaled a taxicab and gave Dolly
Dove's address. He was conscious, somewhat to his surprise,
that he was glad to have a valid excuse for calling upon Quality.
He found he was eager to see the girl who had so profoundly
stirred his curiosity, if no other emotion. She was a queer one,
but she was definitely a beautiful queer one. She seemed utterly
unconscious of herself, of the fact that she was a woman. She

did not neglect adornment, but that seemed only a part of her impersonal efficiency. He could not decide if she were deliberately repressing herself, concealing herself, or if her self-containment and terseness were natural qualities. Anyhow Quality was an interesting study, an individual, perhaps a personage.

He descended from the cab at Dolly's door and rang the bell. The lock clicked and he ascended the stairs. Dolly was standing in the door looking downward inquiringly.

"Oh," she said, "it's you. Where's the Character? I thought you two were kind of Siamese twins."

"Surgery," John said, "solved the problem of separating us. Is Miss Piper at home?"

"She's here," Dolly answered, stepping aside to admit him. "Miss Piper," she mimicked in her treble. "I'll bet it wouldn't make her go all aghast if you were to call her Quality. Or maybe even Toots."

"You've the copyright on Toots," he said.

Dolly clutched her billowing robe. "Hey, Toots," she screamed, "you got a caller. Are you decent?"

Quality Piper came out of her bedroom manifesting no surprise whatever at seeing John. She nodded her greeting and sat down on the davenport.

"Effusive, isn't she?" asked Dolly ironically. "It isn't every caller she greets with wild enthusiasm."

"I'm complimented," John said. "I'm all goose pimples."

Quality merely sat in quiet amiability and waited. John went directly to the reason for his call. "Miss Piper," he asked, "does the name Shiner mean anything to you?"

If he expected her to start, to grow pale, to exhibit some sign of shock, he was disappointed.

"Shiner," she said, "is dead."

"When he was alive," John asked, "was he about five feet two inches tall, with a parrot nose and little blue eyes and mouse-colored hair and a cauliflower ear?"

"Yes," she said.

"He claims," said John, "he's alive."

"You saw him?"

"Yes. This morning. He was hanging around outside my place. He followed me." John described the odd conversation with Shiner. "Frightened, very frightened," he said. "He didn't use your name until I was difficult. He said to mention his name to you and that you would want me to keep a date with him. He said he would sing, which, I take it, is argot for tell all."

"Where?" Quality asked.

"Ben's Den, out Malibu way. Nine o'clock."

"We will go," she said.

"We?"

"Of course," she answered.

"The man was afraid," John said. "His terror was genuine. That means there is something to fear. To meet him, even at a place of his selection, may not be a healthy pastime. Ladies were not included in the invitation."

"You let John handle this," Dolly said. "There's a sign that says Men Only."

"No," Quality said determinedly.

"Want to tell me anything about this Shiner? Not that I'm inquisitive, but it might help in the negotiations."

"Not yet," Quality said.

"And you insist upon coming?"

"I do."

John shrugged. "It's your beautiful, white, swanlike neck you're sticking out," he said.

Evidently she considered this observation unworthy of comment. She ignored its flippancy. "Here at eight o'clock," she directed.

"Is the audience ended?" John asked.

"Yes," said Quality Piper. She stood up, nodded and walked out of the room.

"Boy," squeaked Dolly Dove, "you knocked her for a loop."

"If there was a loop," John said, "it was invisible to the naked eye."

"I know her," Dolly said gravely.

"Cordial, wasn't she?" John said resentfully. "Grateful, too.

She should hire a bouncer. He could have made it more emphatic. He could have thrown me downstairs."

"Don't be young," Dolly said. "Don't be a teetotal damn fool. Now clear out and be back here at eight like she told you."

"I suppose you'll be coming too," John said sullenly.

"Not me," Dolly answered. "I'm too big a target."

A long day lay before John Miller. He returned to his apartment and sat before his typewriter. One script or even two or three were not enough to have in readiness if the Famous Names Group was to produce a show once a week for an indefinite time. He worked until noon with satisfactory results. At half past twelve Zagic Quiros rapped on his door. With Zagic was a boy who appeared to be about eighteen years old. He was lean, with big hands and feet and a shock of ginger-colored hair. He was a gangling, clumsy lad, undeveloped and homely, but somehow the homeliness of his face was attractive. Ungainly he was, as if he had grown too fast. His movements were comically awkward and his shy grin seemed always to be apologizing for his coltish uncouthness.

"This beanpole," Zagic said, "is a fellow by the name of Benjamin Franklin—believe it or not."

"How are you, Benjamin?" John said.

The boy, grinning shyly, stumbled over his feet getting to a chair and sat on the edge of it bashfully.

"He claims," said Zagic, "to be an actor. I saw him once in a bit part. Hobbledehoy kind of thing. This morning a fellow I know was feeding him boiled eggs and sausage, and we got talking. Me, I looked him over and thought maybe. So I towed him along."

John studied the boy. He fitted like a glove John's conception of the juvenile in his script.

"How old?" he asked.

"Twenty-one," said Benjamin.

"But not a ripe twenty-one," Zagic said. "Kind of underdone."

"Can he speak lines?" John asked.

"Listen," Zagic said. "This time I see him he speaks lines the way he looks. Maybe not on purpose, see? But he gets over this idea of an amateur bull in a china shop. He was good for laughs. You kind of felt sorry for him."

"Did you talk to him about the Group?" John asked.

"No. I wanted you to kind of explore him first."

John patiently explained the idea of the Famous Names Group while Benjamin fidgeted and mislaid his hands and seemed to lose control of his feet. John, the more he watched, became enthusiastic. This was the very boy—if he could act, or even project himself as he was.

"Would our plan interest you, Ben?" John asked.

"Yes, sir. Sure it would. It's a bang-up idea, seems to me. I'd go for it."

"Like to try for it?"

"Sure thing. . . . Sure thing," Benjamin assured him.

"Tomorrow night, then," John said. "We'll get the whole Group together at Dolly's. Say eight o'clock. Here's a copy of the script. You'll want to study it."

"I'll learn it. I'll learn it by heart. I bet tomorrow night I don't boot a word."

"It's just a tryout, remember. It's up to you," John warned.

"Yes, sir. . . . Yes, sir. Thank you a heap, Mr. Miller. I'm a lot obliged. I'm a whole lot obliged."

"Right," John said. "Tomorrow night then, at eight." He gave Dolly's address. "Good luck, Ben."

The boy gangled out of the room. Zagic grinned at John. "All he's got to do is just be his natural self," he said.

John frowned thoughtfully. "I wouldn't bet it was his natural self we saw," he said. "Maybe so. Maybe not. Did you notice the kid's eyes? They're smart. Could be he was putting on an act for us."

"So much the better," Zagic said.

"So much the better," John agreed.

"Want to go to the fights tonight?"

"I'm busy," John answered.

Zagic squinted his eyes and leered at John. "Wouldn't be a date with Toots?" he said. "Wouldn't be you're falling for that hand-carved chunk of ice? Now take me. When I go for a girl I don't want to make my pass wearing red flannel underwear and a fur coat. What I want to get from a gal ain't chilblains."

"Scram," John said. "I'm laboring. I'll make a cup of coffee and a sandwich here."

Zagic lingered at the door. "You think maybe Ben Franklin was putting on an act? Could be. But he didn't know anything about the script. How would he know what kind of an act to put on?"

"You found him," John said. "He's your problem."

John worked steadily through the afternoon. At five o'clock he put his manuscript away, bathed, dressed and went out for dinner. He regretted that he had not suggested that Quality Piper dine with him, but the atmosphere had not been clement for invitations. He arrived at Dolly Dove's on time. Dolly's car was standing at the curb. John rang and ascended the stairs. Quality was ready in a trim, tailored suit. Dolly fluttered.

"I ought to go along and look after you juveniles," she said. "My grandmother had second sight. Maybe I got a touch of it. I got the dithers. I got butterflies. You kids'll be careful."

"Caution is the keynote of my life," John said.

Dolly was serious and depressed. "I tell you I got premonitions," she said.

"Nonsense," Quality said tersely.

"My stomach is unsettled. I couldn't eat dinner. You hyper back as quick as you can. I'll have a snack ready." She expelled a breath. "The sooner you get going the quicker you'll be back," she said.

John and Quality descended to the car. "You drive," she directed. John helped her in and took his place behind the wheel. Before he started the engine he sat looking ahead frowning. "Nothing you want to tell me?" he asked.

"No," Quality said.

"I'll be hearing it from this Shiner," he told her. "Why not give me some facts so I'll know better how to handle him?"

"I'll see him alone," Quality said.

"You will not," John retorted. "On that we'll have an understanding. Before we start. You don't get out of my sight. That's the agreement, or you go pitty-pat back to Dolly's apartment. It's an ultimatum."

Quality turned to face him and peered into his determined face. What she saw was convincing. John meant what he said. She did not shrug or give any other sign of dissatisfaction.

"Agreed," she said.

John started the car and presently they were in the traffic heading for Malibu Beach. Quality sat motionless, her hands in her lap. Once or twice John attempted conversation but Quality would have no part of it. She was engrossed by her own thoughts. Either she made no reply at all or granted him only monosyllables.

"This," John said, disgruntled, "could be a pleasant drive."

"It isn't," Quality said.

"Mind if I sing or whistle? Silence frightens me."

"Drive," she said.

John drove. Here was a situation he could not handle. How did one cope with a girl who sat mute and stared before her? It did not help that her profile was lovely, or that her arm which touched his now and then was warm and soft. He might as well have been a hired chauffeur or a robot driver. His chin set with resentment and young, hurt pride. Well, if that was how she wanted it, that was the way she would get it. He did not speak again until they were driving along the beach with the sound of breaking surf in their ears. Minutes later he slackened pace, searching for the sign that would identify Ben's Den where the man Shiner would be awaiting them. He moved the car over into the right-hand lane. The name appeared in neon lights. It was a white house facing the ocean across the boulevard, opposite a sandy gap between beach houses. A road at its right wound up the dark hill.

John turned into this side road and parked across from the eating house. "I'll explore," he said.

"Both," Quality said.

"Have it your way," John answered.

She stepped from the car, not waiting for his assistance. He did not take her arm as they crossed the road. If she wanted to be self-sufficient it was all one to him. They were halfway across when a shrill scream halted them. It came from the underbrush-covered black hillside behind Ben's Den. A tiny figure burst through the bushes in headlong flight. There sounded a shot, and then another shot, not from a revolver, not from a rifle. The running figure tossed up its arms, staggered, fell upon its face.

John, forgetting caution, plunged toward it where it lay in the road. Quality was at his side, keeping pace with him stride for stride. He reached the prone figure, the riddled figure, and turned it over. Shiner's sightless eyes stared up at him. Two charges from a shotgun, probably a sawed-off shotgun, had almost destroyed the little man.

John stood erect. He clutched Quality's arm. He hurried her back to the car and thrust her into the seat. The engine burst into life. He twirled the wheel and spun the car in the narrow road, thrusting its nose into the traffic of the boulevard.

"So Shiner," he said grimly, "will never sing his song."

chapter SEVEN

Quality Piper was not trembling as she might well have been as she sat beside John Miller in the automobile which carried them away from the scene of the murder of the gnome named Shiner. True she was pale and her face was a frozen mask. But there was no tremor. She was in complete possession of herself. Not so John Miller. He was shaken as he never had been shaken before. It was the first time he ever had encountered death in such malignant form—the first time he had ever seen a man shot down in cold blood. He gripped the wheel with tense fingers and knew the meaning of hatred. He hated the unidentified man who had slaughtered the unhappy, terrified little man. He hated the ruthlessness of the act and the dreadful way in which it had been performed. He fought for self-control in silence.

A couple of miles beyond Ben's Den he swung off the boulevard into a side road and circled back toward Santa Monica. He craved lighted, crowded streets; the reassurance that would come from the presence of throngs of normal people. In a convenient space he stopped the car and parked at the curb. He felt the need to cease motion and restore calmness.

"Well?" he asked, not looking at Quality but staring grimly ahead through the windshield.

"Not followed," she said.

"Is that all you have to say?" he demanded.

Quality did not reply, did not move so much as a finger.

"Do you realize the next shot might have been for us?" he asked.

"Yes," she answered.

"Sane men," he said, "don't kill for fun. Even an insane man thinks he has a reason. Shiner was murdered to prevent him from talking to me. What could he have told me that was so dangerous to someone that if was necessary to kill him?"

"It died with him," Quality said.

"Who was Shiner?" John asked.

"What does it matter now?" she said, with an air of discouraged finality.

"Because," John said grimly, "his identity is a starting place. A place to begin the hunt. He was killed because of who he was and what he did and who were his friends and enemies. And because of what he learned. Only by knowing those facts can the police hope to find his killer."

"No police," said Quality.

"There'll be plenty of police," John said. "You can help them."

"No," she said.

"I should have stayed until the police came," John said.

"No."

"I high tailed it," he said unhappily, "because I didn't want either of us to stop a charge of shot. But, secondarily, because I didn't want us to be mixed up in a murder investigation. Not a pure and high-principled bit of conduct."

"But wise," she answered.

John sat erect and turned to face Quality as a supposition that was almost a certainty presented itself to his mind. "I think," he said, "that he was a jockey—a broken-down jockey. It should be simple to trace a jockey named Shiner. Maybe, even, to discover what broke him down and turned him into a wino hiding in some slum. Was he a jockey, Quality?"

"One of the best," she said.

"We'll drive to the nearest police station," John said. "They won't like our running away. But they'll overlook it. A quick identification—and what you can tell will square us with the officers."

"Police!" she said. For once there was emotion in her voice. There was bitter scorn. There was detestation. Quality Piper hated the police.

"You've a grudge against the law?" John asked.

"Damn the police," said Quality Piper, and there was such bitterness in her voice that it appalled John Miller.

"You'll not help them?" John asked.

"Never," she replied.

"Well," John said coldly, "that's that. Me—I'm an innocent bystander. It's your private war. I hereby declare myself out."

Sullenly he started the car and swung away from the curb. He was furious at her. She was an impossible creature and he was fed up with her and her taciturnity and her mysteries. Probably, if he had examined his reactions, he would have discovered that he resented her self-sufficiency; her tacit refusal of his assistance; her cool exclusion of himself from her affairs.

"Right," he said savagely. "You're a lone wolf. Go ahead and do your own howling."

Then she astounded him. She reached out her hand and touched his hand on the wheel. It was a gentle touch, a gesture so foreign to the girl he believed her to be that it rocked him on his foundations. His arm tingled to the shoulder.

"Please, John," she said in a lonely, little girl's voice. "Please, John."

He all but lost control of the car. With two words she had caused a revolution in his mind and heart. In that moment she was infinitely appealing; amazingly feminine and gentle and desirable. A touch of her fingers, the naming of his name, and all anger and resentment vanished. It was a glimpse, a brief lightning-flash glimpse of the girl who lived under the shell with which she protected and concealed herself. It was unbelievable, for it disclosed a sweetness, a tenderness that gave the lie to everything she had seemed to be.

"You win," he said. "Never mind the signals—you carry the ball."

He glanced at her sidewise. The peephole through which he had peered for an instant was closed and sealed. The girl he thought he had glimpsed was not there. Quality Piper, taciturn, inscrutable, master of herself and self-sufficient, had returned. John shook his head. He wondered if he had been seeing things that were not there.

"Drive," she said crisply.

The promised snack was under preparation when Quality and John reached Dolly Dove's apartment. Her negligee was covered by an apron large enough to serve as a circus tent, and she was happy as she always was when her mind was on food.

"Waffles it's going to be," she told them. "I'm the champion waffle maker of the West Coast. Sit and they'll be up in a minute."

"Miss Dolly," John said, "I haven't much appetite."

Dolly's pale, shrewd eyes took in his grimly set lips and Quality's pallor. She shrugged and disappeared into the kitchen. Presently she came back with a dish stacked with golden waffles and a huge coffeepot.

"Not a word out of either of you till you've packed these in," she said. "Something's knocked you off balance. The way to get back on an even keel is to take in ballast."

John buttered a waffle and poured syrup upon it—not because he wanted it but to please Dolly. But with the first mouthful he discovered appetite. Quality, too, was eating silently but in a workmanlike manner. Food, John discovered, did something for one. Dolly was right. One waffle did not suffice. Dolly was delighted to see him devour three with accompanying little sausages, and two cups of coffee.

"What did I tell you?" Dolly demanded. "Now get it off your chest."

"We saw a man murdered," John said.

"Well," Dolly responded, "it wasn't either of you."

"He was mowed down with a shotgun," John went on.

"Then," Dolly said practically, "it was a hired job. So what did you do? I'll guess. You used common sense and skedaddled."

"Just that," John said.

"You didn't get to talk to this Shiner person?"

"No."

"Lucky for you." Dolly was emphatic. "If he'd told you what he knew you'd be the next candidates. From now on you stick to being one-track. Producing a television show's your meat. And there's no hard-boiled private eye in it. . . . It's eleven o'clock. Bill Markey's news broadcast. Let's see if he picked it up."

She turned on the radio and Markey's familiar voice filled the room. He spoke of international affairs, of Washington developments and then proceeded to local news.

"There was a gang murder tonight," he said. "It would be only another killing but for the identity of the victim. A tragic story of descent from fame to the gutter. But a few short years ago the name of the little man whose life was blasted out by bullets from a shotgun was emblazoned on every sport page in the country. The name was Willard Joost, but the world knew him as Shiner. Papers and cards in his pocket made possible the identification. He rode great horses to great victories—in the Belmont Stakes, the Santa Anita, the Derby. Suddenly, mysteriously, he disappeared from the tracks and from the night spots of New York and Chicago and Hollywood. From the day of one of his greatest wins in the Preakness he was seen no more, until his riddled body was found near Ben's Den on the beach. A great little man comes to a pitiful finish. . . ."

Quality got up from her place and walked to her bedroom door. "Good night," she said, and closed the door after her.

John scowled at Dolly, who raised her brows and pursed her full lips.

"There's a curtain for you," Dolly said.

"It lacked punch," John said.

"Drive my car around to the garage," Dolly requested.

"Don't urge me to stay," John said ironically. "I've really got to be going."

"A couple years more," Dolly said, "and your skin'll be thicker. . . . And maybe, if God's good to you, you'll know the difference between a silk purse and a sow's ear." She laid a gross, white hand on John's arm. "It's hell to be young," she said. "For both sexes."

"It's hell to be young," John answered. "It's hell to be middle-aged. It's hell to be old."

"The trouble with boys," Dolly said, "is that they know so much—and all of it is wrong. Go on home, now, and practice aging in the wood."

John Miller walked a couple of blocks slowly, seeking a taxi-cab. His unpleasant thoughts busied themselves, not so much with the murder of the jockey Shiner, as with Quality Piper's connection with that event. A thread ran from the girl to some event in the past, an event so dark that it had spawned a murder. That event, whatever it was, might well account for Quality's reticence, her withdrawal into herself. Her connection with it might be innocent or guilty, but it had turned her into a secretive, enigmatic individual. It even occurred to John that Quality might be a fugitive, and in hiding. Her mannerism, her terseness, her withholding of herself might stem from fear. Yet she did not impress John as being afraid. Rather, it seemed to him, the apt word to describe Quality was determined. Even during the tragic event at Ben's Den she had not lost control of herself. She had maintained a rigid coolness, almost detachment. Where another girl might have been hysterical, Quality scarcely trembled. No, John decided, she was not afraid.

He hailed a cab which took him to McCadden Place. It is not to be wondered that he peered about him cautiously as he alighted. But the street was dark and silent. He mounted the stairs, unlocked his door and thrust it open, but did not step inside. The memory of the blow on his head was fresh in his mind. He reached inside and snapped on the light before he entered. When the room was empty he was ashamed of his caution.

John sat on the edge of the bed and resented the turmoil that suddenly had disturbed his placid life. He resented Quality Piper who had brought the turmoil with her. He wished heartily that he never had encountered Quality. Then, in no pleasant state of mind, he turned off the light and got into bed.

In the morning he got up, made his breakfast and went out for a paper. Shiner had made the front page. The few bare facts of his killing made up the lead; the rest of the column-long story had to do with his history, his triumphs, his unaccountable disappearance at the height of his career. The last winner he had ridden was the famous Bluenose, owned by the Tuscarora Stables. So far as could be learned Shiner had been in no trouble with track officials, or in his private life. He had vanished within two days and no reason for his conduct had ever been discovered.

John telephoned Zagic Quiros. When he was connected and had greeted Zagic, he said, "You know a lot of odd people, Zagic. Is there a horse-player in your collection?"

"Sure. What kind of horse-player you want?"

"Are there different kinds? I want one with statistics. These people study races as Einstein studies mathematics, I hear. They know horses' names and past performances and jockeys and trainers and things like that."

"I know a jackanapes," Zagic said, "that can recite every race since Maud S. trotted a mile in 2:8¾ seventy-odd years ago, with weights and jockeys and track conditions and odds."

"Can you unearth him and bring him to lunch this noon? At the Beverly Hills."

"This horse encyclopedia eats with his knife," Zagic said. "Make it another place where he can display his art without creating a sensation. Make it Marty's Tavern."

"Right you are," John said.

At noon John waited the arrival of Zagic and his friend at the place of rendezvous. Zagic introduced the horse-player as Feed Box Sullivan. The man looked like a truck driver because he he was a truck driver in those intervals when he found it necessary to work for a living. They found a table, ordered drinks, and Zagic asked, "What use you got for Feed Box?"

"Information," John said.

"I ain't no tout," Feed Box said.

"And I don't bet," John said.

Feed Box stared at John as if there was something very queer about him. "Don't bet!" he exclaimed. "What's the idea? Your friend eccentric? What kind of info does he need?"

"About a man. Ever hear of a jockey called Shiner?"

Feed Box narrowed his eyes suspiciously. "I hear of him plenty. I read about him this morning. You keep healthy by not talking about fellers that get themselves blasted. What's your racket, Mister?"

"I write television plays," John said. "It looked to me as if there might be a good mystery play written about this Shiner."

"Sounds screwy."

"He's leveling with you, Feed Box," Zagic hastened to say. "It's the way writers are—screwy like you say."

Feed Box was not completely satisfied, but he shrugged and squinted at John and decided to humor his screwiness. "You ask," he said. "I answer—maybe."

"Start at the beginning," John said.

"Shiner, he starts as a stable boy. Tuscarora Stables. Gets to be exercise boy. After a while they give him a mount. He wins. He's got somethin'. He talks to horses, what I mean. He gets noticed." Feed Box recited a list of horses ridden by Shiner, and the times in which he had finished and the purses he had won. "He's in the money," Feed Box went on. "It gets so you bet on him instead of the gee-gee. I hear he got twelve suits of clothes and five-buck neckties and he learns not to wipe his nose on his sleeve. Then he ups and blows." Feed Box shrugged. "He just hain't there, see?"

"Why?" asked John.

"His top must 'a' come loose."

"No trouble?"

"The way I hear it he's clean."

"Who did he ride for?"

"Different ones—but Tuscarora Stables got first call. No contract I hear tell. But on account he's much obliged to the Tuscarora trainer for givin' him a leg up when he's stable boy. The way the boys tell it Shiner and this trainer are just like a foal and its dam." Feed Box's blue eyes were dreamy. "You ever see a foal and dam playin' around in the paddock? Awful purty sight. About the purtiest sight the' is." An expression of almost maudlin sentimentality was upon Feed Box's face.

"Keep going," John said.

"So when this trainer does the Dutch," Feed Box said, "Shiner's upset. He's on the coast when it happens and gives Sample Room a bad ride in the Santa Anita that day, and he flies back to the funeral."

"This trainer," John asked, "why did he commit suicide?"

"I get it from the horse's mouth he's got a disease that can't be cured. He blasts hisself out with a twelve-gauge."

"Shotgun?" asked John.

"Never hear of no other kind of a twelve-gauge," said Feed Box.

"What," asked John, "was this trainer's name?"

"Best horse conditioner in the country," Feed Box said.

"How long," John asked, "was this suicide before Shiner disappeared? What was his name?"

"Along three, four, five months before," Feed Box answered. "If I remember right. His name? Sure he had a name. Piper it was. Yeah. Marvin Piper. . . . And Shiner never rode agin without a mournin' band around his arm."

John sat rigid and silent for a moment. "Suicide?" he asked.

"That's what the inquest said," answered Feed Box.

John's lips felt stiff as he spoke again. "I'm obliged to you, Feed Box," he said. "I must get along. I've things to think about."

Zagic peered across at his friend. "I shouldn't be surprised if you had," he said.

chapter EIGHT

For the first time the full cast of the Famous Names Group was assembled and made acquainted with each other. In Dolly Dove's living room were America's old Sweetheart, the courtly Kent Farraday, Martha Scruggs, whose famous name had not been determined as yet, Benjamin Franklin, freckled and awkward. These were the actors. John Miller, of course, was there and Zagic Quiros. But there was no doubt as to who was the executive of the little organization. Quality Piper dominated.

"Before anything else," Zagic said, "we got to christen Miss Scruggs. Names are lucky or unlucky. A famous name we got to choose. Scruggs! Ouch! It hurts my ears to listen to it."

"How about Betty Stark?" John asked.

"Who's this Betty Stark?"

"She fought the Battle of Bennington."

"Warriors we don't want. Also I never heard of her. If I ain't heard of her then she ain't famous."

"Florence Nightingale," John suggested.

"No birds," Zagic objected. "Listen. I got one. Jenny Lind. And why? Well, it was good enough for P. T. Barnum and he was the greatest publicity guy ever lived. Look what he did with Jenny Lind! You like it better than Scruggs, Miss Scruggs?"

"I like it," Martha said.

"Everybody agree?"

There was agreement and the roster of famous names was complete. "Now," Zagic said, "I rush out publicity releases."

"Too early for publicity," said John.

"It's never too early for publicity," answered Zagic.

"May we read now?" asked Quality. "This is a tryout for Benjamin Franklin and Miss Scruggs. . . . If you please."

Each member of the group held a manuscript of the play. They sat comfortably about the room awaiting the signal to begin. John was to discover that Quality could express herself when it came to matters of direction or of technique. She wasted no words, but her meaning was clear.

"The scene," she said, "is a living room. Father sits with newspaper under a reading lamp. Enter son. Proceed, Mr. Franklin."

The young man read his first lines. Farraday Kent responded, and the first reading was under way. Each actor endeavored to become the character he portrayed, even though there were no costumes, no movements, and manuscript was used. Quality gave her strictest attention to young Ben Franklin and Martha Scruggs. The girl had personality and intelligence. She understood the character of the daughter and succeeded, even in this first reading, in conveying nuances of voice and manner that established her as a young girl who fancied herself as a woman of the world but whose real naïveté peeped through the surface. It was not overplayed. It was excellent.

But it was Ben Franklin who made the striking impression. His was essentially a comedy role. He never permitted it to descend into farce, seemed to understand the art of underplaying and of timing. John saw his conception of the hobbledehoy son coming to life. This boy, he realized, was a find. He glanced at Quality to see if her satisfaction equaled his own. She was peering at Ben Franklin with an expression which John could not read. It was an intent expression. It seemed to John that she was trying to answer some question. She said nothing either of criticism or commendation.

"Enough," she said.

"Don't you want to run through it again?" John asked.

"Not tonight. . . . Miss Scruggs, Mr. Franklin, I will telephone you in the morning."

The young people understood. They were dismissed in order that the older members of the group might discuss them and their reading and arrive at a decision as to whether they should be admitted to the co-operative.

"May I take you home, Miss Scruggs?" Benjamin asked.

"From now on she's Jenny Lind," Zagic insisted.

"Thank you, Mr. Franklin." She smiled charmingly. "I think we'd better get used to calling me Jenny. . . . Provided, of course, I make the grade."

They said good night and went out together. Those who remained gathered around the table.

"Well?" asked John.

"It moves. It plays," said Quality.

"It seems so to me," said Kent Farraday. "The boy was rather remarkable."

Quality was frowning slightly. "Remarkable," she said.

"Why," John asked, "were you staring at him?"

"An alarm bell rang," she said.

"What do you mean by that, Quality?" John asked. "He was good—good. That boy has a future."

"What kind?" Quality asked.

"He fits the part like a pair of tights," Zagic said.

"Yes," answered Quality. "But."

"But what? I saw nothing wrong, Miss Piper. I was impressed." This from Kent Farraday.

"There's something," Quality said.

"Toots has broken out with an intuition," said Dolly.

"What did you find wrong?" John demanded.

"Nothing," Quality answered. "But an alarm bell rang."

"Warning of what?" John asked a bit impatiently.

"A boy," Quality said, "can be a good actor." She paused and stared at the carpet. "And a bad actor," she finished. She shook off the mood that depressed her. "I think we should risk him," she said.

"Risk?" John asked.

"To me," she said, "he is a calculated risk."

"Maybe it's something you ate," Zagic said.

"I hope so," she replied.

"With that settled," John said, "how about the girl?"

"Excellent," was Kent Farraday's opinion.

Quality nodded assent.

"No inklings about her?" John asked with a touch of sarcasm.

"None," answered Quality.

"So," said Zagic, "we got a troupe. We got actors. We got a play. Everything we got except money. Do we get black masks and rob a bank?"

"Mr. Farraday," John said, "this means a great deal to you."

"My young friend," Mr. Farraday said, "I doubt if you can understand how much it means."

"And to you, Miss Dove?"

"Not the way it does to Kent," Dolly said, and her pale eyes regarded Farraday with understanding and sympathy. "I'm fixed. I can eat. . . . But another way it means a lot to me. An awful lot."

"After hearing this script read tonight," John said, "I'm sure we could sell to one of the networks. I don't want to do that— but I feel an obligation to you folks. I don't want to stand in the way of a comeback for you, Mr. Farraday—or you, Miss Dove."

"Now listen," Zagic said, "the chances are a network would take only the script. They'd do their own casting. Maybe they wouldn't go for this idea of the Famous Names Group."

"Perhaps I could stipulate that," John said. "Shall I put it up to them?" He paused and looked from one to the other. "I'll put it to a vote. Miss Dove?"

Dolly pursed her lips and frowned and hesitated. "No," she said.

"Mr. Farraday?"

The old actor's face worked. It was his last chance, perhaps, this script. A network might accept him with the play. It might not be possible to finance. The decision he was asked to make might send him back into obscurity and poverty. He threw back his shoulders and lifted his chin.

"No," he voted.

"Quality?"

"No."

"And Zagic?"

"Nix," said the publicity man.

John brushed the back of his hand across his eyes and spoke with some difficulty. "You," he said slowly, "are magnificent people." His jaw set with determination. "I'll raise that money to carry on—or bust," he said.

"Well," said Dolly, dusting her hands, "that's that. Now I'll crochet a snack. We'll feed the butterflies in our stomachs so they won't flutter so much."

She and Quality went into the kitchen leaving John and Kent Farraday and Zagic in the living room. They were glum. Fifteen thousand dollars was an enormous sum to raise.

"Mr. Farraday," John asked, "are you sure you don't want to change your vote?"

"Mr. Miller," the old actor said, "no man is completely bankrupt if he retains his self-respect."

The three men went down the stairs together. "We're all going the same way," Zagic said. "What say we walk a little? Seems like I could sleep better if we tied on a nightcap."

"I would relish it," said Kent Farraday. "Not for medicinal purposes as you suggest, Mr. Quiros, but to promote sociability and to lead us to a better acquaintance with each other."

"Mr. Farraday," John said, "I would like to ask a question. If the subject is repugnant to you, I will drop it."

"No subject, Mr. Miller, which is of interest to you could be repugnant to me," Farraday said in the grand manner.

"At our first meeting before Mike Romanoff's door," John said, "I got the impression that you had been waiting to speak to Humphrey Salmon."

"That is true," Farraday said. "I so far forgot my pride as to seek a word with that man."

"He acted," John went on, "as if there was something deeper than mere drunken resentment at being accosted. As if, Mr. Farraday, he held a spite against you."

"There is no enmity," Farraday replied, "more bitter than that of an individual who has wronged another for the man he has wronged."

"Would you care to tell me more?"

"I fear it would boot nothing. In a moment of dire need I humiliated myself to plead for, at least, partial restitution. Why do you ask these questions?"

"Because," John said, "he's a problem. He seems to be meddling in our affairs."

"That," Farraday said, "could be because of me."

"No," John replied thoughtfully. "He wants our show."

"How would he know about it?"

"When I went home that night—after we dined in Romanoff's—someone was in my apartment. He smacked me with a blunt instrument and stole my brief case in which was a copy of our script and an outline of our project. No ordinary prowler would have taken those papers. I reason from cause to effect. I punch Mr. Salmon; Mr. Salmon responds by sending a friend to slug me. But I think there's more to it than trying to get possession of our show. It isn't big enough."

"We don't know yet how big it may be," Farraday said. "Salmon is a shrewd man. No fish is too small for his net."

John walked along in silence, pondering. Finally he asked another question. "Mr. Farraday, did you ever encounter a jockey who was called Shiner?"

"Who was brutally murdered last night? When I knew him he was not a jockey. He was a humble stable boy. I can't say I knew him. I remember watching him exercising horses. The name stuck in my memory because his employer thought he was a promising lad." He sighed. "Those," he said, "were the old days, when I had a wider acquaintance. When, if I may say so, I was sought after."

"Would you also remember the name of his employer?"

"Of course. The Tuscarora Stables."

"And the trainer, who thought Shiner was a promising boy?"

Farraday sighed. He did not turn to look at John. "It is, indeed, a small world," he said.

"Marvin Piper," John persisted, "had a daughter."

"I knew her as a cunning little girl," Farraday said. "I would not have recognized her that night but for the name."

"Which," John said, "brings us back to Humphrey Salmon. Was he visible then? Was he in any way connected with the Tuscarora Stables or with Marvin Piper?"

"Of a connection I would not know. Salmon was known at the tracks. He owned a few horses. It was possible he knew Marvin Piper as most horsemen knew a great trainer and a splendid man."

"Who, nevertheless, killed himself," John said grimly.

"It was said he had an incurable illness."

"I do not think Quality Piper believes her father had an incurable illness," John said. "It would account for many things if Quality believed her father was murdered." He paused again, considering if he should make the disclosure and decided it was best to do so. "Quality and I," he said gravely, "saw Shiner murdered last night. He was killed to stop his tongue. He had something to tell, and he intended to tell it to me. We went out to meet him at Ben's Den. We were not fifty feet from him when he died."

"Sweet, suffering, hard-scaled crocodiles!" Zagic exclaimed. "What have we stuck our snoots into? Me, I'm just a publicity guy without a punch in either hand. I want out."

Farraday halted and faced John Miller. "Miss Quality was there! She saw that dreadful sight! Shocking! Shocking! . . . The poor child. How did she react, sir?"

"She reacted," John said bitterly, "with silence."

"Now I really need a drink," Zagic interjected.

"The conclusion one is forced to draw," said Kent Farraday, "is that Miss Quality is right. That her father suffered from no malady. And the inescapable fact is that he was the victim of an assassin."

"Right," John replied, "and the next conclusion is that the

thing that drives her is to find her father's killer. It explains her."

Zagic expelled a breath noisily. "Which," he said huskily, "kind of, sort of, after a manner of speaking, pushes us up to another bloody unsettlin' point."

"Which is?" asked John.

"That Miss Quality Piper is the logical selection by all form sheets as the most likely to succeed in going to bed on a slab in the morgue."

"Quite," John said succinctly.

"What I need," Zagic said, "ain't just a noggin of rum. It's a consecutive flock of 'em, leadin' up to a blackout. Me, I want to forget."

chapter NINE

The Sunset Studios in Culver City was a sprawling collection of buildings set at odd angles. It appeared to have grown aimlessly rather than to have been planned. There were no great sound stages such as one finds on the lots of MGM and Columbia and Warner Brothers. A minimum of great picture art had been given to the world by Rolf Agnew, who was its genius. Every motion picture company must have at least one Genius, spelled with a capital G. But Rolf's talents did not run to great spectacles or epoch-marking dramas. His forte was comedy or even farce. The brief masterpieces which he produced were seldom flaunted in lights over the marquees of theaters. They followed the news reels and preceded the feature. But Mr. Agnew was highly regarded in the profession because he possessed a desirable quality. He made money. High art has emanated from Hollywood; it has made fine contributions to the ephemeral literature or drama of our times. But even pure art in that city is subjected to the yardstick implied in the question—What did it do in the box offices? Which, after all, is not a thing to be caviled at, because virtue deserves its reward, and the more reward it receives the more virtue it contains.

Rolf Agnew operated his studios to make money. In this he was successful, and in addition he gave the exquisite pleasure of belly laughs to millions of his fellow countrymen.

John Miller waited in the outer office, which was located in a sort of cottage up a cul-de-sac. He had made an appointment with Agnew by telephone. Quality Piper had told him that the Sunset Studios was a suitable place in which to make his pilot film from the standpoint of equipment, efficiency and cost. But he wanted to see for himself. He was not kept cooling his heels. His appointment was for ten o'clock and promptly at that hour he was admitted to the presence.

The presence was a genial, burly man whom nature might have intended to be a roustabout but had confused its ingredients. The body was that of a stevedore, but nature, in an absent-minded moment, had equipped it with imagination and shrewdness and a sense of humor. Physically he did not fit his office, and his office did not fit the general idea of a place of business. It was a pleasant living room, furnished and decorated with taste. It was rather a place in which to receive one's friends socially than a place in which to manage a concern whose success depended upon the ability to cut corners, to avail one's self of economies and to get the best of bargains.

Rolf Agnew, one sturdy leg over the arm of his chair, was comfortable. He grinned and waved John Miller to a comfortable chair.

"So," he said genially, "you see gold in them thar television hills."

"I'd like to prospect for some of it," John answered.

"Contrary," said Agnew, "to glowing rumors you don't get to it with a jackass, a pick and a setting of sour dough."

"So I understand," John said. "On the other hand a man might find it without floating a bond issue. Experts tell me I have to have twenty-five or thirty thousand dollars to make a pilot film."

"Shucks, Mr. Miller. You've been talking to the boys who do things in the grand manner including court etiquette and genuine Rembrandts on the wall." He snorted. "Anything the lavish lads can do for thirty thousand I can do for fifteen."

"Including actors' salaries?" John asked.

"Providing you don't want Clark Gable and Greta Garbo."

"My actors draw no salaries."

"Amateurs?" Agnew asked with raised brows.

"No," John said, "partners."

"Say that again," Agnew said, ceasing to rock in his chair.

"My outfit," John explained, "is a co-operative. We're all owners."

"Sounds screwy," Agnew said, but he was interested. "What kind of actors did you hornswoggle into that kind of a deal?"

John's eyes twinkled. "Here's the cast," he said. "Dolly Dove, Kent Farraday, Jenny Lind, Benjamin Franklin."

Agnew's eyes bugged. "You sure went out with a shovel and robbed graves."

"The name of our company," John said, "is the Famous Names Group."

"Complete with epitaphs," Agnew said, but not scornfully. "Son, maybe you dived in and came up with an idea." He waggled his shaggy head. "There have been some startling resurrections in this television racket. Dolly Dove! Old Kent Farraday!"

"They're not forgotten."

"Son," Agnew cautioned, "you're in Hollywood. An idea around this town is something you don't broadcast. You're safer toting a roll of bills into a sailor's dive than trotting around this burg with a notion that'll pay off. Next morning you wake up and some quick-thinker has cobbed it and put it into production."

"The name," John said, "is copyrighted. And I don't trumpet the idea. I'm telling you because the story goes that you deal off the top of the deck."

"That's the rumor, is it?" Agnew said. "Huh. . . . Besides this troupe of yours, have you got a script?"

"Scripts for four shows," John told him.

"So you got actors and you got a script. What's holding you back?"

"Cash," John answered.

"I've heard of it. Got a script with you?"

John opened his brief case and tossed a folder on the desk.

"It's a slack day," Agnew said. "Want I should read it?"

"If you've the time."

Agnew sat back and read swiftly with practiced eyes. When he had finished he turned back and reread a couple of scenes.

"It's got a chance," he said cautiously. "Cash, eh? Now I tell you what, Mr. Miller. I like your Famous Names angle. I like your script. I'll make your pilot film for you."

"On what terms, Mr. Agnew?"

"In this business everything's a gamble. You make, for instance, *Ivanhoe* with an all-star cast and color and all the doodads. It's still a gamble. Maybe you get back your nut only; maybe you make millions. It all depends if the ball drops on the right number. . . . So I make a bet on you. For fifty per cent of this charade I furnish studio, crew, lights, sound and quite a chunk of know-how."

"Sorry, Mr. Agnew. We're parting with no slice of it. All or nothing."

Agnew nodded. "You also are a gambler," he said. "But you'll think it over. Now come out and see what we have here. Maybe somebody's working." He clicked a switch and spoke into the box on his desk. "Gerty," he said, "any company working?"

"Cops and Robbers," a voice answered.

"Ever see a television show being born, Mr. Miller?"

"Never."

"Come along then. This is a whodunit. Got a good rating. Bill Boyle is the private eye."

They walked out of the office and debouched upon a paved road between brick structures. A couple of hundred feet along Agnew led John up a ramp to a broad platform leading to enormous doors capable of admitting a locomotive. Just as they reached this portal a bell rang and a red light flashed.

"That blocks us," Agnew said. "They're turning. Won't be but a couple of minutes." He pointed to a housed vehicle in the road. "That's the sound truck," he explained. "Records the dialogue for the sound track." He frowned. "Music," he said. "Wish we could get along without music, but we can't. Background music. Petrillo! For using music he grabs five per cent of the gross."

75

It was only a matter of minutes before the red light over the door extinguished itself and Agnew pushed open one of the tall leaves to enter a huge interior cluttered with lumber, furniture, scenery, electrical equipment. The *Cops and Robbers* company was working toward the far end of the room. To John it looked like a confused mob scene, a clutter of technicians in overalls, two or three people seated in camp chairs, half a dozen men whose functions he did not understand, a girl at the side, seated, with papers on her lap. This, he guessed, was the script girl whose duty it was, among a multitude, to see to it that the star did not wear a four-in-hand tie in one scene and a bow tie in the next; or that a smoking cigarette on an ash tray was there continuing to smoke in the succeeding scene which might be taken an hour later. Under her eyes was the breakdown of scenes. A very important and responsible job. It was Quality Piper's job in her studio.

Agnew was speaking. "There's the mixer," he said, pointing to a box at the side. "It takes noises, such as dialogue, music, incidental sounds and regulates them and blends them together."

Cables snaked over the floor leading to lights on standards, to long booms from which microphones were suspended, to the many electrical devices necessary to the correct lighting of a scene. In a glow of light beyond the milling technical people was the set, an office scene. Behind the desk sat the star of the show, bending over him was another actor. They were in brief discussion. A girl stepped in front of them before the camera and a gadget in her hands made a slapping sound. This was the slate identifying the scene for the cutting room. Silence fell and the clustered group stood motionless. A buzzer sounded and the outer doors were closed again to traffic.

"Quiet," ordered the director.

"Turning," said the mixer in charge and pressed the red button on his sound panel, the button controlling a ganglia of electrical nerves. It started the sound-film recorder, the synchronized camera motor, shut off ventilating fans and the possible ringing of a telephone bell, and started the warning of the red light and buzzer outside.

After about three seconds someone called, "Speed." The director called, "Action."

Then, before the scene could start, the director halted it, calling sharply, "Kill that junior and put a silk on one of the broads."

This was jargon to John Miller. Later inquiry told him it meant to put out a tiny spotlight and hang a diffusion cloth over an oblong side light. This was to eliminate a hot spot at the left of the desk.

When, again, conversation was permitted Rolf Agnew continued John's education. "One reason the amateurs bump their bottoms," he said, "is that it takes pros to handle lighting. You can have a good story and a top cast, but if you get bum lighting you're up the creek without a bucket. And lighting for television is another colored cat from lighting for the motion pictures. A scene that might do in a theater could give nothing but black figures groping in a fog on your home screen. This is a business where you have to know your stuff. And you have to punctuate your action just as you have to use periods and commas and exclamation points in writing. You do it with close-ups and with off-stage sounds and so forth and so on."

"But do you need this mob of people to do the trick?"

"Young man, I'm a penny pincher. If I could get along without one of them he'd be sitting at home." He quirked his head. "Listen," he directed.

Staccato orders were being given. "Tip that broad so it doesn't hit full flood. Try a single silk. Gobo the baby. Take the junk off junior in the corner. Swing the one with the snoot for a little backlight. Gimme a drip net. I want a baby on a stick right there. . . . O.K. Save 'em!"

"Those things," Agnew said, "make the difference between a picture that knocks 'em dead, and a flop. You can't do it by guess and by God. It takes savvy and experience, and it costs money."

"You're making a swell sales pitch," John said with a laugh.

"I'm making no pitch. I don't give a hoot whether I get your business or not—much. I'm trying to make you see a great light.

77

I'm trying to butt it into your skull that second best is no good."

"I'm converted," John answered.

"My good deed for the day," Agnew said. "Now I can tie a knot in my handkerchief. Seen enough for lesson one?"

"More," John admitted, "than my digestion can handle."

Agnew led John back to the office. "Anything more I can contribute?" he asked.

"I'm grateful, really grateful, Mr. Agnew, for your graciousness."

"I'm a gracious feller," said Agnew. He cleared his throat, "Always, when mebbe there's a dollar in it for the old man. . . . Think over my seductive offer, Mr. Miller. It stands till further notice."

John took a taxi back to Hollywood. He wanted to digest what he had seen and heard over a good luncheon so he told his driver to take him to the Beverly Hills Hotel. By good fortune there was a small table to which he was shown by the headwaiter. He ordered a cocktail and settled back comfortably. The room was filled with the usual patronage of chattering patrons, with beautiful girls, with notables from the motion-picture world and with hangers-on who hoped to attract the attention of the notables.

Business conducted itself even here. Telephones had been plugged in at tables so their occupants could keep in constant touch with their offices, or discuss problems, or make propositions. In Hollywood a man's importance seems to be measured by the amount of telephoning he does—especially in public places where he can be observed plying his trade. One thick, foreign voice was bellowing across the continent to New York. "You should do quick what I order. . . . You should get dis writer. You should on a plane put him today. Tomorrow he must be here. . . . Vat! He don't vant to come! What I care what he vants. . . . Iss dis a man that runs up and down elevators who is speaking, or is it Lorenzo the Great? Tell me that. I vant this man. I vant him in the morning. What he asks, pay him. Otherwise you got no job any more. Understand that? No job."

He banged down the receiver. "Jacks-asses," he roared, and commenced wholeheartedly to spill soup on his vest.

John grinned. Incredible, perhaps. Comical undoubtedly. But this man was a great director—a power, a waver of magic wands, and a decreer of life and death who had no faint doubt that the world was blessed with the presence of no greater man than he.

John heard another voice speaking over the telephone. It was a low, musical, beautiful, good-humored voice, a voice which, once heard, was not to be forgotten. Especially not to be forgotten with the telephone for a reminder. John sat with fork suspended, every faculty alerted. He turned his head slowly. The girl who spoke into the telephone was slender but luscious. Her hair was spun silver. Her eyes were violet; her face was one of peculiar and individual beauty. There was an odd but gracious charm, not only of appearance but of manner. If her head, her shoulders, her arms, her breasts were equaled by the unseen portion of her figure, then, from top to toe she was one of the most desirable women John Miller ever had seen.

He listened with grim intentness. What she was saying was inconsequential chitchat, but her voice was not inconsequential. John had heard it once before, only once, and it had come to him over the telephone. He could not be mistaken in that gay, contralto voice. He would take his Bible oath he was listening now to the girl who had talked to him over the wire so shortly after he recovered consciousness after being struck down in his apartment!

There she sat, charming, alluring, with every indication of being innocent as a playful kitten. She replaced the receiver and turned to her companion, a young man in a conservative sports coat. From his appearance as seen from the back, just another young man. He turned his head so that John could see his profile. John did not know him. His features were good. There was nothing about him to suggest faintly that he was anything but a rather pleasant-looking young man of some position, either socially or in business. He seemed sure of himself, but not cocky. He could be a young executive occupying a lucrative position, or, more likely, the son of a wealthy father.

79

As John studied the couple it was inconceivable to him that either of them could have discreditable connections or be involved in a world where bludgeons were regarded merely as tools of the trade.

John got up from his chair and walked to the door where the headwaiter stood at his post. He passed a bill into the headwaiter's palm.

"I wonder," he said in a low voice, "if you can tell me the name of the young lady at the table against the wall—the one with the silver hair?"

The headwaiter smirked. "Surely," he answered. "That is Miss Loretta Kimball."

"An actress?"

"Oh, no, sir. Not an actress. Just a young lady, sir. A very nice young lady who has a great many friends."

"Would she," John asked, "be a friend of Mr. Humphrey Salmon?"

"That I would not know. I have never seen him with her. All I can tell you about her, sir, is that she comes here frequently for luncheon, and seldom with the same gentleman."

"Thank you," John said, and returned to his seat. He sat staring at Miss Kimball. She became conscious of his attention and their eyes met. There was no sign of recognition. She smiled with spontaneous good humor—as if she liked the world and everybody in it and was willing to smile out of the abundance of her contentment. Not a provocative smile, nor a coquettish smile. Merely a casual smile signifying nothing but a warm liking for everybody and everything.

John hurried through his lunch, paid his check and sat smoking a cigarette. By an effort of will he prevented himself from staring at Loretta Kimball, but he listened with intent care. What he heard was only pleasant chatter; the give and take of two cultured young people who, obviously, enjoyed each other's company.

"This has been nice, Freddie," he heard her say. "You're an agreeable person. But I must hurry along. I've a very, very important engagement at home, and I mustn't be late. My hairdresser is coming."

"What," asked Freddie, "can a hairdresser do to improve you?"

"She's not for improvement but to help me keep what I've got," she told him. "And to give me all the gossip. Between her and my masseuse I'm the best-informed girl in Hollywood."

She stood up in one lithe, graceful movement. "No," she said, "you mustn't come along. I'm going to walk home—alone. I like to reverie. Do you ever? It's fun. Give me a ring—huh?" It was very cunning the way she said "huh."

She floated out of the room, and John noted that there was nothing disappointing about the part of her that had been concealed by the table. He followed. She walked around to the lobby with little, staccato steps, looking neither to right nor left. No one spoke to her as she turned past the desk to the front door of the hotel. Apparently she was working, already, on her reverie. At the foot of the steps she spoke to the starter, shaking her head when he suggested a taxicab. She clicked down the curving walk to the Boulevard, waited for the light to change and crossed to the other side. Once safely through the traffic, she turned to the left, chin high, face rapt. John followed at a discreet distance.

She walked briskly a few blocks and then turned into a driveway which wound up the hill and disappeared between a pair of stone gatehouses between which the way was barred by huge, ornamental iron gates. By some magic the leaves of the gates opened as she approached them, and she vanished.

John stopped and gaped. He stood before the entrance to an estate in the city. The house he could not see, but it was easy to imagine that it would fit its opulent setting. To live in a home like this meant money, a great deal of money; and everywhere money means power and influence.

John repeated her name: Loretta Kimball. It meant nothing to him; he knew no one of that name who stood on the heights in Hollywood.

A voice spoke at his elbow, soft and courteous.

"You were interested in the young lady?" it asked.

John turned to face a man in his thirties, an immaculately tailored man with the ugliest, most brutish face he ever had encountered. The voice and the face could not belong to the same individual. The tones were cultured and the manner urbane, but the features were those of a Silenus who had degenerated into a preliminary prize fighter.

"Who wants to know?" John demanded.

"Let's not be at cross purposes," the man said. "I detest cross purposes."

"And what," John persisted, "if I was interested in the young lady?"

"No one will object," was the reply, "so long as you keep your interest in the past tense. You saw her, you were attracted, you followed her. Quite natural, I'm sure. Store it away in your memory as a pleasant episode." The smile that accompanied these words was an ugly grimace. "But keep it in storage."

"And if I don't?"

"Now, now," said the Gargoyle, "please don't try to irritate me. It is very disturbing to be irritated, so I never permit it to happen."

"But if it does happen?" John asked.

"Let's not contemplate that. . . . It has been charming to encounter you, sir. End of episode."

The individual turned on his heel and sauntered away leaving John in a state of mind that bordered upon quandary. His mood was bellicose. He was all for demanding explanations, forcing issues. But wiser counsels prevailed. And, after all, he had not been guiltless. He had followed a strange young woman. . . . It was wholly possible that a girl living in such a mansion might be equipped with a bodyguard. Unsuspected by herself she might be under that sort of guardianship when she went out alone. John drew a deep breath and went on his way. His immediate mission was to discover who lived behind those iron gates.

chapter TEN

It was no difficult matter for John Miller to discover that the owner of the palatial estate into which Loretta Kimball had disappeared was Jabez Winkleman, President of Pan-Pacific Oil. But to identify the girl was not so easy. Her name indicated that she was not a daughter. He went home and sat at the telephone but none of the contacts he made was able to give him information. Not even Dolly Dove, who knew the motion-picture world and its gossip in its most intimate details, could enlighten him. Miss Kimball did not gravitate in that world.

"What's this caper?" she wanted to know. "For why are you lathered up about this Kimball sugar plum?"

"I might," John told her, "want to nibble it."

"I got other plans for you," Dolly snapped, "but if you got to know I'll telephone Mattie."

"Who is Mattie?"

"Runs a syndicated gossip column. Mattie Service. She's a topflight keyhole peeper. Sit tight and I'll call you back."

"Find out," John directed, "if she's a little playmate of Humphrey Salmon."

"Snooper," Dolly said.

In half an hour she called back. "This Kimball sugar plum," she said, "is a hunk of enigma. She nests in old Jabez Winkleman's house. Little birds twitter that she's Winkleman's niece, or secretary, or a combination, or a relative of his wife. The wife's ironclad, so there's nothing naughty. Jabez belongs to the old school that would wreck a bank but wouldn't notice Ava Gardner in a bathing suit. If she's a working girl the hours are short. She eats with nice people in the conservative set and goes out to Dimity Farms to feed lumps of sugar to Jabez' ponies. Period."

"What's Dimity Farms?"

"It's a place where race horses have babies and eat expensive grass and learn table manners."

"Horses," John said frowning, "keep galloping into the picture."

"Was I helpful?" Dolly asked.

"Not very," John told her.

"Give me an easier snooping job next time," Dolly said. "Like finding out if Stalin was a Communst. Goo'-by."

Presently the telephone rang again. It was Rolf Agnew speaking. "Listen, Miller," he asked, "who don't like you and why?"

"I suppose numerous people dislike me for various reasons," John answered. "Why do you ask?"

"The word's out against you," Agnew said.

"Meaning what?"

"Sometimes," Agnew said, "the word speeds around in this town that certain people come off on you if you touch 'em. They got a form of leprosy. The hint works down from the top and nobody knows who started it on its way. It says hands off this character. No touch."

"And this word has gone out against me?"

"Emphatic," said Agnew.

"It came to you?"

"Within an hour after you left my office."

"In what form and from whom?"

"I didn't say," Agnew answered. "But it was known that you came to see me, and why. Eyes must be on you, Miller. What makes you sticky?"

"I'm just a writer with a script. I never kicked anybody's dog."

"If," said Agnew, "there was such a thing as a blacklist in

Hollywood, you'd be at the head of it by two laps. Sure you didn't rob Warner Brothers' safe, or tweak Louis B. Mayer's nose or pin a Kick-Me sign on Harry Cohn's back?"

"I never molested any of these gentlemen."

"Anyhow," Agnew said, "you're a skunk at a strawberry festival."

"So," John asked curtly, "I can't play in your yard?"

"That," answered Agnew, "I didn't announce. Take me, I ain't pint size in this racket. I don't get told. Unless there's a cogent reason. I'm too bulky to shove easy. Before I slam the door in somebody's face I ask why I should. So I'm asking you."

"Could this come about," John asked, reaching the quick decision to spread his cards, "because I bopped a citizen named Humphrey Salmon on the button a while ago?"

There came a change in Agnew's voice. "What name did you mention?"

"Humphrey Salmon."

"I heard you the first time," Agnew said. "So you dusted Salmon, did you? Where occurred this fistic episode?"

"In front of Mike Romanoff's."

"With spectators?"

"A few."

"When Salmon stops this punch," Agnew asked, "how did he react?"

"He got up off the sidewalk and strolled away."

"He's a hunk of man. You must pack a wallop. What caused the fracas?"

"He pushed an old gentleman by the name of Kent Farraday. Whom I never had seen before. Nor had I ever seen Salmon. But it irritated me."

"You picked a jim-dandy to slug," Agnew said. John heard a chuckle. "In my book, you could hunt through the telephone book and not find a punching bag would draw louder cheers from me."

"Has Salmon power to send out the word against me?" John wanted to know.

"He's got a say-so," Agnew answered. "Nobody can put his finger on exactly why."

"Salmon seemed not to hold resentment. He came up to me at Santa Anita the next day and apologized."

"So!" Agnew exclaimed. "That ain't good."

"Maybe it was his idea of humor. I think he evened things up after our meeting. I stepped into my apartment, and the next I knew I was picking myself off the floor with a lump on my head. And my brief case missing. My guess is that Salmon sent a representative by the name of Sligo McNulty to express his appreciation with a cudgel."

"All of which," Agnew said, "are circumstances which alter cases. You mind the offer I made you?"

"Yes," John said.

"It still stands," Agnew stated, and hung up the telephone in John's ear.

John uncovered his typewriter and inserted paper, but it remained blank. Concentration denied itself to him; his mind flickered and he could not compel it to steadiness. Too many considerations disturbed him. He found himself in argument with his conscience about his obligations to Dolly Dove and Kent Farraday and Quality Piper. Agnew's offer would insure them their chance at resurrection in the amusement world. Agnew, he felt instinctively, was a trustworthy man. Agnew would retain the idea of the Famous Names Group and would not displace its members with others of his own selection. It would be possible to go to work at once in Agnew's studio and the pilot film could be made a reality in a matter of days. It would, in effect, mean selling his script to Agnew and becoming merely a writer of a television show. It would mean abandoning the co-operative idea and becoming, to all intents and purposes, employees, not partners. It would mean giving up the chance of large profits in return for only a minor share in the proceeds and a salary. It is true that if the thing succeeded he would have made a reputation as a writer and the actors would once again have some measure of that fame which is dearer to them than money.

Money! If he declined Agnew's proposition where could he raise the fifteen thousand dollars necessary to produce that first film—the pilot film? He couldn't earn it; he couldn't borrow it. He allowed himself to dream—to dream of some wonderful opportunity to invest his few dollars and realize an enormous return. But that was nonsense. It was more practical to hope to get a tip on some longshot at the track. But money must be had. Lack of money barred the door against him.

His flittering mind settled for an instant upon Quality Piper and upon the murdered Shiner—and the voice over the telephone which he was certain was the voice of the lovely Loretta Kimball. This atmosphere of crime, intrigue, of murder, of possible murder in the past, of danger to himself or to Quality Piper in the future was not clement to cogent planning. He abandoned the effort to fix his mind upon his typewriter, thrust on his hat and clumped down the stairs to the street. He wandered aimlessly and unhappily. He suffered from that agony which comes to all writers—that black terror that he had emptied his reservoir; that his mind had lost the gift of imagination and creation and that he never would be able to write again. He was tempted to stop in at the nearest bar and to launch upon a project of drowning his troubles—of seeking alcoholic nirvana. But he was not a drinking man and the very thought of it revolted him.

"All this," he said to himself furiously, "is damn nonsense." But if it were nonsense he saw no way to resolve it into sense. Maybe companionship would help. He went into a drugstore and telephoned Zagic Quiros, but there was no answer. He called up Dolly Dove. She would be something solid to lean on—something cheerfully solid. Dolly's piping voice answered.

"Oh, it's you," she said. "What gives?"

"I've got a large, black, bad-tempered raven sitting on my shoulder," he said.

"That's literary, probably. It can't be anything else. What

does it add up to?" He could, in his mind's eye, see her shrug her more than ample shoulders.

"I'm in a state of mind," he said.

"Well," Dolly said, "lug it up here and I'll contrive to get you loose from it."

Twenty minutes sufficed to carry him to the apartment, where Dolly answered the door to him. She was an enormous cloud of lavender. It might have been a hostess gown or a night robe or a costume for a masquerade. It was grotesque but somehow it was very human and, in a ridiculous way, soothing. When one looked at her in this absurd gown the first impulse was to laugh because it was so incongruous, so fantastic. But the next emotion was quite something else. Because the gross woman was so naïvely human. She looked like an enormously inflated doll, but, obviously, she was unconscious of ridiculous appearance and childishly delighted with herself.

"Stylish, ain't it?" she asked.

"Striking," John said.

She narrowed her eyes at him. "You think I'm a fatheaded old ninny, don't you? Eh? You think I look like somethin' the cat dragged in. You think I got no taste riggin' myself out in this floatin' voile creation. . . . You kind of took me by surprise, Johnnie. This get-up ain't a public showing. It's private. This is the kind of thing I used to wear when I was slim and everybody used to gasp when they saw me floatin' around. So, afternoons when I'm alone, I kind of reconstruct myself and pleasure myself by pretending I'm like I used to be. It tickles me to death and it don't do anybody any harm. When I was eighteen, Johnnie, you'd of sucked in your breath if you'd seen me in this creation."

John sucked in his breath. Dolly patted his arm with a white hand like a dumpling. "Much obliged," she said. "Now what's griping you?"

"It's gone," John said. "You've exorcised it."

"What'll it be? Tea or beer?"

"Tea," John answered.

"She's out," Dolly told him.

"Quality?"

"Her." Dolly frowned. "Out with a young fellow. He come and got her and off she went. I didn't catch his name. She didn't give any explanation."

"Does she ever?" John asked.

"You'd be surprised," Dolly said. "He didn't look like the kind of a boy she'd be interested in, neither. But you never can tell. . . . Now what about this upper-crust girl you had me to phoning all over about?"

"Just how," asked John, without explaining his interest in Loretta Kimball, "does a man from the wrong side of the tracks get to meet one of Jabez Winkleman's household?"

"Only way I can think of," Dolly said, "is to rescue her from a fate worse than death. After that she'd have to recognize you socially. Anyhow that's the way love stories recommend." She squinted at him. "You got some stealthy purpose in wanting to meet this denizen of the society pages or was it love first crack out of the box?"

"Business, not pleasure," John said.

"How does she get into the act?" Dolly asked.

"Remember," John asked, "the voice over the telephone. After I got slugged in my apartment."

"I hardly ever, very seldom, almost never forget anything," Dolly answered.

"Loretta Kimball," John said, "was that voice."

"Rats," Dolly said inelegantly.

"There are not," John declared, "two voices like that in the world."

"A niece or a granddaughter or a ward or a secretary to Pan-Pacific Oil don't get that kind of grease on her hands."

"This one did," John said positively.

"Well," Dolly said judgmatically, "I calc'late the Duchess of Luxemburg could let her foot slip. She show any sign of recognizing you?"

"None. I tailed her home. I stood outside the gates looking after her when up comes a cross between Lon Chaney and Bela Lugosi and puts up a Keep Off the Grass sign. He was gentle and polite. But he meant business. So it looks as if Mr. Jabez Winkleman isn't careless with his whatever-she-is. Her extra equipment includes a bodyguard."

"That," said Dolly, "could be. Or not. If she's this telephone voice then folks more likely to deal in bodyguards might be footing the bill."

"That could be," John agreed. "So, it's obvious, I must meet her socially."

"You use your influence," Dolly said, "to get me in the Social Register, and I'll invite her to a frolic."

John changed the subject. "Rolf Agnew called up," he said. "He told me the word's gone out against me."

"He'd know," Dolly said. "That's bad. Did Agnew want out?"

"Agnew," John said, "don't like to be elbowed. He said his offer stood. He'll finance us for fifty-one per cent. And give us a deal off the top of the deck. Maybe we should accept."

"You," Dolly said, "are thinking about Kent Farraday and me—the out-of-season twins."

"Yes," John answered frankly.

"Then quit it," Dolly said briskly in her squeaking little voice. "Kent and I'll ride the plow till we finish the furrow."

"But, Dolly, where'll we get the necessary money?"

"Not out of me," Dolly said promptly. "I'm tight. . . . How much money you got, John?"

He told her. "'Tain't much," she said. "Now, take me. I'm a finagler. In this troupe of ours I'm vice-president in charge of monkey business. I was elected to it."

"Unanimously," John assured her.

"Then," Dolly said, "you hold out enough to get past on with three meals a day, and pass over the rest. Say two thousand dollars."

"What will you do with it?" John asked.

"That," said Dolly, "is for both of us to find out. Maybe toss it to the sparrows. But they'll have to be awful smart sparrows. When I feed a bird it's because I got a mortgage on its feathers. . . . Now you set while I brew a pot of tea. I got some cinnamon buns and a batch of ginger cookies. If I got to resume financial skulduggery I want to do it without my insides screechin' for a government subsidy. While I'm in the kitchen you write out that check."

"Yes'm," John answered.

When America's ex-Darling returned with refreshments John's state of mind was more optimistic than it had been for days. If she had nothing else to contribute Dolly Dove was a tonic to abolish mental depression.

chapter ELEVEN

Zagic Quiros battered on John Miller's door at an unseasonably early morning hour. John had only put the coffee on, so he doubled the supply and fried four eggs instead of two.

"Why this sunrise call?" John asked.

"I'm instigated by Dolly," Zagic told him. "She wants to look at horses."

"Santa Anita?"

Zagic shook his head. "Seems like there's a kind of kindergarten for gee-gees that she's got a yen to see. Where they feed them on solid gold oats and grass with this chlorophyll in it. Looks like Dolly wants to make a two-dollar bet but she craves to do research before she risks her money."

"Today?" John asked.

"This morning. They'll be ready at ten."

"They?"

"Including Quality Piper," Zagic said.

The two young men reported at Dolly's apartment. Dolly's car had been brought around from the garage and was waiting at the door. The women were ready. Quality in a severe tailored suit and Dolly in a vast garment of plaid which she firmly believed gave her a horsey appearance.

"Why horses?" John asked when they were seated in the automobile.

"On account," said Dolly, "of I'm tired of people." She sat in the front seat with John, who was driving. Quality and Zagic sat behind. He was disgruntled.

"Me," he said, "I like somebody to talk to."

"Talk to yourself," Quality said.

"No fun," Zagic retorted. "I ask myself a question, see? What's the good? I always know what I'm going to answer."

They drove through Hollywood, out Sunset Boulevard and then northward into the country beyond. Dolly chatted shrilly about nothing. Zagic interjected tart observations. Quality sat completely composed and looked at the scenery. If the scenery looked back at her it was rewarded for the effort. Three quarters of an hour after their start they arrived at a closed gate which Zagic got down to open. Before them spread an area of rolling farm land, criss-crossed by white fences enclosing fields of grass each occupied by grazing horses. Straight ahead was a cluster of barns. To their left was a white cottage, and beyond that was another group of stables. Everything was neat, clean, so well tended that it seemed almost sanitary. Dolly told them to stop at the cottage which was at once the office and the dwelling place of the superintendent of the stables. A tiny electric vehicle little larger than a kiddy car buzzed past them, then stopped and backed.

"Didn't expect you so early, Miss Dove," said a short, stout man in a dilapidated straw hat.

"Boys and girls," Dolly piped, "this is Wally Sweet. Wally, meet Miss Piper and Mr. Miller, and the character is Zagic Quiros."

Sweet regarded Zagic with interest. "Now there's a name," he said approvingly. "Got something outstanding. Bet it ain't in the studbook. Finding names for colts that the studbook authorities'll allow is a chore."

"I've always wondered," John said, "who named horses."

"It takes cockeyed genius. Want to drive around, or walk?"

"Walk," Quality said.

"Ohmigod!" Dolly exclaimed in horrified tones. "Walk."

Nevertheless she alighted from the car and waddled over to

the fence inside which were two mares each mothering a spindle-legged foal. Sweet pointed. "That's Sweetbread," as if he were pointing out Queen Elizabeth. "Sire of her foal is the great Irish horse, McGonigle's Pride." The colt kicked up its uncertain legs and frolicked. Its mother followed anxiously, a jealous eye on the other occupants of the field. "Belong to Jabez Winkleman," Sweet informed them.

John glanced quickly at Dolly and then at Quality. Dolly's face was bland and serene; Quality's face was merely interested.

"Winkleman'll be out this morning," Sweet said. "It's his day. Never misses a Thursday."

"So I hear it bruited about," Dolly said innocently.

"Looks like his car turning in," Sweet said, peering across the fields to the gate. A black, chauffeur-driven car came majestically down the lane and turned toward the office. It stopped behind Dolly's car and a tall, spare old gentleman with big ears and a leathery face stepped to the ground. He turned with a courtliness which one would not expect from his grim, deacon's features, and handed a young lady to his side. Dolly clucked and glanced sidewise at John Miller. Jabez Winkleman's companion was Loretta Kimball.

Sweet stepped forward to greet them. Winkleman nodded curtly; Loretta dimpled and smiled, and glanced inquiringly at the little waiting group.

"Mr. Winkleman," Sweet said in introduction, "an old friend of mine whose name you'll remember—Miss Dolly Dove."

"Indeed I remember," said the old gentleman.

"And Miss Piper, Mr. Miller and—"

"The character's name is Quiros—Zagic Quiros," Dolly said.

"And Miss Kimball," Sweet continued.

Quality Piper and Loretta Kimball studied each other. Loretta's gaze was open and direct and smiling; Quality glanced once at Loretta's face, let her eyes travel swiftly down the girl's figure and then travel away. But her inspection had been complete.

"Piper," Jabez Winkleman observed. "That name is familiar to me."

"A common name," Quality said.

"But," Jabez replied, "it belonged to an uncommon man." He turned to Sweet. "How are Sweetbread and her baby?"

"In the pink, sir," Sweet answered.

The old gentleman stooped, scrambled through the fence followed by Sweet, and walked across the grass toward Sweetbread and her foal. The mare picked up her ears and arched her neck. The colt stood close to his mother and stared. Winkleman walked around them studying with wise, knowing eyes, nodding in response to something Sweet had to say.

John, more interested in Loretta Kimball than in horses, noted that she looked at him with faintly wrinkled brows.

"Mr.—Miller, isn't it? Haven't we met before?" Loretta asked.

"I would have remembered it if we had," John responded.

"Oh, I remember," she said. "I saw you at luncheon at the Beverly Hills." She smiled and nodded. "You stared at me."

"Who wouldn't?" John asked.

"And you were waiting for a car when I came out," she went on. "I notice people. I believe you walked in the same direction I did." Her eyes were twinkling with gay malice.

"I imagine that happens often," John answered.

"It's really a nice compliment," Loretta said. "I don't mind in the least."

"A thing," John said, "that you can safely enjoy—being so well chaperoned."

"Chaperoned!" she exclaimed with raised brows. "Now what in the world can you mean by that? I'm never chaperoned. Uncle Jabez—I call him uncle though he really isn't—lets me roam simply wild."

"Then," John said, "it must have been just a public-spirited citizen, or a volunteer Sir Galahad, who warned me off."

Her eyes narrowed the merest trifle and she paused an instant. Then she shook her head and moved her shoulders. "If it's a conundrum," she said, "I'm a poor guesser." She turned in friendly way to Quality. "You like horses?" she asked.

"Yes," answered Quality.

"I really know nothing about them," Loretta said, "though I

95

come here often with Uncle. I suppose you know all about them—blood lines and conformation and all like that."

"Yes," said Quality.

John stood aside comparing the two young women. The impact of Loretta Kimball's beauty was instant. It hit you between the eyes. It was a gay beauty, of which she seemed to be unconscious even though it was enhanced by every device of modiste and beauty parlor. Quality's beauty was almost latent. There was no sudden impact. One had to observe, and penetrate the wall of reserve which she had erected around herself before awareness of her loveliness came. Her effort seemed to be to conceal her beauty rather than to flaunt it. Judges in a beauty contest would have chosen Loretta instantly, but John was not sure they would have been right. In the jargon of the advertising world, Loretta knew how to sell it. John wondered what the choice would be if Quality applied equally efficient salesmanship.

Jabez Winkleman and Sweet were approaching the fence after their inspection of Sweetbread and her baby. As they stooped to pass through the bars a motorcar stopped at the gates and a man alighted to open them. He drove through, closed the barrier behind him and continued down the lane. It was a sports car of robin's egg blue. It stopped behind Winkleman's limousine and Humphrey Salmon stepped to the road. He stared for a moment at the company, then lifted his homburg and advanced smilingly. "Ah, Winkleman!" he exclaimed. "Glad to see you." He glanced across the fence. "I hope you find Sweetbread and family well this morning."

"Quite satisfactorily so," Winkleman said without warmth.

"And Miss Dove! One sees you so seldom. . . . I've met Miss Piper, of course—and Mr. Miller. The other gentleman, though, I do not know."

"The name's Quiros," said Zagic. "Of the old Czechoslovakian family."

"I like Brooklyn myself," Salmon said. "My apologies. Winkleman, I never have been presented to Miss Kimball, though I've admired her from afar."

"Then no introduction seems required," Winkleman said, and Loretta smiled her habitually warm and inviting smile.

"Would you nice people," asked Salmon, "like to see Manchu? You know I bought him in England. Only arrived a few days ago."

"Paying for him," Winkleman said crisply, "eighty thousand dollars."

"Doing my part in the rehabilitation of Europe," Salmon said lightly. "Would you care to see him? Where's he stabled, Sweet?"

Sweet waved his arm to the left. "Doesn't feel at home yet," he said. "Maybe later would be better."

"Nonsense," Salmon said sharply. "It's only a step. Shall we walk?"

"All but me," Dolly said. "I ride in one of those kiddy cars."

They strolled along the road, Dolly squeezed into one of the tiny electric vehicles, and turned to the left just before they reached the exercise track, to a group of stables and tack rooms built around an open, hard-packed square.

"Fetch him out, Sweet," ordered Salmon.

"It might be better—" Sweet started to protest.

"I said fetch him out," Salmon ordered peremptorily. "Do I have to do it myself?"

He strode away through a space between buildings. Sweet shrugged and followed after pausing to say, "Salmon's got his own stable boy in charge."

Presently there came sounds of conflict, of snorting, plunging, kicking. Into the open space came a great roan horse, not led but dragging a bow-legged man in overalls who clung to the halter. The splendid animal reared, ears flat to his head, kicked, lunged. Zagic sought safety on top of the fence.

"Hold him down," snarled Salmon. "How can we look at him when he's all over the place?"

The great horse stood quivering, nostrils flaring. Loretta shrank back against her uncle; Dolly did not leave the kiddy car but clearly she was apprehensive. Quality stood erect, unmoving, inscrutable, staring at Manchu with no sign of nervousness in manner or bearing. John stood not far from her watching her as she stood but with wary eye upon the infuriated stallion. The groom clung to the halter grimly. Half the time his feet were off the ground.

"Hold him down, confound you," Salmon said.

"Shameful!" Quality uttered the one word quite audibly.

"I suppose you'd know how to handle him better," retorted Salmon.

"Yes," said Quality through compressed lips.

She stood a dozen feet away from the rearing, kicking horse. Quite calmly she stood, her lovely face expressing nothing, though her eyes were hard.

"Disgusting!" she said.

"Come away from there, Quality," John urged, taking a step toward her.

Everyone else had retreated to places of greater safety. . . . Salmon, enraged either by Quality's word or by the behavior of the roan stallion, raised the whip in his hand and struck the animal savagely upon the flank. Manchu squealed, reared, lunged out with iron-shod hoofs. His power sufficed to jerk him free from the groom and with trailing halter he plunged. John shouted, dived in a flying tackle that swept Quality from the stallion's path to the hard earth. Manchu, such was his impetus, could not wheel in time. The fence stood before him. Too late he tried to leap. The upper bars caught him across the knees and he somersaulted, crashed to the hard-packed earth of the exercise track and lay still. His beautiful neck was broken.

Winkleman, Quiros, Sweet, appalled, ran to John and Quality. John sat up dizzily. Quality stirred, placed her palms on the ground. Sweet raised her to her feet.

"Are you hurt, Miss? Are you hurt?" he asked.

"No," Quality said.

She stood erect, not swaying. She gave no heed to the grime that defaced her suit, seemed unaware of it, unaware of torn fabric. She looked down at John, turned to look at the broken fence and the dead horse. Her face was white, but not with pain. John scrambled to his feet shaken and breathless. Without looking at him Quality stretched out her arm and touched his shoulder. It was a gesture more eloquent than words. When she spoke it was to Humphrey Salmon who stood rooted to the ground, face purple. Quality pointed at the carcass of Manchu.

"That," she said, "was murder."

"An eighty-thousand-dollar murder," Sweet said between clenched teeth.

For a minute there was tableau. No one moved. Then John, limping a bit, walked across the intervening space toward Humphrey Salmon. "Mister," he said, "I'm not interested in the murder of eighty-thousand-dollar horses. But I am concerned about the murder of a million-dollar girl. Was it impromptu, or was it planned? . . . I saw you lash that horse, Salmon. . . . Like this." He snatched the whip from Salmon's hand and slashed the man across the face, once, twice. He threw down the whip and waited as Salmon backed away. His fists were clenched, waiting, hoping for attack. But Salmon did not attack. He raised his hand to his face, marred by two red weals. Then, eyes stony, he turned on his heel and walked away, trudging as if he carried a heavy burden.

"For that," Zagic said in a voice that quivered, "he'll kill you."

"For that," John answered, "I wish he would try."

Dolly was fussing over him, brushing him with her handkerchief, pinning the flapping rent in the knee of his trousers.

"Young man," Jabez Winkleman said, "you are impulsive. Sometimes impulse is admirable."

Sweet was almost in tears. "What a tragedy! What a tragedy! A beautiful horse, a wonderful horse. . . . Damn that man! Damn him!"

Loretta Kimball looked up into John's eyes. As she stood there she was amazingly appealing, wonderfully sweet, completely human and desirable. "I like a man," she said, and hesitated for a word, "a man who is adequate."

Quality said nothing.

"A drink will do us good," Sweet offered. "Shall we go to the house?"

"And, maybe, if you got it," Dolly suggested, "a ham sandwich. It's past noon."

They retraced their way to the cottage, Dolly filling the tiny electric car. In the office Sweet offered drinks. Winkleman refused, Quality declined. Loretta did not like whiskey.

"No ham?" Dolly wanted to know.

"Uncle," said Loretta. "That nice place down the road. Cannot we have lunch there together?" She put the question to Quality. Somehow it was a challenge. Quality lifted the intangible gauge of battle.

"Yes," she said.

"Then follow us," Loretta said. "We know the way."

The party drove away from the office, through the gate and down the road. Again Dolly Dove sat beside John Miller. Quality and Zagic occupied the back seat.

"I," Dolly said presently, "didn't plan on this."

"But you planned," John said.

"You wanted to meet the Kimball lollypop," Dolly said. "Well, I'd say you got introduced."

"So I did," John said slowly, with knitted brows. "And I can't believe she's—" He groped for an epithet.

"A lady hyena who yowls over telephones at night," Dolly suggested.

"It's incredible," John said.

"When," Dolly replied, "you been around as many places as I been, there ain't anythin' that comes even close to being incredible."

A couple of miles of further driving and John guided the car into a driveway in the wake of Winkleman's limousine. Inside the waiters put tables together for the party. The only zestful appetites were Dolly's and Loretta's. Quality picked at her food, and even the inviting dishes were repulsive to John. From the social point of view the luncheon was not a success.

"Uncle," Loretta said in what was the desperation of a hostess with a difficult situation on her hands. "Shouldn't we invite all these nice people to the doings tomorrow evening?"

"Of course," Winkleman responded.

"Five o'clock. On the grounds. There'll be an orchestra and cocktails and food. . . . And the swimming pool, and dancing for those who like it. Do say you'll come."

"Now that's right nice," Dolly said. "I dote on parties."

"And I'm sure," Loretta said, her eyes upon Quality's figure, "that Miss Piper dotes on swimming pools."

It was another challenge. Again Quality lifted the glove. "Yes," she said.

"And you, Mr. Quiros and Mr. Miller?"

"Tickled pink," Zagic said.

John smiled crookedly. "If," he said, "the Gargoyle will let me in."

"You should worry," Loretta said with her most fetching smile, "if he'll let you out again."

John wondered if there were covert significance in this saying.

They re-embarked in their cars and drove toward Hollywood. Zagic had pre-empted the driver's seat, compelling John to sit behind with Quality. Somehow he felt ill at ease, embarrassed. How did one behave toward a young woman whose life you had probably just saved? He need not have worried. Quality did not mention the matter, did not thank him or indicate by word or manner that she was under obligations.

He essayed light conversation without success. In desperation he said clumsily, "I'm looking forward to seeing you and Miss Kimball in swim suits tomorrow. Is it a competition?"

"Yes," Quality said.

"Who'll win?" John asked.

"You be judge," she said, and then surprised him by being almost garrulous. "That's what it's for," she added.

chapter TWELVE

"Quality," said Dolly Dove, "has got me in a wing-ding."

"As how?" John Miller asked.

He and Zagic Quiros were in Dolly's apartment ready to escort them to the cocktail party in Jabez Winkleman's grounds.

"Well," Dolly asked, "where is she?"

"Probably getting a facial," John guessed.

"Last night she's out with a young man. Same one I told you about before. Today she lunches with him. What goes on? Questions she don't answer. This boy is younger than she is and he don't even know how to tie a necktie." The shrug that accompanied this was of earthquake proportions. "What man'll attract what woman you never can tell. Take my first husband. He's a little runt about the size I was when I'm eighteen. With ears, and what he talks about wouldn't interest a guinea pig. And all the glamour of a slab of salt pork. So I marry him. Could I tell you why? Then I start taking on flesh and he gets skinnier. I could wear him for a locket. So I have to chuck him on account that people snicker when they see us together."

"He must have had some fatal attraction," Zagic said.

"Sure," Dolly said, "but what was it?"

"It's in the papers," Zagic said, "about eighty thousand dollars' worth of horse breaking his neck."

"But not," Dolly said, "about John laying a whip across Salmon's face. After a while a man can forget even eighty thousand dollars. But the other sticks in his memory. Like Winkleman said, John, you were impulsive."

"He tried to murder Quality with that horse," John said grimly.

"If anybody hit me with a horsewhip," Zagic said, "there'd be a tussle. This Salmon took it. He's bigger 'n you. He's yellow."

"I don't think so," John said thoughtfully. "Just licking me wouldn't be enough—provided he could manage it."

"It didn't look good. He should have swung on you."

"A man," John said grimly, "who can take what he did and walk away is bad medicine. When he turned and slunk away cold shivers ran down my back. It scared me worse than if he'd drawn a gun."

Dolly nodded. "You got it right, John," she agreed. She sighed gloomily. "Maybe I better quit meddling. This thing out at the stables didn't turn out the way I planned. . . . You wanted a close-up of this Loretta Kimball, so I finagled it. So Quality almost gets trampled and a wonderful horse is dead. And no life insurance company would sell you a policy. All loss and no profit."

"I got to meet a beautiful girl," John said.

"Yes," Zagic said, "and if she's mixed up in anything gummy, then I'm a Senegambian medicine man."

"It was her voice over the telephone," John insisted.

"You just didn't hear good," Zagic said.

The outer door opened and Quality came into the room, neat as a pin, self-possessed, unsmiling. She merely nodded.

"Now where you been?" Dolly demanded.

"Lunch," Quality answered.

"You got an appetite if you can lunch from ten in the morning till four in the afternoon."

Quality smiled faintly but gave no explanation. She passed through the room and into her bedroom to dress for the afternoon's affair. Presently they heard the water running in the tub. It was a full half hour before she came out, dressed, hatted, ready to proceed to the Winkleman party.

"You took your good time," Dolly said.

"But it was worth it," John exclaimed.

Quality did not acknowledge the compliment even with a faint smile.

"Chatterbox," Quiros said.

"Shut up, Character," Dolly snapped. "Let's get the show on the road."

John Miller drove. This time Quality sat beside him, a small handbag on her knees.

"Your swim suit in that?" Quiros asked.

"Yes," Quality answered.

Quiros contented himself with a whistle. "What you expect," Dolly demanded, "red flannel underwear? There's a war on."

"What war?" John asked. But Dolly only snorted at masculine obtuseness.

The great bronze gates which barred the world from Jabez Winkleman's estate were not accustomed to admit a car of the vintage and cost of Dolly's little vehicle. They opened reluctantly. John drove up the steep, circling driveway to an open space where an attendant pointed out a parking space. The area was already occupied by a number of automobiles which indicated the quality of the guests already arrived. Another attendant conducted them into and through the house, opening glassed doors upon a cloister surrounding a lushly planted patio. In its center was an oval pool surrounded by chairs and tables and chattering guests. Loretta Kimball advanced to greet them with cordial smile and extended hand.

"How fetching you look, Miss Piper," she exclaimed.

"And you," Quality rejoined.

John, peering from one to the other, thought that it was seldom two lovelier, contrasting girls stood side by side. Quality dark and still; Loretta blonde and vivacious.

"I wonder," he said, "which of you would win the apple."

"Apple?" asked Loretta with slightly raised brows.

"I was thinking," John explained, "of the first recorded beauty contest. Which brought on the Trojan War. Paris would have a tougher decision to make today."

Jabez Winkleman, the somberest of all the gaily clad company, stood up to greet them. His manner was grimly gracious as if he found it difficult to unbend, but John found his handclasp to be firm. "Miss Dove," he said with something approaching dry courtliness, "will you sit here beside me? Not so long ago I was not the least ardent of your millions of admirers."

"He was quite daft about you," Mrs. Winkleman said—a buxom, wholesome woman with twinkling, kindly eyes.

Dolly chuckled. "Who'd 'a' thought in those days that a bridegroom would have to use a derrick to hoist me over the threshold!" she said.

"I believe," Mrs. Winkleman said, "you already know our guest of honor—Dr. Scruggs. And Miss Scruggs."

"Sure we do," Dolly replied. "Hello, Doc. You're not so hard to look at either, darling." She patted Martha Scruggs on the arm.

They made a little group about a table. Loretta led Quality away to conduct her around the pool, introducing her to guests as they made their progress. It was as if she were deliberately inviting comparison, giving the people assembled there an opportunity to observe and to determine which of the pair was the lovelier. It was not a blatant challenge but John was able to recognize it as a challenge and wondered if there were any reason for it save that rivalry which is inevitable between two lovely women.

As John studied the men and women who made up the party he became aware that he and Dolly and Quiros and Quality— and possibly Martha Scruggs—were the only people present with any connection with the motion picture world. No famous actors or actresses were there. This was not the artificial society which admits to its ranks because of notoriety or the ephemeral fame of the silver screen. It was society based upon family and position and tradition, solid, conservative, admirable. He heard names spoken which recalled the golden history of California; names which called to memory accomplishments and high services to the nation. In these people was no trace of snobbery because they had so long been accustomed to their quality that there was no need to assert it.

"Classy," Dolly whispered in John's ear.

John's eyes crinkled. "My grandmother Van Rensselaer would have approved of it," he whispered back.

"My gawd!" Dolly exclaimed. "Do you belong? I'd never have thought it!"

"Hush!" John warned. "I'm a dark-complexion sheep."

In the background an orchestra played with restraint. A bevy of the younger people scurried toward the Grecian temple in miniature which was the bath house, and presently emerged, laughing and chattering to disport themselves in the pool. Last of all came Loretta and Quality. It was as if they made an entrance as, side by side, they walked to the opposite end of the pool where arose the structure from which projected diving boards, low and high. John grinned as he thought how shocked his grandmother would have been forty years ago, and he reflected an instant upon the changes wrought by time and events or evolution upon morals and manners, prejudices and shibboleths. He reflected upon how some intolerances had been replaced by easy tolerance and how other intolerances had emerged to take their places. Apparently every age must grow its own crop of intolerance, sweeping away the ideas and prejudices of its parents. In but a few short years the human body had become respectable; a thing not to be concealed by unsightly fabrics, but frankly accepted as a fact and not hidden as a pornographic mystery.

What the world had lost in prudery it had gained in beauty.

Loretta ran up the ladder to the highest platform, calling back over her shoulder gaily to Quality. She walked out upon the pliant board, pulling a cap over the radiance of her hair. She walked out to the end and stood there immobile for seconds. Every eye was lifted to her, and not an eye, young or old, but was moved by the slim graciousness of her figure, its sheer perfection of line and contour—topped by her lovely, laughing face. She turned again and called a word to Quality. Then she raised upon her toes and stretched her arms before her. It was a sight to clutch at the heart. Her body resolved into motion. She called to her aid the resiliency of the springboard and then she was in the air in bird flight, arms wide spread in that dive named after the most graceful of birds, the swan. She entered the water perfectly, leaving its surface almost without ripple. Then she emerged, shaking her head and laughing, and swam with strong strokes to the edge of the pool, where she paused and looked upward expectantly. Again John sensed a challenge.

Suddenly he was afraid, afraid for Quality—lest she would not, or could not accept this gauge of battle. Quite unaccountably it would have been to him a tragedy if Quality had flunked the trial or if she were not equipped to compete. The exhibition of Loretta Kimball had been the confident feat of an expert. And he had no reason for hoping that Quality would be able to vie with it.

There was a hush. It seemed to John that the audience was asking the same questions that troubled him—wondering if Loretta would be able to score a triumph uncontested.

Slowly, with accustomed gravity of face, Quality commenced to climb. John's heart beat with excitement. Dolly Dove's hand touched and gripped his own. She was suffering the same suspense, the same anxiety as he. The girl reached the platform, stepped slowly but without faltering or hesitation to the end of the board, and stood motionless as Loretta had posed. Someone in the crowd exclaimed. As well he might. It was a slender, perfect statue that stood there above their eyes, not insouciant and challenging as Loretta had been, but somehow combining dignity with beauty in a most effective way. She did not smile downward. It was as if she were unaware of the dozens of eyes upon her. Slowly she spread her arms, flexed the board, lifted to her toes and launched herself through the air. If Loretta had demonstrated perfection, Quality equaled her achievement. Birdlike she, too, arched through the air, seemed to glide there for instants and then entered the water as an otter might have done. A gasp ascended from the spectators and a ripple of applause. It is possible those who watched sensed something more than two beautiful young women at play—a contest, perhaps a grim contest in which some unperceived prize was at stake.

Dolly's hand relaxed and she breathed deeply. "Was I fit to be tied!" she whispered. "Darned if I wasn't almost praying."

The girls climbed from the pool and, still side by side, dripping like two mermaids, walked to the table at which Jabez and Dolly and John were seated. Loretta was chatting with animation; Quality merely listened with a faint, inscrutable smile.

"Children," said Mrs. Winkleman, "you were wonderful."

"Quality was superb," Loretta said generously.

Again that faint smile moved Quality's lips. "Score tied," she said.

"Which," laughed Loretta, "calls for a play-off."

"Definitely," Quality said, and this time she smiled the first genuine unrestrained smile John had ever seen upon her face.

The girls ran toward the bath house, towels draped over their shoulders.

"Two champs," Zagic said in awed tones.

"Nix to you," Dolly piped. "Never room but for one at the top."

"A profound observation," said Jabez Winkleman.

"I just coined it," Dolly answered.

John was conscious that Jabez Winkleman had been studying him with shrewd eyes, appraising him, possibly reaching conclusions regarding him. The old gentleman leaned forward and addressed him directly. "Young man," he asked, "what business are you in?"

"I," said John, "am a writer."

"A precarious trade," Jabez observed.

"All trades are precarious," John answered. "I've even heard that life itself is apt to be."

Jabez cleared his throat. "Since yesterday," he said dryly, "I apprehend that yours has become more so. . . . Um. . . . I observed certain qualities in you, Mr. Miller. Notably a quick mental and physical reaction. The ability to resolve decision into action. Regardless of consequences." Again he cleared his throat. "These excellent qualities," he said, "might be nullified by rashness. However, young man, I prefer a man who acts decisively, even with rashness, than one who hesitates lest he be guilty of imprudence."

"He who hesitates is in the soup," Dolly Dove interjected. "That's another one I just made up on the spur of the moment."

"The great Napoleon," Jabez said, "whose morals I deplore but whose efficiency I admire, is said to have observed that he would rather have a general who made ten quick decisions, nine of which were wrong, than an officer who made ten hesitant decisions and was nine times right."

"Napoleon," John said, "knew how to select his marshals."

"Upon what are you engaged at the moment?" Jabez inquired.

"I have written a series of television acts," John told him. "We are trying to get them produced."

"And if you succeed?"

"If we succeed," John replied, "I, personally, will have established some reputation. But also Miss Dove, who has been long inactive, and Mr. Kent Farraday, whom you may remember, will regain their old fame and prosperity. Naturally we all hope the venture will be profitable."

"How profitable?"

"That," John said, "is impossible to estimate." He smiled at Dolly. "I'm afraid you will think us impractical, sir, but the imponderables are more important to some of us than the cash."

"What imponderables, young man?"

"To Miss Dove and Mr. Farraday," John said, "a resurrection in the profession they love. A return of departed fame. The violins will play for them again. They will listen once more to applause which has been long silent."

The old gentleman nodded grudgingly. "I think I understand what you mean. It is a thing I have observed, that there are individuals who prefer what you call fame to the possession of wealth. I will not call it absurd."

"I think, sir, that all human beings are motivated by the same thing—the desire for applause. Some crave the plaudits of audiences, of the public. Others, as yourself—if you will not think me impertinent—crave the applause of themselves. Miss Dove gives a great performance and is admired for it by millions, perhaps. You, Mr. Winkleman, make a tremendous business success—and win your own admiration. You don't need the money you acquire by your coup, so why else should you try for it except to exalt yourself in your own opinion? The difference is only a difference of audience. Miss Dove plays to multitudes, you play to one."

Winkleman was not annoyed by this frankness. He even nodded his deacon's head thoughtfully.

"Young man," he said, "in addition to being decisive you are also acute. . . . I shall be pleased if you will call upon me at your convenience. It would pleasure me to broaden our acquaintance, Mr. Miller."

"That," said Loretta Kimball, who, with Quality, had returned to the group during this colloquy, "would please me, too, Uncle." She smiled invitingly, almost intimately at John. "I'd like to know him better myself."

"You," Jabez said in his dry-as-parchment voice, "might go farther and do worse."

John's eyes turned without command from him to Quality's face. It told him nothing. It was bland rather than withdrawn. It was as if she listened with trite politeness to something in which she had no personal interest.

"Quality," Loretta said (the girls seemed to have arrived at a first-name basis), "I want you to meet a perfect darling. I just saw him come. I'm taking a chance by introducing him to you, but I feel generous today. . . . Oh, Mike Strange, come over here and meet the sensation of the hour."

Quality accepted introduction to the young man who appropriated her promptly and led her toward the tables set forth with refreshments. Loretta looked up into John's eyes and grinned impishly.

"That," she said, "wasn't so much generosity as it was low trickery."

"Am I flattered?" John asked.

"Hungry?" Loretta asked.

"For flattery?" John countered.

"Aren't we all. Shall we look at the gardens? They're well worth seeing."

"With you, Miss Kimball, I'd look at toadstools. . . . You have a startlingly lovely speaking voice. Once heard, never to be forgotten."

She smiled up at him and he felt the impact of it to the soles of his feet. "Let's sit here," she motioned to a rustic bench, "and I'll talk a streak to make sure I impress the sound of it upon your memory."

"Every voice," John said, "has a quality of its own, but yours has more of it. Some voices one would not recognize on the telephone, but even over the wire yours could not be mistaken."

"That," Loretta said, "sounds to me as if it had a significance."

"Hasn't it?" he asked.

"Are you suggesting that you have heard me speak over the telephone?"

"Not suggesting," he answered. "Stating."

"How ominous you sound. Should I be startled?"

"It was I who was startled when I heard you speak again," John said.

She was quick to perceive. "That," she said, "is why you followed me home the other day. Because you thought you had spoken with me before. How very disillusioning!" She smiled at him again, disarmingly, charmingly. "Now I thought it was for quite another reason."

"You telephoned me at my apartment," John said baldly.

She only laughed at him. "Never having seen you, Mr. Miller—to be knocked off my feet by your manly beauty; and never having heard of you, illustrious as you may be in—in an inconspicuous way—why should I be so infatuated as to telephone you, a total stranger?"

"Possibly," John said, "you were ordered to do so."

"Do I look the sort of girl to take orders?"

"No," John replied.

"So," she replied with a cunning little shrug, "let's talk about something more profitable. . . . I'm a very forward girl who is not afraid to make overtures. Uncle Jabez invited you to call and see him. That opens this house to you, does it not? And it is open to so few men who interest me. I'm inviting you to call on me."

He laughed at her almost gaily. "Object matrimony?" he asked lightly.

"Not at the moment," she laughed back. "Make a note of our private telephone number." She told it to him.

There was a rustling in the ornamental shrubbery behind them and a man stepped from the flowering bushes. "Miss Kimball," he said with grave courtesy, "aren't you neglecting your guests?"

"I'm not neglecting this one," Loretta said.

"Ah," John said softly, rising to his feet, "the Gargoyle."

"I'm quite accustomed to my face," the man said in his cultured, amiable voice, "so I do not resent references to it. . . . You are a resourceful young man, sir. My compliments. . . . Miss Kimball, I'm sure you will wish to rejoin the party."

"And who are you?" Loretta asked. "Puck of Pook's Hill?"

"Older than that, Miss Kimball," the man said. "Orpheus the sweet singer." His smile distorted his repulsive face. "Be advised, Mr. Miller. You will find it more agreeable at the pool."

John hesitated an instant, then he replied in a voice equally as courteous as that of the Gargoyle. "It doesn't seem a clement time to argue the point," he said.

"Very gracious of you, Mr. Miller," the man said. "It's a pleasure to deal with a gentleman of perception."

He withdrew as he had come.

"Doubtless a hamadryad," John said to Loretta.

"John," she said, using his given name quite unconsciously, "I never saw that man before. . . . I'm afraid."

"Now, now," John answered her, "he doesn't exist. He's folklore."

He extended his arm to her deferentially; as her fingers rested upon it he felt them to be trembling.

"There are bad and dangerous things in folklore," Loretta said.

"Like werewolves and succubi and things that go bump in the night?"

"And vampires," she said. "Aren't vampires the worst of all?"

"They have their weak points," John assured her. "They can't cross water and garlic makes the way impassable to them."

Suddenly she was herself again, alluring, happy, amazingly lovely as she turned her face up to him.

"Then," she said in her contralto, rich voice, "let's go and find a sprig of garlic."

chapter THIRTEEN

Young Benjamin Franklin was a find. Martha Scruggs, not yet accustomed to her new name of Jenny Lind, was proving to be more than satisfactory in the role of the sister who deemed herself a sophisticate but constantly betrayed her naïveté. The scenes which Kent Farraday and Dolly Dove played together combined subtle humor with side-splitting farce. Quality Piper drilled them and drilled them so that even John Miller thought she was too much of a martinet. But she made them work for her without resentment. It is doubtful if a television script ever had been rehearsed so thoroughly. Even Zagic admitted that the troupe was good.

"But," he objected, "what good's being good if it never gets past being a parlor charade? You got to get it on film. We're ready to shoot and our gun's loaded but it ain't got any trigger. That's a kind of a metaphor or something. By trigger I mean cash money."

"Be patient, my friend," Kent Farraday said in the grand manner. "With faith one can move mountains. We must not permit our faith to abate."

Ben Franklin surprised them. He spoke with sincerity, not like the clumsy hobbledehoy he seemed to all of them. "Right, Mr. Farraday," he said. "We got to stick it out. If we got to tighten our belts—well, let's grab hold of them and tighten. No use arguing. We got to hang on. I've got confidence."

"That," commended Kent Farraday, "is the spirit of a real trouper. Young man, I commend you."

John warmed toward the young man, but chancing to glance at Quality, he saw that she was peering out of the corners of her eyes at the boy with an expression John could not read. Certainly it did not express unbounded enthusiasm. Possibly it indicated merely personal dislike for the boy; but Quality was not one to let personal dislike override efficiency. It troubled John vaguely.

The rehearsal was over, and as usual Dolly Dove was generous with refreshments. Zagic Quiros spoke with his mouth full.

"Ain't it," he demanded, "about time I started to do my stuff? Look! We got a thing the papers'll fall for. Comeback for Dolly Dove. Comeback for Kent Farraday. Also in the cast we got Benjamin Franklin and Jenny Lind. It's a natural." He frowned at Quality. "What," he demanded, "can you do besides dive? Me, I'm looking for angles. Could we get a photograph of you on that springboard—with the set of legs you wear 'n' all we could bust into the rotogravures. You got any other talents you been hidin'?"

"Never," Quality said sharply, "mention my name."

"Whoa!" Zagic did not like it. "You're an asset. In this publicity game you got to use assets. Listen!" he became impressive. "Now take me, I'm a student. I got to be. Take art, for instance. What for do artists paint pictures?" He paused for oratorical effect. "Why, to be looked at, for sure. So the conclusion I come to is the more folks want to gawk at a picture the greater art it is, see? Well, you hang up a tony landscape with trees and right beside it you hang a girl that forgot to put on her clothes. Now I ask you. Which one'll have a crowd standing in front of it? There's your answer. There ain't any art higher than leg art. But also there's novelty. What could be noveler than a director with legs? In that alone there's a story."

"No," said Quality.

"Oh, Miss Piper," Martha Scruggs interjected, "I thought you and Miss Kimball were just too lovely yesterday. I mean the way you shared the limelight. I'd have expected two girls like you to be jealous, but you weren't a bit. It was—it was *charming*."

John blinked and peered at the girl incredulously. Such naïveté could not exist in the modern world. She had been there; she had seen a battle, bitterly fought to a draw, and she thought it was simply too, too sweet! Dolly was grinning.

"Dearie," she said, "you better crawl out from under the cabbage leaf."

John had pondered the episode at Jabez Winkleman's pool. The significance of it must have been evident. The feminine malice of it was so thinly veiled. Loretta Kimball, confident in the possession of skill and rare beauty, had planned the thing to embarrass Quality Piper, to outdistance her, to shut her out of the beam of the spotlight. It was no gracious gesture to share with Quality that had prompted her to that exhibition of her body and of her artistry. She had done it all so gaily, so insouciantly, so effectively. It must have shocked her to her very toes when Quality mounted that ladder, advanced to the tip of the springboard and duplicated in grace and perfection the swan dive she just had executed. But this John would say for Loretta: she had carried it off like a thoroughbred. Astounded as she must have been, disappointed as she certainly was, she had exhibited no sign of either. As for Quality she had allowed no natural triumph to appear in face or manner. She had taken it in stride.

"That gal," Dolly Dove pronounced, "is a this and that."

"Why, Miss Dove!" exclaimed Martha Scruggs. "How can you say that? I thought she was perfectly sweet. My papa was her uncle's doctor."

"Ain't that," asked Zagic, "what they call a *non sequitur?*"

"What in the world do you mean?" Martha asked.

"Is every girl that's uncle was a patient of your dad's just perfectly sweet?" Zagic asked.

"It helps," John said dryly.

Benjamin Franklin was sitting on the settee beside Martha Scruggs. He was patently admiring her. "How about my taking you to dinner tonight?" he asked in a voice meant for her ears alone, but Dolly overheard.

"Get smart, Ben," she said. "Come down sick and be her pa's patient before you make a pass. That's the what-d'ye-call-it to open the door."

"You're making fun of me," Martha said without resentment. "But just the same papa is *very* particular whom he accepts as patients."

Kent Farraday cleared his throat in preparation for a pronouncement. "Miss Piper," he said, "what I admire about your directing is that you avoid the trite. You are not uninventive in small matters. We actors," he spoke the words as if he were saying "we prime ministers of England," "stand in dread of scenes in which we merely stand or sit and pass lines back and forth, in which there is no relieving action. In these spots there are all too many directors, lacking imagination, who resort to such overworked devices as lighting a cigarette, or taking a drink. I'm thinking of that scene between myself and my son. You perceived the need for the punctuation of action. But what you required us to do was not artificial. You foresaw what might be needed. I am seated at my desk. The dialogue commences. Quite naturally I lay down my pen and turn as though resenting an interruption. Excellent. Does my son light a cigarette? No indeed. Quite as an embarrassed boy might do he runs his finger around inside the back of his collar and awkwardly drops his hat. The feeling of the scene is set. Mediocre direction calls attention to itself. A wisely, artistically directed scene appears spontaneous, uninfluenced from outside."

"Thank you," Quality said briefly.

"Go to any B picture," Farraday continued, "or watch a horse opera on your television. You will see what I mean." He smiled. "Or your Western. Whenever the Western faces a quandary it brings on the galloping horses."

"She does it with gestures," Zagic said, getting to his feet. "Good-by, playmates. I got a heavy date."

They all trooped down the stairs. John Miller went directly

to his apartment. As he fitted his key in the door he heard his telephone ringing. It continued to ring until he reached his desk and lifted the instrument.

"Mr. Miller?" asked an unforgettable voice.

"It is, indeed," John answered.

"Mr. Jabez Winkleman's secretary speaking," said the voice.

"Greetings, secretary," John said.

"Mr. Winkleman," said Loretta Kimball formally, "hopes it will be convenient for you to call tomorrow at ten."

"It will be convenient," John replied, "to call upon Mr. Winkleman at ten. It will be more than convenient to call upon Mr. Winkleman's secretary at any hour of the day or night."

"You will be expected, then," Loretta said impersonally.

John gathered that she was speaking in the presence of her employer or her uncle or whatever relation he might be to her, and that light conversation would not be prudent. He sat in his comfortable chair with the evening newspaper, wondering what the old gentleman had in mind—why he should have troubled to make an appointment. Jabez was an important individual, who, John was certain, did not receive inconspicuous young writers without a purpose. He was flattered as any young man must be, but also he was puzzled. However, there was no purpose to be served by speculating. All would be revealed at the interview in the morning.

His real worry was the Famous Names Group. They were ready. The play had been rehearsed until the actors were ready to go before the cameras. One day in the studio to give the technicians opportunity to light the scenes and to familiarize themselves with the script was now all that was necessary to complete the pilot film. In one more day that could be accomplished and the film sent to the cutting room, where sound, clip shots, close-ups would be assembled and the whole put in the can ready to meet its fate. Everything was ready but money.

If that essential commodity delayed its coming, how long could the company be held together; how much longer would its morale remain high and its keen edge maintained? They might go stale, there might be desertions, the whole thing might fall apart for lack of the not inconsiderable sum necessary for its production. It might, for the sake of all, be necessary to accept Rolf Agnew's offer.

He went out to dine in a state of mind bordering upon discouragement, whiled away the evening at a motion picture and came home to toss upon his bed until sleep closed his eyes.

In the morning he arose reluctantly and prepared his lonely breakfast. It would be useless to try to work with a mid-morning engagement which might be important. He read the papers, dressed, decided to consume the intervening time by walking to Jabez Winkleman's home. He strolled slowly through a morning inclement with chill and fog. A few minutes before the designated hour he arrived at the forbidding bronze gates, which, upon supplying his name, opened to him and he trudged up the steep, winding path to the front door of the residence.

A manservant opened to him, and, once more stating his name, he was conducted down a tapestry-hung hall to the open door of a room that seemed more a library than an office. Jabez Winkleman sat behind a priceless desk. The old gentleman did not rise nor extend his hand, but motioned to a chair.

"Mr. Miller," he said in his precise voice, "I did not send for you captiously."

"I am sure of it, Mr. Winkleman."

"How old are you, young man?"

"Twenty-six," John answered.

"Educated where?"

"Andover and Dartmouth."

"How did you reach Hollywood?"

"I wrote a few short stories. They attracted attention. I was offered a position as writer by one of the studios."

"Were you successful?"

"Not conspicuously." He explained: "Patience is a quality very necessary to a young man in my position. The powers hire you, and then they seem to forget you. It is not easy to have attention direct itself upon you. Your paycheck comes regularly but otherwise you are ignored."

"Inefficient," said Mr. Winkleman.

"Perhaps," John said, "it is deliberate. Possibly to find if you can stick it out."

"Which," Jabez said, "you did not do."

"I am not patient," John said. "Besides, I found a thing I wanted to do."

"Television?" Jabez asked.

"Yes, sir. An idea for a series of plays. Which developed into an idea for a sort of stock company, a co-operative."

"You have," Jabez said, "qualities I am surprised to find in a writer."

"I believe," John said with a smile, "that Julius Caesar was an author. Disraeli wrote novels. Winston Churchill's career started as a writer."

Jabez' answering smile was wintry. "And Mark Twain had to be rescued from financial follies. . . . I made this appointment with you, Mr. Miller, to offer you an opportunity. I am a man of business. I have built a considerable concern. I have done this because, among other reasons, I have known how to pick my subordinates and to delegate authority to them. You have assets which can be useful to me. Would you care to enter my employ?"

"In what capacity, sir?"

"That we should have to determine—where you would fit in. There would have to be a period of education. I can offer you an attractive salary—for a beginner."

"The business world," John said, "does not attract me. I want to succeed in the profession I have chosen. I do not believe I would be happy as an employee discharging monotonous tasks. Besides, Mr. Winkleman, I have obligations to my associates." He paused a moment considering if it would be wise to speak of the other problem in which he found himself involved. He studied Jabez' deacon's face. It was stern, humorless, but intelligent and somehow, it impressed with its integrity. John determined to be confidential.

"Your interest in me, Mr. Winkleman, has its origin in the melodramatic events out at the stables."

"Yes," Jabez said.

"Those events," John continued, "have a background."

"Quite evidently so."

"Without my volition," John said, "I have become involved in something malignant. There has been at least one murder, possibly two. I believe there was, under your eyes, a deliberate attempt to commit another murder."

"Of Miss Piper?" Jabez asked.

"Yes. . . . I have made an enemy—"

"Of Humphrey Salmon," said Jabez. "How does he fit into the background?"

"That I have not discovered, or even that he does fit. Miss Piper believes her father to have been murdered. A man named Shiner, a former jockey, was brutally killed before my eyes, to stop his mouth. I think he was about to tell me something about Miss Piper's father's death."

"Would her father," asked Jabez, "be Marvin Piper, the trainer?"

"Yes, sir."

"A good man, Mr. Miller. An upright man. I knew him well. He is said to have killed himself."

"His daughter," John answered, "does not think so."

"Upon what does she base her conviction?"

"I do not know."

"Does she believe Humphrey Salmon to be involved?"

"I think so, but she has not accused him. She is not a talkative young woman."

"But one," Jabez said with a faint smile, "who is not to be taken lightly." He paused. "As events have shaped themselves, Mr. Miller, do you believe Humphrey Salmon has guilty knowledge?"

"I am convinced of it," John replied.

"Has it occurred to you, young man, that your—er—rashness of the other day has placed you in some danger?"

"Naturally."

"Yet you mean to persist?"

"It would not abate my peril if I did desist. If Salmon is the sort of man I believe he is he will have to save his face. Which means, if he can arrange it, a slab in the morgue for me."

"Quite," said Mr. Winkleman unemotionally. "Er—Mr. Miller, my offer to you is withdrawn. At least temporarily."

"Because I am a bad risk?" John grinned at the old man.

"No," answered Jabez grimly. "Because I think you may be of greater use to me in your—shall we call it avocation?"

"Avocation?"

"Your private war with Humphrey Salmon," Jabez said. He rustled the papers on his desk and did not look at John. "I have some reason to disapprove of Mr. Salmon," he said. "Yes, Mr. Miller, you may prove to be very useful to me, indeed." He stood up in dismissal. John walked to the door, but turned as Jabez spoke. "Young man," he said, "you will be welcome in this house—socially. Though I am somewhat inclined to advise you against availing yourself of that welcome. . . . Thank you for calling, Mr. Miller."

John left the house far more bewildered than he had been when he entered it.

chapter FOURTEEN

"To look at me," Dolly Dove said to John Miller, "you wouldn't think I was much on literature, eh?"

"Well, frankly, no," John said. "I thought your art was culinary."

"While I'm waiting for a leg of lamb to roast," Dolly said, "I read."

"Shakespeare?" John asked.

"Not me," Dolly said scornfully. "Westerns are my meat."

"Leading up to what?" John asked.

"Leading up to," Dolly said, "a man by the name Wilbur Stork."

"And who was Wilbur?"

"Only readers like me remember," Dolly said, "on account of he wrote in magazines you never heard of. Maybe fifteen—twenty years ago. He wrote about a ranch that was called the Diamond K where nobody was employed that wasn't a hero. And where the boss hero was a scalawag with the name of Curleyhead Considine."

"And so?" John asked.

"And so, and in consequence of me being elected by you folks vice-president in charge of skulduggery and finance, I snooped. This Stork author is around seventy-five years old. He's extinct. For those stories he never got more than a hundred dollars apiece. Well, maybe there have been literary critics more literary than I am, but when it comes to material for movies I got experience to guide me."

"Find a place to light," John told her. "I'm up in the air."

"Two thousand dollars," Dolly said, "was like finding the Comstock Lode for this Stork. So, while you were spending your time getting into trouble and running after the wrong girl, I hunted up this Stork and made a dicker with him. Remember your two thousand dollars? . . . Well, you haven't got it any more. With it," she went on, peering at him somewhat askance under her plucked eyebrows, "I make a dicker."

"Now," John said, "you've got me really interested."

"So we now own the motion picture and radio and cheap edition rights to Curleyhead Considine, with this worn-out author getting a fair split of the profits, if any."

"And there," John said, with sinking heart, "goes our capital —bang."

"Could be," Dolly answered uneasily. "But on the contrary possibly not. One thing you kind of forget, Johnnie. I'm a has-been but I ain't a never-was. In places and by people I still get treated polite, and I can walk into offices that maybe even Perle Mesta would have to wait on a bench outside of. For old time's sake."

"Continue," John said.

"That's all," Dolly answered. "To be continued in our next. Just wanted to break it to you that your two thousand nice dollars have gone down the drain—maybe."

John grinned wryly. "Well," he said philosophically, "they weren't much good to me anyhow."

Dolly changed the subject abruptly. "If," she said, "there were two bundles on the table there, and in one of them was wrapped up Quality Piper, and in the other was this Loretta Kimball—and you were given your choice to take, which would it be?"

"That," said John, "is what is called a hypothetical question."

"I know about them," Dolly asserted. "Invented by a San Francisco shyster by the name of Delmar when Harry Thaw was being tried for murder. It got, if memory don't flutter, this Thaw sent to the bug house instead of to the hot seat."

"But I," John said, "am not on trial."

"That," piped Dolly, "is what you think."

"Incredible as it may seem to you, Dolly," John smiled, "it's possible neither of them would want to be chosen."

"Which, of course," Dolly said tartly, "you're too dratted vain to believe. What would become of the world if every boy your age didn't estimate himself so high he thinks he can get any girl he has a yen for? It would be bad for eugenics—and you needn't grin, on account of I know bigger words than that. Sure. If young men didn't have that notion, and was humble, they'd all go for second-class girls they'd think they were worthy of, or maybe third-class—and the race would slide downhill. Nope, Mr. Miller, he-vanity is one thing we got to rely on if we aim to improve the breed."

"You're a philosopher, Dolly. But what about the tenable theory that it's the women who do the pursuing and selecting?"

"Bosh," Dolly said. "A girl can't select and hunt down what ain't available. A man's got to stand in reach of the rope before he can be lassoed. . . . And you're trying to give me the Chinese runaround and get my mind off the main subject. Which would you pick?"

"At the moment—neither," John said a bit impatiently. "I've more pressing things to think about than girls."

Dolly emitted a treble snort.

"And," John said, "while we're on the subject—and as a sort of corollary—who is this gentleman with whom Quality Piper has so many engagements? Probably she is somewhere with him at this very moment?"

Dolly's face became worried. "I don't know," she said somberly. "I simply don't know. She doesn't state. I can't pry it out of her."

"Then," John said with a wide grin, "I'd suggest that you work her over a little before you plow my field."

John put down his teacup on the table beside the plate on which only one delicious doughnut remained.

"How sore are you going to be," Dolly asked, "if I've lost your bankroll?"

"Not very," John answered. "Call it a donation to charity. This Wilbur Stork will have meals instead of just mealtimes."

Dolly bestowed upon him her highest compliment. "Johnnie," she said softly, "you're a trouper."

The point had arrived where John felt it necessary to economize, so, instead of riding back to his apartment in a taxi, he took the long walk. Day was merging into evening when he arrived at the entrance to the building and he was about to turn in when the door of a waiting taxicab opened and Sligo McNulty stepped out to confront him.

"Hello, Mr. Miller," Sligo said. His right hand was in his jacket pocket.

"Got another proposition for me?" John asked.

"Nope. Invitation. Gilt-edged, engraved invitation."

"Well, well!" John exclaimed with mock surprise. "From whom?"

"Mr. Salmon wants to see you," Sligo said.

"But," John answered, "I don't want to see Mr. Salmon."

"I got something in my pocket here that says you do," Sligo retorted.

"Why, Sligo, I thought you were just a chiseler. No idea you were a gunman, too."

"I'm versatile," Sligo said. He motioned to the taxi. "Your car's waiting, me Lord."

John half turned as if to obey; then his left hand darted out and gripped Sligo's left wrist while he pivoted on his heel and drove his right fist into Sligo's stomach. Sligo said, "Awk!" and doubled up like a jackknife, dropping to his knees and was ill. John stooped over him, jerked the automatic from his pocket and slipped it into his own.

"I read in a book," he said, "that a high-grade gunman never gets in reach of his victim's hands. That makes you second-class. "So Salmon wants to see me, does he?"

Sligo was too occupied to speak. John stirred him with his

foot and then stepped to the open door of the taxi. "Know where to go?" he asked the driver.

"Sure," said the man in a disinterested voice.

"Then," John said, "go there, and no capers."

"Me," said the man, "I just drive cabs. I don't waltz with nobody." He eyed John over his shoulder for a second. "You're kind of sudden, ain't you, Buddy?" John thought he detected a hint of admiration.

"Instinctive reflex," John said, "slightly conditioned by contact with effete civilization."

"My gawd!" exclaimed the driver. "One of them. He et a dictionary."

John slammed the door. He glanced at Sligo who had not yet seen fit to arise from a kneeling position. The driver meshed his gears and drove. His skill as a chauffeur was of so high an order that John understood why he should be employed on such an errand as this. The cab stopped in the parking space before a tall office building.

"This it?" John asked.

"You're there, Professor," said the driver.

John alighted and entered. He studied the list of tenants in the lobby and found that Humphrey Salmon Enterprises was on the sixth floor. The elevator carried him upward and he walked to a door with Salmon's name on the glazed glass. When he opened it he found himself in the reception room of a suite of offices that were impressive. He walked to the desk behind which sat a businesslike young woman.

"Mr. Humphrey Salmon, please," he said.

"Your name?"

"John Miller."

"Have you an appointment?"

"Oh, definitely," John told her.

She spoke into the telephone and then nodded to John. "Mr. Salmon will see you, sir. Second door on the left."

The surroundings in which John found himself suggested prosperity and efficiency, with no suggestion of anything of which to be afraid. It was reassuring. In offices such as this, occupied, busy, there could be no violence of which to be apprehensive. It was odd, John thought, that an invitation to visit such a layout should be delivered at pistol's point.

He did not knock but opened Salmon's door and stepped quickly inside. It was a large room, luxuriously furnished. The walls were embellished with old hunting prints and an excellent Currier and Ives depicting the ancient trotter, Maude S. Salmon sat behind a huge Circassian walnut desk. He did not rise, but he did lift his brows.

"Where," he asked, "is Mr. McNulty?"

"Slightly ill," John answered. "On the sidewalk in front of my apartment. He gave me an automatic as a souvenir of our meeting."

Salmon shrugged. "At any rate you are here," he said. John noted that the weal left by the whip had not faded from his cheek.

"Of my own volition," John said.

"You are always striking people," Salmon complained.

"There are something over a hundred million people in the United States," John answered grimly, "that I never struck. I'm selective."

"I was afraid," Salmon said, "that an ordinary invitation would not have been accepted by you."

"It wouldn't," John answered.

"Mr. Miller, you have struck me twice. Once with your fist; the second time with a whip. At the race track I assured you that I held no resentment. You were justified. Strangely enough I have no desire for reprisals for the second occasion. It was a moment of intense excitement—a regrettable moment. You acted upon a false premise, but again there was justification."

"You deliberately tried to murder or to maim Miss Piper with an enraged stallion," John charged grimly. He paused an instant. "Why?"

"If," Salmon said, "I had any intention to harm Miss Piper I would have chosen a more efficient method."

"There is," John retorted, "such a thing as spur of the moment. It might have come off. No charge could have been made against you." He paused again, and then said, "None of this explains why you wanted to talk to me."

"I'm trying to explain. I do not like enemies. They are a nuisance. Primarily I wanted to tell you that you have not made an enemy of me."

"Why," asked John, "should you care?" John smiled thinly. "Was the idea to make me careless?"

"I want to do business with you," Salmon said. "Among other things I am an author's agent. I'm good at it. I would like you for a client. You have great promise."

"How would you know that?" John asked.

"You have just done a very excellent script."

"How would you know that?" John repeated. "Did you read the script? One was stolen from my room the night of our first encounter."

"Such things get around among the trade," Salmon said.

"Not good enough," John said. "Mr. Salmon, I wouldn't do business with you if it were a choice between that and starvation."

"I'm sorry, Mr. Miller—very sorry."

"I'm still wondering why you wanted me to come here," John said. "Certainly not to solicit me as a client. I would be small peanuts to you. Of course you had a purpose."

"I have no other purpose," Salmon said gravely.

"Such, perhaps—in the argot of the underworld—to put me on the spot."

"Absurd, Mr. Miller."

John jerked the automatic from his pocket and tossed it on the desk. It scarred the polished walnut. "Return it to Sligo McNulty," he said.

"Why not," Salmon asked imperturbably, "keep it as a souvenir?"

"Not my type of *objet d'art*," John said. "Our business seems to be over. Or is there something else?"

"Nothing else, Mr. Miller. Thank you for coming."

John turned away, presenting his back to Salmon. It required resolution. The pistol lay so handy on the man's desk. He strode to the door, opened it and stepped out into the corridor. Nothing happened.

One thing was clear in John's mind. The conversation he had just completed with Humphrey Salmon was meaningless. Salmon must have had a compelling reason to bring him here—to step so far outside the character he was careful to present to the world as to send a gunman with his invitation. There was a reason for bringing him to this place at this time. John felt a chill between his shoulder blades. It was not so much a premonition as a certainty that he was walking into something. Some reception had been prepared for him, but at what moment it would come or what form it would take he could not guess. As he stood before the bronze doors of the battery of elevators, it seemed foolish to be apprehensive. This was one of the most select office buildings in Los Angeles. True, it was late afternoon and most of the businesses housed there had been closed for the day; but even so it was an unlikely scene for violence.

His finger pressed the button and his eyes followed the arrow on the indicator over the door. A light flashed, the elevator door was thrust open by its operator, and John stepped inside. He was alone with the girl in a sort of metal vault where he could not be reached until those doors opened again to permit his exit. For that interval, while the car descended, he was safe from any attack.

The car stopped; the operator opened the door and John stepped out into the marble lobby. His feet sounded loud upon the floor as he walked toward the street. Standing at the cigar counter was a gentleman with an exquisitely tailored back who turned as John came abreast of him and nodded agreeably.

"Good evening, Mr. Miller," the gentleman said courteously.

"Good evening, Gargoyle," John replied.

"Not meaning to be offensive, of course?"

"Definitely not," John answered. "Merely descriptive."

"Pretty is as pretty does," said the man. His smile was a grimace which removed his words from the realm of triteness. "I have been waiting for you."

"I rather thought someone would be," John answered.

"There is," said the Gargoyle, "a rear entrance to this building. To reach it one must go through that door behind you to the basement. Will you permit me to guide you?"

"Why?" John asked, bending his will to compel his voice to remain steady.

"Because," said the Gargoyle, "in my opinion it will be more clement."

"And if I refuse?"

"I'm afraid there would be an argument."

"Which you would win?"

"Which," was the answer, "I would win." He flicked back his coat and before it fell into place again, John glimpsed a revolver in a holster hanging at the man's side. "Shall we go? You precede me." He smiled his hideous smile again. "I'm not Sligo McNulty," he said.

"So you saw that?" John said.

"Excellent reflexes. . . . Please follow directions."

John walked erectly to the designated door. A flight of steps led downward. "To your right, please," said the Gargoyle. "Then straight ahead." They continued through the gloom of the basement and every instant John thought to hear the roar of a gun and feel the impact of a bullet. He continued to walk.

"Up the half-stairs and into the street," was the next command.

John found himself in a narrow street that was alike to an alley. There was no automobile waiting there.

"If I were you," his conductor said, "I would walk three blocks to your left before turning. Then a block to the right, where you will be able to call a taxicab." Again came that distorting grimace. "And in future, Mr. Miller, please obey only your more rational impulses."

John's legs felt suddenly boneless. His voice was not altogether steady as he spoke. "What is this, anyhow?" he asked.

"A slight variant," said the Gargoyle, "in the profession of baby-sitter. Good evening, Mr. Miller."

The man turned leisurely and strolled away. John was not sure, in his relief, that he could walk to the corner, much less the number of blocks he had been advised to cover.

chapter FIFTEEN

John was perplexed. The Gargoyle was an enigma to him. At their first encounter the man had seemed menacing in spite of his gracious manners; on the second encounter at Jabez Winkleman's party he had been humorous in a sinister way; in the third encounter in the lobby of the office building in which Salmon's offices were situated, he had been facetiously paternal. The three pictures failed to register, as color printers say. They did not fit into a pattern. Of one thing John felt he could be certain: that the Gargoyle had thwarted some intention of Humphrey Salmon's by guiding him out of the building by a devious route. Something unpleasant had been prepared for John had he left the building by its main entrance. But what had been the grotesque man's motive in befriending? John could not guess—or whether he was friend or foe.

In his mailbox, when he reached his apartment building, he found a single letter, the address in script, bold, full of character, each letter perfectly formed. He opened the envelope as he walked up the stairs and paused at his door to read. It was informal.

"Dear John," it opened. "Uncle has a horse running at Santa Anita tomorrow. Would you care to join us for luncheon in the Club House? The car will call for you at eleven-thirty. Please telephone." It was signed "Loretta Kimball."

Without taking off his hat John sat down on the davenport, read the note a second time and hesitated. Had the invitation been inspired by Jabez Winkleman? Was it a mere expression of Loretta's willingness to proceed further with their acquaintance, or was it another move on the bewildering checkerboard? Whichever it was John could perceive no disadvantage to him in accepting. He tossed his hat on the desk and dialed the private number Loretta had given him. Her unforgettable voice answered.

"John Miller speaking, Miss Kimball," he said.

"Couldn't it be Loretta?" she asked.

"I'm not venturesome," he said, "but a little encouragement helps. Loretta, I found your note. I'll be delighted to go out to the track with you."

"Pray for good weather," she said. "Uncle's horse isn't a mudder. Tomorrow at eleven-thirty."

"In my best necktie with my hair combed," John said.

Fifteen minutes later the telephone rang. This time it was Dolly Dove.

"Hi, Johnnie," came her twittering voice. "Want to be chauffeur tomorrow? Santa Anita. I got one straight from the horse's mouth. Toots and the Character and me."

"Sorry, darling," John answered. "I'm in demand. You're a quarter of an hour late."

Dolly's sniff was audible. "Lemme guess. The blonde snake-charmer."

"I never noticed the reptiles," John answered. "But it is Miss Kimball and Mr. Winkleman. Going in style including uniformed chauffeur."

"I'll have to exhume Kent Farraday," Dolly said disappointedly. "Better put wax in your ears."

"I didn't know Ulysses was a friend of yours," John laughed.

"Ulysses I don't study," Dolly answered, "but I'm a specialist on sirens. You betting on Winkleman's nag?"

"If," John said, "it's a dry track."

"I might risk two dollars on him," Dolly said. "Good-by."

Promptly at eleven-thirty next morning the Winkleman car arrived for John. Its only occupant was Loretta Kimball—if one did not count the chauffeur who opened the door for John.

"You're prompt," he said to Loretta.

She was staring with some distaste at the street and the façade of the apartment house. John grinned. "There'll be a bull market in my social standing when the neighbors see me in this equipage," he said.

"On the gloomy side, isn't it?" she asked.

"It has one attribute that brightens it up," John answered.

"Yes?"

"Its cheapness," John said.

"Surely," she said, "you can afford a better neighborhood than this."

"I suppose I could. But I'm a penny pincher. A penny saved is a penny earned. Suppose I earn five hundred dollars a week. I suppose I could afford to spend a hundred of it for rent. But I don't. I spend fifty a month. That increases my earnings by three hundred and fifty a month. That's four thousand a year. In forty years it would amount to a hundred and sixty thousand. And I could retire." His grin was amiable.

She smiled back with equal amiability. "Let's see. I guess you to be twenty-seven. In forty years you'll be sixty-seven, with maybe eight years more to live. So you've traded forty years of comfort for eight years of security." She shook her head. "Not for me," she said firmly.

"When you're old and broke," John said, "because you've spent your substance in riotous living, I'll come around and make faces at you."

"But I'll have had fun," she answered, and then almost fiercely, "Nothing is going to stop me from having fun."

"Probably nothing will," John said. "But then you have a capital asset that I lack."

"I?" she asked, wide-eyed.

"Beauty," John said.

She turned and looked at him with half-narrowed eyes. There was a measure of calculation in her glance, and something besides that he could not read. "That," she said, "is cynical—as if you thought beauty were a marketable commodity."

"Isn't it?" he asked. "Whether you like it or not; whether you think it's nice or not, there you are. Let's take two girls of equal virtue and intelligence. One of them is homely as a mud fence. The other is as lovely—say—as you are. Which one is the odds-on favorite? The beauty gets a more desirable husband, or a more richly endowed penthouse. Because she displays more marketable wares."

"I suppose that's true," she said. "Beauty is opportunity. If you're a smart girl and wait till the right knock comes on your door. But there's a catch. Or why would so many lovely girls tie themselves to clucks?"

"What's the catch?" he asked.

"The idiots," she said tartly, "fall in love."

"Which you mean not to do."

"Which," Loretta said firmly, "I definitely mean to do. I wouldn't miss it for gold and precious stones. I only hope I have good luck." There was a trace of uneasiness, even of bitterness in her amazingly musical voice.

"Good luck?" John asked.

"I hope he'll be—eligible. I hope he'll be free. I hope he'll be in a position to love me and to marry me."

"But if he isn't?" John asked.

Her hand touched his, gripped it. "Then," she answered gravely, "I'll make the best of it. I'll toss my bonnet over the windmill."

"Interesting," John said and peered down into her eyes. "But there's always the alternative of marrying for money or position—and making the best of it."

"I've thought about that—of the necessity for that." She compressed her inviting lips. "It wouldn't deprive me of love."

"How amoral!" John said amusedly.

"Be shocked if you want to."

"I'm not shocked. I'm just speculating."

"There's no law against that," she said, and her shoulder pressed against his arm. It might have been inadvertent.

135

"You're not opening possibilities?" he asked.

She smiled up at him, and there was impact in her smile. "You're a startlingly attractive man," she answered.

"Whoops!" John exclaimed.

"Suppose," she said, withdrawing a little, "we pass on to another topic."

"Leaving this one on the agenda?" he asked.

"Why not?" She changed the subject abruptly. "If I didn't love horses I'd never take this miserable drive again."

Was Loretta, John asked himself, being merely honest; was she having fun with him; or did he actually, as Dolly Dove had suggested, need to block his ears with wax from a siren's song? On the whole, reverting to that warning voice over the telephone; to her challenge to Quality Piper at the party; to the appearance of the Gargoyle in the garden, he was inclined to vote for the wax. So far, in the puzzle which perplexed and sometimes frightened him, Loretta was the one point of contact with the murder of Shiner, the jockey, and with the motive for that killing. His attitude toward her must be one of business, not pleasure. If it were her intention to lure him, then he must permit himself to be allured. Being young and not especially despising himself, he gave no thought to the danger that her allurement might be too strong for him to withstand.

They were driven to the foot of the stairs which rose to the club house and entered the lounge. It was a lavish and beautiful spectacle. It seemed to John that millions of flowers must have given their lives for its embellishment. Never in his life had he seen before such masses of lovely blossoms. They blanketed the walls, overflowed from tables. The great room had been transformed into a florist's dream.

Already many people were there, being served with preluncheon beverages. Well-known faces, lovely as the flowers—if a trifle more artificial—were to be seen in almost equal profusion. There were actors, magnates, producers on display, and a scattering of citizens with no claim to eminence, but with connections which gained them admission to the club house. Loretta paid the notables scant attention though many of their eyes followed her enviously. She was not of their world, seemed rather scornful of their world.

A table in a select spot awaited them outside. Once again it was opposite the tote board, almost upon the finishing line. It was set for four, but they two were the first to occupy it. The great oval inside the track again was ablaze with flowers. Beyond it rose the mountains—a magnificent backdrop for the scene. No more impressive setting for the sport of kings could be devised by man.

"Beautiful, isn't it?" asked Loretta.

"The most seductive gambling hell in all creation," John answered dryly.

"Don't be saturnine," she chided laughingly. "The object of all this is to improve the breed of horses."

"Go down to the windows when they open," John said, "and see how many of these people are interested in equine eugenics. To them blood lines are statistics on a form sheet."

"Few of the great owners are betters," Loretta defended.

John went on teasing her. "When they improve the breed of horses what do they accomplish?" he asked.

"Beauty, for one thing," she answered.

"That's one score for your side," John admitted. "But what about that is useful? When breeding produced Man o' War what did it contribute to the world? Was civilization advanced a single stride? Did humanity benefit?"

"Get off the soap box," Loretta said gaily. "Do we have cocktails? What's on the menu?"

"Shouldn't we wait for Mr. Winkleman?"

"Maybe we'll catch a glimpse of him. It's doubtful. . . . Oh, there are some of your friends! That exquisite Miss Piper, and Miss Dove. Who's the distinguished old gentleman with them?"

"That," John answered, "is Kent Farraday. In his day he was as great a screen actor as Clark Gable is today."

Loretta stared at the old gentleman with narrowed, speculative eyes. "It must," she said, "be a horrid thing to have stood at the top, famous, envied—and then to have it all disappear and to be forgotten."

137

"No," John answered gravely. "Not if you have integrity. Not unless vanity is the one great moving force in your life. It isn't the aura of glamour and applause that makes a man great; it is the character and ability of the man that creates the glamour and applause. He is as great when they disappear, in himself, as he was when they were present. It is only tragic if your vanity cannot endure the loss of the trimmings."

"I couldn't stand it," Loretta said. "I couldn't." She continued to peer at Kent Farraday. "He has a splendid head. He—he looks like a great gentleman."

"He would like to hear that from your lips," John said gravely.

Jabez Winkleman came down the steps stiffly. "Afternoon, Miller," he said to John. "Sorry I couldn't drive out with you." He smiled dryly. "Better probably. Two young people don't need an old man to wag a tiresome jaw." He drew out a chair and sat down. "I'll have a sandwich with you. Then would you like to go down and see Wheat Field?"

"Very much," said John. "It's a dry track so I'm plunging on your horse. Two dollars across the board."

"I'm venturing," Jabez said, "two dollars on the nose." He glanced over the people sitting at their tables. "Aren't those your friends, Mr. Miller? Miss Dove and the young woman who dived so beautifully?"

"Calling on horses," John said dryly, "doesn't seem to be a lucky social event for Miss Piper."

"Do let's ask them," Loretta said enthusiastically. "Then I can meet that wonderful-looking old gentleman."

"Old gentleman?" Jabez said. "Since when, my dear, have elderly gentlemen attracted you? . . . His face is vaguely familiar."

"He," John said, "is Kent Farraday."

"Indeed it is," Jabez responded. "Years since I've seen him on the screen. Dolly Dove and Kent Farraday. How the sight of them carries me back."

They finished their luncheon. The stands were filling rapidly with people chatting, studying form sheets, moving from table to table. Numbers were appearing on the tote board—horses and odds in the first race of the afternoon. Jabez laid down his napkin and stood up. "Shall we go?" he asked.

John and Loretta followed him. He stopped at Dolly's table, but it was Loretta who spoke to them first. "How nice to see you here, Miss Piper," she said with a graciousness that was the merest fraction beyond the line of being overdone. "And Miss Dove. . . . Can it be this is Mr. Farraday? To meet you makes the afternoon perfect."

"Your public has arrived!" exclaimed Dolly shrilly, with a touch of acid in her voice. "Let's see you turn handsprings."

"I would delight to turn handsprings for so lovely a young lady," Farraday declaimed. He smiled at Dolly. "You don't begrudge me this moment of adulation, surely."

"Your joints," Dolly squeaked, "are too stiff for doing nip-ups."

Jabez extended his hand to Farraday. "Time has been kind to you, sir," he said in his stiff, deacon's manner. "We are going down to see my horse Wheat Field. Would you all like to come with us?"

They trooped down the stairs, even Dolly to whom pedal locomotion was repulsive, and walked to the stables. A hundred feet along they paused before a stall over whose half door was thrust the head of a golden gelding, eyes gentle, ears cocked inquisitively. For him Wheat Field was an apt name. Quality Piper, as if drawn by some affinity, stepped close to the door. Wheat Field arched his neck, cocked his ears in an instant's hesitation and then bent his head to nuzzle Quality's cheek.

"The like of that," said a wizened little man in leather puttees, "I never seen!" He stared; his eyes widened with incredulity. "Miss Quality! It's Miss Quality. No wonder Wheat Field gives you the kiss of welcome. . . . Miss Quality, don't ye remember Danny? Sure, you ain't forgot Danny."

Quality's face was transformed. It became young and happy. All self-restraint vanished, all discipline. "Oh, Danny! Danny!" she exclaimed softly, and took the leathery face between her hands and kissed the wrinkled cheek. "Oh, Danny! Danny!" Tears were in her voice and in her eyes.

"Me old eyes," Danny whispered, "never thought to have the joy of restin' on your bonny face again."

"Why," exclaimed Loretta, "it's a reunion!"

"Yes, Miss Kimball," Danny replied, coldly polite, "it's a reunion the like of which comes but once to any man."

"Quite touching," said a sardonic voice from the right. John Miller turned to see Humphrey Salmon standing there, his eyes crinkled in a mirthless smile. "Good afternoon. I trust Wheat Field is fit, Mr. Winkleman."

He took a step toward the stall, but Danny interposed his small body. "Keep away from my horse, you." His gray eyes were sparking; even in daylight they seemed chatoyant. "You ain't fitten to come nigh a horse like Wheat Field. Don't you dast to touch him."

"Why," Salmon elevated his brows, "what is this?"

"Well you know what is this," said the little man.

"Danny!" Mr. Winkleman did not lift his voice but it carried command. The little man backed away and stood with his shoulders against the door of the stall. The golden gelding nuzzled his neck.

There was the sound of a small, soft thud, and a tinkle. Loretta Kimball had dropped her handbag and its contents escaped to the trodden ground. Salmon bent swiftly, swept the trinkets into the container and handed the bag to Loretta. Then he bowed nonchalantly and walked away in the direction of the club house. Loretta held her handbag under her arm, pressed tightly to her body. "We'll miss the first race if we don't get back," she said nervously.

John Miller was not surprised by her sudden tension. The thing had been boldly contrived and audaciously carried out under their eyes. Probably none of them but himself had seen Humphrey Salmon, as he fumbled with the spilled contents of Loretta's purse, add to them furtively a folded bit of paper. The opportunity had been contrived. Obviously to John the meeting had been arranged. The girl had dropped her bag to give Salmon opportunity for some communication.

Jabez Winkleman did not return with them. Quality patted

Danny's shoulder and whispered something in his ear. They walked back chatting to their tables.

"Good luck, Johnnie," whispered Dolly Dove.

"In what?" John asked.

"I've got eyes in my head, too," Dolly said, and sat down, spreading her clouds of pastel skirts around her. She was grinning maliciously.

Opportunity did not come to John until the third race in which Wheat Field was running. It was an exciting finish. Three horses came into the back stretch neck and neck. Loretta, urging on the golden gelding, flushed, excited, left her purse on the top of the table. John stood behind her as she clapped her hands together, crying out encouragement. His hand reached out. Swiftly he snicked open the bag. His fingers explored and came out with the folded note. He thrust it in his pocket just as Wheat Field flashed over the finish line winner by half a length.

chapter SIXTEEN

It was natural that John Miller should feel some restraint during the drive back to Hollywood. In his pocket reposed a scrap of paper abstracted by him from Loretta Kimball's handbag—placed there by Humphrey Salmon. This established to his satisfaction that Loretta's voice had indeed been the one he heard over the telephone on the night of Shiner's murder. It established that there existed between Loretta and Salmon some concealed connection of a guilty nature. No opportunity had been given him to read the paper, and Loretta had not discovered its loss.

Loretta settled back in her corner of the seat and explained her silence by saying that she was exhausted. John was relieved that conversation was not required of him. As their journey approached its end Loretta did not suggest that he stop in at Jabez Winkleman's home for some refreshment. Instead she suggested that she drop him in McCadden Place. He deduced that she was eager to be alone to read the communication from Salmon.

As the car stopped at his door Loretta ceased for a moment to be distrait and extended a warm hand. "It's been a lovely afternoon," she said. "So nice it mustn't stand alone. You'll telephone me, John."

"In the morning," he assured her.

"If this keeps on," she said provocatively, "we may not have to telephone each other."

"Don't be turning a young man's head," he said. She lifted her face and he kissed her, not too perfunctorily.

He ran up the stairs, opened his door and withdrew the folded paper from his pocket. On it were scrawled only a few words: "Same time. Same place. Without fail." There was no signature. There was no information there—only a peremptory command to an assignation. He concealed the note in the pages of his dictionary. It might become a significant piece of evidence.

He scratched up a lonely meal and sat down at his desk to work upon a script. Unaccountably invention flowed. He lost himself in composition. Hour followed hour until he was exhausted, pleasantly exhausted and with a rewarding sense of accomplishment. Once in bed he slept like a top.

He had not set his alarm clock but the ringing of the telephone bell awakened him. It was Dolly Dove's twittering voice.

"Had breakfast, Johnnie?" she asked.

"Just woke up," he answered drowsily.

"Make yourself a cup of coffee and hot foot it up here," she directed. "We've got a date."

"With whom?" he asked.

"Don't ask silly questions," Dolly said. "Just light a fire under your behind."

John stumbled into his kitchenette, put on the coffee, broke a couple of eggs and laid three or four strips of bacon in the spider. With food under his belt he felt more eager to face the day. He bathed, dressed and ran down the stairs zestfully. Life was good. After two blocks' walk he secured a taxicab which carried him through the gracious morning to Dolly's apartment. Dolly was ready all but the hat. Quality Piper was ready in a severely tailored suit.

"Never," Dolly greeted him, "miss a chance for another cup of coffee."

"Why the turmoil?" he asked.

Dolly saw fit to be tantalizing. "Gulp your coffee," she said.

"I'm not inquisitive," John said. "I'm co-operative. I dote on being waked up in the middle of the night. I love to be ordered around. 'Mine not to reason why; mine but to do and die.'"

"Yeah," Dolly said amiably. " 'All in the valley of Death rode the six hundred.' I recited that in the fifth grade. We're going out to sink the hook into Rolf Agnew. Stuff him and hang him over the mantel."

"Why Rolf Agnew?" John asked.

"On account of," Dolly said, "he's sniffin' the bait."

"All right," John grinned, "I'm in no hurry. What bait?"

"Curleyhead Considine," Dolly twittered. "I been working while you slept. You and I, Johnnie, are going along to haul in the line. Toots is coming to see the fish don't steal the bait."

Quality had contributed no word to the dialogue beyond a brief good morning. She sat serenely betraying no sign of impatience. She watched John drain his coffee. "Shall we go?" she asked.

"What's keepin' us?" Dolly squeaked and bounced to her feet.

John drove the car. Quality sat beside him, while Dolly occupied the back seat.

"Enjoy the races?" John asked.

"Yes," she replied.

"Bet on Wheat Field?"

"Yes," she said.

"Now that we've covered that fully," John said ruefully, "what topic do we attack next?"

"None," Quality answered.

"Mind if I whistle?" John asked.

"Can you?" she asked with what he hoped was a flicker of interest.

"Like a bird."

"Then whistle," she said.

John was a whistler. He puckered his lips and emitted trills and runs and warbles to arouse the envy of a canary.

"Diggity!" exclaimed Dolly Dove. "He must have hatched out of an egg."

Then John was astounded. Quality was whistling too. Following him with amazing skill, her whistle blending with his, harmonizing, executing trills and cadenzas with sheer artistry. John turned to stare at her. She seemed unconscious of him—completely absorbed, eyes shining and happy.

"Dog my cat!" Dolly exclaimed.

"What else can you do?" John demanded. "You dive like a swan; you whistle like a mockingbird. Can you do card tricks or tell fortunes?"

"Yes," she said.

"Tell mine."

She turned and looked at him gravely. It seemed to John that it was the first time she really had been aware of his existence. She shook her head. "Not yet," she said firmly.

John drove on silently. Quality was an enigma. She lived within a shell, but now and then, at rare intervals, she emerged for an instant. When she did so there was a glimpse of quite another person, not a coldly efficient machine, not a girl suppressing all emotion, enigmatic, almost forbidding, but warm, alive, eager. He remembered her as he had seen her yesterday before Wheat Field's stable when the wizened little man had greeted her. Then she had been sweet, gentle, affectionate, capable of deep emotion.

"Who," he asked, and was surprised at his own question which was spoken without conscious volition, "who is Danny?"

Instantly she shut herself away again. "An old friend," she said coldly.

They came to Culver City, turned through Rolf Agnew's gates, gave their names to the guard and were waved on. John remembered the way to the office and stopped just inside the cul-de-sac where the cottage was from which Agnew directed his enterprises. The receptionist remembered him, and smiled. "Mr. Agnew will see you," she said. "Go right in."

Agnew sat shirt-sleeved, one leg over the arm of his chair. He straightened himself and stood up. "Long time, Dolly," he said.

"Long time, Rolf," she responded.

"So you're in this, Miller? And who is the young lady?"

"Miss Piper, Mr. Agnew," John introduced.

"Quite an army," Agnew said. "Sit, everybody."

"We need an army," Dolly twitted, "if we want to hang on to our eye teeth."

They seated themselves. Agnew tapped a folder on his desk. "I've read this tripe," he said.

"Some folks," Dolly said, "got a passion for tripe. Cook it six ways myself."

"It's got possibilities," Agnew said.

"If," Dolly snapped, "it didn't have certainties you wouldn't have sent for us to come here. Quit jabbin' with your left and let's go into a clinch."

"Right," Agnew grinned. "Make your play."

"It's not the stories," Dolly said, "it's the character—this Curleyhead Considine. Sure, the stories set him up. But here's a character the kids'll go for strong. It he hits—which he'll do—there won't be just ten or twenty shorts, but a hundred or two hundred or five hundred. It'll go on forever."

"You hope!" Agnew jeered.

"So," Dolly said, "we're not peddling just a bunch of stories. We're peddling a continuous performance."

"All right. You've sung your song. What's your proposition?"

"Twenty-five thousand dollars cash," said Dolly promptly, "and five per cent of the gross on movie shorts and television."

"How," demanded Agnew, "did you escape from your keeper?"

"That's the price," Dolly said firmly.

"No," interjected Quality.

"No—what?" asked Agnew.

"By-products," said Quality.

"What are they?" Agnew demanded.

"Curleyhead cap pistols," Quality said.

"Yeah?"

"Curleyhead cowboy suits."

"Yeah?"

"Curleyhead camping kits."

"Now what," Agnew demanded, tossing his hands in the air, "is the girl talking about?"

"Royalties on the sales of," Quality said.

"Go into that a little further," Agnew said with sudden interest.

"Millions of boys," Quality said. "Tremendous market."

"I grant that, but what of it?"

"If," Quality said, more prodigal with words, "Curleyhead becomes a popular juvenile hero. Form clubs. Curleyhead Corrals. Passwords and grips. Plug Curleyhead products."

"I see," Agnew said. "You mean make a dicker with manufacturers to produce these doo-dads and charge 'em a royalty for using Curleyhead name?"

Quality contented herself with an affirmative nod.

"Maybe you have something, Miss Piper. It would depend, of course, on Curleyhead becoming a knockout boys' hero."

"We," said Quality, "retain those rights."

Agnew peered at Quality with respect. "But consider this, Honey," he said. "I take all the risk. I buy this Curleyhead. Then I spend my money to produce shorts. Not peanuts. My organization markets. I'm the fellow that makes this Curleyhead a hero. I take all the gamble and spend all the money—and you sit back and scoop the gravy."

"Yes," said Quality composedly.

"Young woman you've got a nerve that would stampede elephants."

"Yes," agreed Quality.

"Now you listen to me. I'm Rolf Agnew, the old penny pincher. It's how I've made my dough. By cutting corners and not missing bets. I'm in the driver's seat. You play my way or there's no game."

"No," Quality said promptly.

"I don't doublecross and I don't cheat. I make what I think is a fair offer. You make money. I make money. Everybody's happy."

"Then offer," said Quality.

"I'll take a chance on the Curleyhead stories. They may go. That's my worry. Now here's what I'll do: You folks have got up a thing you call the Famous Names Group. Miller's written the scripts. You've no cash to produce a pilot film. Right?"

"That's right," John said.

"So," Agnew said, "I'll make your pilot film. I'll give it the best possible production. For and in consideration of all rights to Curleyhead. That's my offer. Take it or leave it."

"Leave it," Quality said succinctly. She stood up and nodded and moved toward the door. John's heart stood still. Dolly Dove was eying Agnew through narrowed lids. She got up to follow Quality, and John with a gone feeling in his stomach could not do otherwise. Quality opened the door.

"Hey," Agnew said at the last instant, "don't go off half-cocked."

"You," said Quality, "delivered an ultimatum."

Agnew was rueful. "An ultimatum," he said, "is what you back down from if you don't want to risk a bloody nose. Come back and sit down."

The three returned to their chairs and waited.

"What's your counter-offer?" Agnew asked. "Do you want to consult?"

"Toots is handling this," Dolly said. "We ride with her."

"Shoot, Toots," Agnew said with a wide grin.

"Twenty-two thousand five hundred cash," she said. "Three per cent of the gross. Half the royalties from by-products."

"I'll go for half the royalties," Agnew said after consideration. "Make it two per cent of the gross and full costs of making your pilot film."

Quality smiled at him and nodded. "That," she said, "is what I came to get. Agreed."

Rolf Agnew got up impressively. He walked ponderously to Quality's chair and patted her on the shoulder. "Toots," he said, "with me you jump into the king row. . . . Where'd you find her, Dolly?"

"The cat dragged her in," Dolly said tartly.

"Gimme the loan of that cat," Agnew told her.

"When," John asked, "can we start to grind?"

"Monday morning, if you'll be ready."

"Four days," John said. "We'll be ready."

"What," asked Dolly, "about the word being out against John?"

"There's one word that goes in these studios," Agnew said, "and that's the old man's. . . . I'll have contracts drawn. Ready to sign tomorrow. Hope this turns out good for all of us."

They shook hands all around. Agnew showed them to the door and they climbed into the car. John sat for a moment motionless behind the wheel.

"Start her up," Dolly commanded.

He grinned. "I can't remember how," he said. "I've got to come down to earth. It's really so, isn't it?"

"Yes," Quality said.

"Now," Dolly said, "we can turn the Character loose with publicity."

"I want Kent Farraday to know it first," John said.

"The whole kaboodle are coming to dinner tonight. You can break it to them all at once."

John started the car, meshed the gears and drove out of the lot.

"Want to whistle again, Quality?" he asked gaily.

"Too soon," Quality said.

"Too soon—why?"

"Wait," she said, "till the pilot film is in the can."

chapter SEVENTEEN

The ensuing days were filled with detail. First there must be a set, a living room inside which all action in the first episode of the series would take place. Such a set was available. With slight refurbishing it could be made to do. Furniture was selected from Agnew's storeroom. There was the matter of wardrobe which turned out to be a minor problem. Each actor supplied his own costume from clothing worn by him in his normal life. The general plan of lighting was set in conference with electrical experts who bore odd technical designations. There was the gaffer, and the best boy and the crewmen. The camera crew who were to photograph the play must be acquainted with all details and the prop man must know what articles must be provided and when. Technical matters must be taken up with the sound mixer and his assistants. There was an infinity of matters to which careful attention must be given. John would have been bewildered in the welter of details, but Quality was efficiently calm, never flustered, with a talent for smooth direction and executive ability that caused John to feel his own inadequacy. He was discovering how useless a writer was after the production forces took possession. It was one thing to write a play, to create characters on paper; but quite another thing to bring them to life on celluloid.

When Saturday night came John was in a state of mind, exhausted and irritable and apprehensive. Now that the moment had almost arrived when the success or failure of his idea was out of his hands and in the hands of people who would play the several parts, of technical men who would translate words and acting and business to a pilot film, he suffered agonies of doubt. He was stale. He looked at the whole matter with jaundiced eyes. Such black moods come to every man who creates—when he looks at his work with disgust, almost with loathing and convinces himself that it is not good. He sulked in corners.

Dolly Dove's wise eyes noted. She waddled over to him and twittered. "Johnnie," she said, "you got the heeby-jeebies."

"I wish I was out of it. I wish I never had thought of the damn thing."

"Sure. Everybody feels that way when there's nothing for him to do but wait for the verdict. What you need is some comedy relief."

"I," John said, "couldn't laugh at a man slipping on a banana peel."

"So," Dolly went on, "tomorrow's Sunday. No work here. What we're going to do is relax. You and me and Quality. And Farraday. He's got a peaked look. We're going on a bust. We're going to drive somewhere for the day, and the first one that mentions the Famous Names Group is going to hear words, syllables, phrases and paragraphs from me that will curl their ears."

"I'm spending the day in bed," John said crossly.

"You," retorted Dolly, "are going to do what you're bloody well told, and like it."

"I concede the match," John told her. "What time do we start and where are we going?"

"Be at my place at eight-thirty. I haven't made up my mind where we're going."

They went out to Dolly's car and John drove them home. Dolly asked him to stay to dinner, but John declined. Large-winged moths were fluttering their wings against the walls of his stomach. He wanted to walk and walk and walk. So he set out for McCadden Place briskly. His endeavor was to detach his mind from anything connected with television. He found it was agreeable to think about Quality Piper. He wondered how it would be to spend his life with so taciturn a girl, and decided that it would be highly interesting. He wondered if she would be a different sort of person if her mind was free and her life uncomplicated by the murder of Shiner, by her narrow escape when Humphrey Salmon's great stallion had gone berserk and had come unhappily close to killing her or himself. He sensed that the death of her father was constantly in her thoughts. He wasn't certain whether the berserk horse had been loosed against him or against Quality. Murder must have a compelling motive. The motive for Shiner's killing was clear to him. The little man had been shot down becaese he was about to communicate something to Quality. To someone it seemed necessary to eliminate the jockey. That led him to scrutinize the past. Shiner had intended to disclose the secret of why he had vanished at the very peak of his career. It was logical to suppose that the killing of Shiner stemmed from the death of Quality's father—who believed with all her heart and soul that he had not taken his own life, but had been murdered.

It required no deep reasoning to arrive at this conclusion, or that the compelling purpose of her endeavors was to find the truth about her father's death—and to bring to justice his killer. If that were so then Quality stood in danger. He gave consideration to Loretta Kimball. She was a link; in some manner she was implicated. There was something between her and Salmon who wrote notes to her commanding an assignation. Loretta had, with a boldness, made it rather plain to him that she was attracted by him. The question was whether it was a real thing, or whether she was acting upon orders. For what purpose he could not guess. It was difficult to find the place in the jigsaw puzzle which she occupied. She was an individual who need not throw herself at any man. She possessed rare beauty and a high connection. So desirable was she that she could pick and choose. Then why was she throwing herself at his head? Either she was bad or she was good, and by some indiscretion held over her head by Humphrey Salmon was com-

152

pelled to take his orders and to carry them out. But, as John had studied her, she manifested none of the dread that must inevitably assail a victim of blackmail. Never was she worried or distrait. But whichever it was, she had, because of her lovely speaking voice and characteristic inflection, unveiled herself to John as the one definite coupling with Salmon—the one definite person who established a connection of Salmon with the brutal slaying of Shiner. No man, young or old, can quite compel himself to believe that such a girl, with grace and charm and beauty, can be allied with crime. It was incredible.

He reached his apartment and opened the door. Glancing at his watch he saw that it was seven o'clock, time for local news on the radio. Automatically he turned it on and then divested himself of his outer clothing and put on a comfortable robe. With half an ear he listened to the broadcast while he put coffee in the pot, and decided to supplement it with bacon and eggs and toast. While he waited for the coffee to come to a boil he listened.

"An explosion, which may have been due to carelessness or to murderous intention, wrecked the apartment of Danny Whitcomb late this afternoon. It may have been leaking gas from the stove, or a bomb placed in the kitchen during the absence of Whitcomb and his wife. Whitcomb was removed to the hospital where there is doubt of his recovery. Mr. Whitcomb is well known in racing circles. He is trainer for Jabez Winkleman's stables. This afternoon Wheat Field, belonging to Mr. Winkleman, scored an impressive victory at Santa Anita."

For a moment this announcement did not alert John. Then he remembered—remembered the affectionate greetings exchanged by a small man named Danny and Quality Piper—and Danny's evident enmity toward Humphrey Salmon. He snapped off the radio and reached for the telephone. Dolly Dove's childish treble answered.

"It's Johnnie," he said. "Is Quality there? I'd like to speak to her?"

"What gives?"

"Is Quality there?" he insisted.

153

"I'll call her," Dolly answered.

There was brief silence and then Quality's voice came over the wire.

"Did you," John asked, "listen to Mason's seven-o'clock broadcast?"

"No," Quality said.

"Was the last name of the little man you were so glad to see at Santa Anita this afternoon—Whitcomb?"

"Yes."

"There was an explosion in his flat. The police say gas stove or bomb. I gather they incline to bomb."

"Not Danny! Oh, not Danny!"

"He was taken to the hospital in a precarious condition."

"What hospital?"

Johnnie gave her the name.

"I'll go there at once," Quality said.

"And I'll meet you," Johnnie said.

She did not dissent. "Thank you," was all she said.

John put his clothes on again, turned off the flame under the coffeepot and went out to find a taxicab.

"Don't pull back on the reins," he told the driver.

Twenty minutes of skillful driving carried John to the entrance to the hospital. He found Quality waiting at the information desk. "He's in emergency ward," the attendant told them. "I don't know if you can see him."

"May we see the doctor in attendance?" John asked.

The attendant spoke into a box. A voice replied that Dr. Nevins was in the ward, and not available at the moment.

"Two visitors of Daniel Whitcomb."

"Don't know how long it will be," said the voice, and then, "The doctor has just left the ward. He will be down in a minute."

It was more than a minute before Dr. Nevins appeared, ready for the street, hat upon head and bag in hand.

"Dr. Nevins," called the receptionist.

The doctor approached, glanced at Quality and John curiously. "What is it?" he asked briskly.

Quality, characteristically, left the speaking to John.

"We came," he said, "to find out about Danny Whitcomb—to see him if possible."

"He is under opiates," Dr. Nevins said. "May I ask who you are? Relatives?"

"A very old friend," Quality said.

"What is his condition?"

"He's in shock. Secondary burns about the face." He frowned and hesitated. John knew that he was holding something back.

"Are the police here?" John asked.

"Waiting for him to become conscious."

"So it was not gas."

"I think," Dr. Nevins said, "the officers will want to see you."

"Meantime," John inquired, "what is his condition—I mean his chances for recovery."

"He will," said the doctor, "get well."

"Can he be moved?" Quality asked.

"For what purpose?" Dr. Nevins asked.

"To take him out of the ward. Private nurse. Every attention."

"That can be arranged," the doctor said. "Would your name be Quality?"

"Yes."

"He mutters that name constantly," said the doctor.

"I," she replied, "am Quality Piper. Will you see to it, Doctor, that he has everything?"

Dr. Nevins spoke to the receptionist. "Have the police informed that there are visitors for Danny Whitcomb," he directed.

Presently a plain-clothes officer got off the elevator and came to them.

"Lieutenant Fogg," said the doctor.

"This," John said, "is Quality Piper. I am John Miller."

The lieutenant was a dapperly dressed young man, and John liked his face.

"You came to inquire about Danny Whitcomb," he said, rather than asked.

"Yes," John said.

"Why?" asked the officer.

"Because," said Quality, "I love him."

Her voice must have convinced Lieutenant Fogg, for he relaxed and laid aside the formally severe attitude of an interrogating policeman.

"How did you hear of Whitcomb's—accident?" There was a distinct pause before he spoke the word accident.

"It came over the radio," John said. And then, "It wasn't an accident?"

"It was not an accident. Miss Piper, he keeps muttering a woman's name. Would you be Quality Piper?"

"Yes," she answered.

"At first," Lieutenant Fogg said, "he only mumbled your name. Then he said something that sounded like Sunflower. After that he was restless. 'I must tell Quality,' he muttered several times. What did he want to tell you, Miss Piper?"

She shook her head. "I don't know," she answered.

"He is being moved to a private room," Dr. Nevins said.

"Will a policeman be left on guard?"

"That is hardly necessary."

"I think it highly necessary," John told him. "Do you recall the murder of an ex-jockey named Shiner?"

"I remember. What has that to do with it?"

"Both Shiner and Danny," John told him, "worked for Miss Piper's father. Both wanted to tell Miss Piper something, and were prevented. I think a policeman should be placed at his door."

"What did he want to tell Miss Piper?"

"We don't know. I believe it was something to do with the death of Miss Piper's father."

"Hospitals are safe places," said Lieutenant Fogg. "Nobody could reach Whitcomb there to harm him. Murderers don't break into hospitals."

"But," said John, "it's been done."

The lieutenant spoke, "Miss Piper, was your father the great trainer of race horses?"

"Yes," Quality replied.

"Both Shiner and Danny Whitcomb were his employees at the time of his death?"

156

"Both," said Quality.

"He shall have police protection," the lieutenant said. And then, reassuringly, "His injuries are severe and painful, but not lethal." He turned to Dr. Nevins. "How long before Whitcomb can receive visitors?"

"Not," said the doctor, "before the day after tomorrow."

"So," said Lieutenant Fogg, "there's no reason for you to stay here. I'll want your addresses. We may want to question you again. . . . After Whitcomb returns to consciousness."

Quality spoke again, and to Dr. Nevins, "The best of everything," she said.

"At whose expense?" the doctor asked.

"Mine," Quality said.

"You may run along now," Lieutenant Fogg permitted. "You will be notified if we want to talk to you again."

"My father was murdered," she said.

"The inquest did not say so," said the policeman.

"I say so," Quality responded.

The lieutenant frowned. "It looks," he said, "as if we'll have to backtrack."

"Yes," Quality said.

"If things are as you suspect," Lieutenant Fogg said gravely, "and one witness has been killed and a second has had a narrow escape, you may be in danger."

"I am," Quality said unemotionally.

"Do you ask for police protection?"

"No," Quality said.

"I won't detain you further," said the lieutenant. "Good evening."

They walked to the door with Dr. Nevins. "Spare nothing," Quality said.

"There may be considerable expense," said the doctor.

"Spare nothing," Quality repeated.

They parted in the parking space. Quality and John walked to Dolly Dove's car which had brought Quality to the hospital.

"Shall I drive?" John asked.

"No," answered Quality.

She drove with an efficiency that John admired. It seemed that she did everything with perfection.

"I hope," he said, "that your mind is relieved."

"Yes," Quality answered. And then she uttered a single word. "Flowers," she said.

They drove in silence which Quality broke. "Dear Danny!" she said.

"You have great affection for him?"

"Yes," Quality said.

They drove to a florist's and entered. "Horseshoe," she said to the clerk. "Roses."

"Isn't that sort of—rather—" John objected.

"Yes," Quality said. "Bad taste. But Danny will love it."

John pondered an instant. "I think," he said, "it is in very good taste." He felt drawn toward her; sensed a tenderness able to appreciate and to understand. She was not buying flowers for herself, and, laying aside niceties, had chosen what Danny would like most.

"You're quite a person, Quality," he said.

She turned her head at the sincere compliment and looked at John. She made no reply, but John thought she was pleased.

They ordered the horseshoe, Quality paid for it and they went out to Dolly's car. Quality drove over to Sunset and headed for Dolly's apartment. They passed the entrance to Jabez Winkleman's home. John spoke again.

"What do you think of the Winkleman set-up?" he asked.

"Loretta?" she asked.

"Very well. What about Loretta?"

"A bitch," Quality said promptly.

John jumped as if a pin had been thrust into his leg. He peered at Quality's profile. He could not have been more surprised, possibly shocked had the epithet come from his mother's lips.

"Naughty! Naughty!" he said. "Papa wash the mouth with soap."

"You asked," Quality said. "I answered."

"Maybe I'd better take another topic."

"Yes," said Quality.

"Such as what?"

"Being followed," she told him.

"We? Being followed!"

"Since the hospital," she said.

John peered through the rear window. "That large, black car?"

"Yes," she said.

"Three men in it," John informed her. "Can you shake them off?"

The black car was half a block behind them, maintaining its distance. Ahead was a stretch of two clear blocks without traffic. Quality moved the car over to the middle of the boulevard. Suddenly the black car accelerated speed.

"They're coming up fast," John said.

The black car was now but two lengths behind. In a second it would pass them. Quality thrust with all her might against the brake pedal. John was thrown against the windshield. In the same instant Quality veered the car toward the righthand curb. There was a clatter of sound as bullets were discharged from a sub-machine gun. Quality, by sudden braking and swerving, had ruined their timing and disconcerted the gunner. The bullets went harmlessly ahead of them, only one striking the hood. And then the assailants were gone.

John sank back on the seat, rubbing his bruised forehead. Quality moved over to the curb and stopped the car.

"Quick thinking," John said a bit huskily.

"Only chance," Quality said.

A second car, unnoticed, pulled up behind them and a man alighted. He walked to the open window of Dolly's car and leaned his elbow. It was the Gargoyle.

"Nice going, Miss Piper," he said, and then to John in his amiable, cultured voice. "Don't you remember things, Mr. Miller? I warned you not to stick out your neck."

"How came you in this pea patch?" John asked weakly. Reaction had set in.

"Why, I chaperoned you from the hospital."

"You weren't a great help. If you meant to help."

"In a sense," the Gargoyle said, "you were expendable. To my regret, of course. Now will you please go home and hide in the cellar for a few days?"

"No," said Quality succinctly.

"How do you come into this?" John demanded.

"Just a man working for wages," answered the Gargoyle.

"For what employer?" John asked.

The Gargoyle was reproachful. "Now you wouldn't expect me to answer that," he said. "Start your motor, Miss Piper. It would be just too, too lovely if you both would stop complicating my job."

"Did you see the men in that car?" John asked.

"Oh, I saw them all right."

"And recognized them?"

"Two of them," said the Gargoyle.

"What are you going to do about it?"

"Nothing," said the Gargoyle. "Spur the horses, Miss Piper. If you won't be careful do be as careful as you can. Really I'm hoping our next meeting won't be in the morgue, with you occupying adjoining slabs. Good night, and untroubled dreams."

He straightened, walked slowly back to his car.

"Who," asked Quality, "was he?"

"A cross between a hamadryad," said John, "and a jack-in-the-box."

"I wish," Quality said, "he had taken off his shoes."

"Why?" John asked.

"So," Quality said, "I could have seen if he had goat's feet."

chapter EIGHTEEN

Quality Piper and John Miller and Kent Farraday were driving in the direction of Santa Monica to a destination not yet disclosed by Dolly Dove. In the baggage compartment of the car were baskets of lunch, the food prepared by Dolly's own hand. Dolly and Farraday occupied the back seat; Quality rode with John, who was driving.

They passed the campus of the university. "Pretty fancy," John said.

"Yes," replied Quality.

"Now I," John said, "learned my multiplication table in more austere surroundings. Andover and Dartmouth."

"Smith," Quality said.

"You," John said, "don't know the first rudiments of conversation. The primary rule is this. I say, 'How are you feeling today?' You answer that you are very well indeed. But you don't stop there, or the conversation dies. The correct thing is for you to say you're in perfect health, and then ask a question, like 'Which do you prefer? Kippered herring or sauerkraut?' That keeps the talk alive. You can go on that way for hours."

"Why?" Quality asked.

"Because, by some happy chance, if you keep the ball in the air it's possible to stumble upon an interesting topic. You talk and talk and in that way disclose your innermost soul to your companion. He gets interested in you and you get interested in him. And one thing leads on to another until you arrive at wedding bells and four children."

"Why four?" Quality asked.

"Improve the breed," John said. "Able and intelligent and nice-looking people should have more children than scavengers. So in a jillion years the scavengers will be crowded out and the beautiful and wise will populate the earth."

"Eugenics!" said Quality.

"I hear," John said, "that you can transmit physical characteristics to your offspring, but not mental. Is that true?"

"Bosh," said Quality.

"Does that finish the topic?"

"No," Quality said.

"All right—contribute to it. Alterations in the human race come slowly. Maybe a hundred thousand years. Now take horses: You breed for speed and get it. But suppose you bred for intelligence. Each generation being on a higher plane than the last. In a million years horses will probably be able to talk, and dogs and foxes. With scientific breeding we might, in a jillion years, have a horse in the White House—or a dachshund."

"Or," said Quality, "a jackass."

"Darned if you're not learning," John applauded. "Probably horses and dogs and coyotes will organize and demand equality. Imagine how entertaining it would be if your next-door neighbor were a mongoose."

"Or a panda," said Quality.

"There would be leaders," John went on. "Revolutionists like the suffragettes. Parading with banners demanding equal rights for quadrupeds."

"For cripes sake!" exclaimed Dolly. "Come on down and rassle with me on the grass. I'm not outfitted to blunder around in some tarnation philosophical stratosphere. What I'm interested in is tomorrow and Thursday and Friday, and the price of pork chops and how in hell I can gyp the Income Tax Bureau." She sniffed. "What happens a million years from now don't cut any grass with me."

They passed Malibu and continued on the road that skirted the ocean; passed the place where Shiner had been shot down, and a couple of miles beyond stopped at a beach house isolated from its neighbors.

"This is it," Dolly told them. "Borrowed it for the day. I got a principle," she said. "Never pay for a thing you can get for nothing."

They garaged the car and went into the house which was familiar to Dolly. "You men take that room to the left. Toots and I will use the other." Presently John and Farraday appeared in trunks and waited. For some mysterious reason it takes a woman longer to get into a swim suit the size of a bandanna handkerchief than it does a man to bathe, shave and don full dress attire. Dolly and Quality came out at last.

"Now look at her," Dolly said, "and look at me. You wouldn't think I used to have legs almost as pretty as hers. Much admired, they were, only in those days we weren't let to show them so much." She sighed. "That's what an appetite does for a body."

There was, indeed, a contrast. Dolly, notwithstanding the modesty of her suit—a relic from Mack Sennett's bathing beauty days—looked as if she had been raised by yeast. Hers was not a human body but a terrain to be surveyed by cartographers. Quality, as she waited silently, was breath-taking.

"Let this be a warning to you, young man," Dolly said. "When you're selecting a wife the first thing to do is study her appetite. Providing you like slim ones. A slender girl with a big appetite is a bad pick. In a few years she'll bulge. The difference between me and Toots is thirty years and a passion for calories. . . . Lucky it's a grand day."

They took blankets and went out upon the sand. They could see distant figures basking or fishing, but no one was within a hundred yards of them. They arranged themselves comfortably. Dolly looked with distaste at the cold waters of the Pacific and then spoke in her falsetto voice to Farraday.

"Kent," she said, "you made slews of money in your day. Like me. What did you do with it?"

"Saved it," Farraday said. "It was necessary, of course, to maintain a proper establishment in keeping with my position, yet I was economical."

"Then how come," Dolly demanded—it seemed to John callously—"they say you're on your uppers?"

"A lack," Farraday said, "of worldly wisdom, and an absence of suspicion."

"Somebody snatched it, eh? While your back was turned."

"An investment counsellor," Farraday said, "in whom I reposed complete confidence. So much so, as a matter of fact, that I gave him a power of attorney."

John knew that a great many motion picture actors retained an investment counsellor, or entrusted their business affairs to someone accustomed to the habits of money and securities, so he was not surprised at Farraday's statement.

"And this financial wizard," said Dolly, "scooped the jackpot."

"To my great discomfiture," Farraday replied. He turned his eyes toward John. "The name," he said, "of the man I trusted unwisely was Humphrey Salmon."

"I guessed we were coming to that," John said.

"Why," asked Dolly, "didn't you sue the daylights out of him?"

"To litigate," said Farraday, "is vastly expensive. Also I was reluctant to expose myself to the world as a gull. One has a certain dignity. I did not care to be laughed at."

Dolly's teeth snapped together. "Listen," she said. "If anybody gypped me out of a thin dime I'd raise a rumpus you could hear in China and anybody could laugh that had a mind to."

John stood up, reached his hand down for Quality's and drew her to her feet. They strolled down to the water.

"Cute, huh?" Dolly said to Farraday.

"A charming young couple," Farraday agreed.

"You're worried," John said when they were at some distance from the others. "Is it Danny, or hoodlums trying to do us in?"

"Danny," she said.

"But the hospital reports that he is doing well."

"After he gets out," Quality said.

"They'll try again, you think?"

"Yes."

John looked about. The spot where they stood was lonely and exposed. Suddenly he felt apprehension and knew that it had been unwise to give this opportunity to whoever it was who felt their elimination was necessary.

"We," he said, "are a pair of sitting ducks . . ." He bent his brows and peered out to sea. "Someone is afraid of you, or of me, or of us."

"Of me," she said flatly.

"Why?" he asked.

"Because," she said, "I never give up."

He looked at her, at her lovely, intelligent face, her determined chin, the glow in her eyes. He knew she would never give up. He knew that nothing could move her from any purpose she had formed. She was admirable. It came to him suddenly that she was steadfast—that she would hate forever or love forever. He knew, as he looked at her perfection, that a thing had happened to him. It came to him suddenly. He realized that he desired her with all his heart—that it was no passing fancy, but a deep, abiding desire to have her for his own. Not because of her still beauty, though that was a part of it, but because of what she was—of what she could be to the man to whom she gave herself. Enigmatic, taciturn she might be. Encased in a shell she undoubtedly was. But she was the one woman in all the world for him. For some man the shell would be broken and the enigma solved. Suddenly he knew that man must be himself.

"Quality!" he said.

Some urgency in his voice caused her to turn and look into his eyes. He bent toward her. He could see that she comprehended, knew what he was about to say.

She shook her head, "No," she said. It was a positive *no*.

"Do you mean not now?" he asked. "Or never?"

She did not reply to either question. With one lithe, supremely graceful movement she stood up, and without a word strode back toward Dolly Dove and Kent Farraday. She had moved not more than a dozen paces when there was a sound from the wooded hill that rose upward from the boulevard. It was not a backfire. Cars do not backfire on sheer, wooded slopes. It was the detonation of a rifle. Sand flicked at Quality's feet and she halted abruptly. John flung himself upon her, thrust her to the sand, covered her body with his. In quick succession there came two other shots, not in the voice of the weapon that had fired first. Then there was silence.

Quality struggled to rise. "No," John said. "Not yet."

So they waited, pressed close together, his body interposed between her and danger. He could feel the warmth of her and the steady pulsation of her heart.

"Up," she said.

He raised himself upon his elbows and Quality prepared to rise.

"Three shots," she said.

"Three," he answered.

"One rifle, two pistol," she told him.

"Anyhow they missed," he said shakily.

They were staring at the hillside from which the rifle shots had come. They saw a man round the corner of the beach house and walk toward them across the stretch of beach. Again John placed himself as a shield before Quality and waited. The man came deliberately, closer and closer, until his features disclosed themselves. It was the Gargoyle.

"Good morning," he said in his amiable voice.

"Good morning," John replied.

"Miss Piper, I presume," the Gargoyle said. "Might I be introduced? Last night it would have been inconvenient."

"I don't know your name," John told him.

"Gargoyle will do. It's a favorite of yours."

John performed the introduction ironically. "Miss Piper," he said, "may I present the Gargoyle?"

Quality nodded.

"It would be so nice," the man said, "if people would only be smart. If they would only learn." He was almost pathetic. "You make it so hard for me. I'm dreadfully busy with a multitude of things to do. Yet you go bumbling around. Can't you, please, tuck yourself into a nice, safe basement for a few days?"

"No," Quality said.

"Not if I say pretty please?"

"No," Quality answered.

"Then," the Gargoyle told her, "I'll just have to make the best of it. But you really are a nuisance."

"No," Quality said.

"Then what are you?"

Her eyes were amused, sardonically amused. "Probably bait," she said.

The Gargoyle grinned—if the horrible grimace could be called a grin. He faced John Miller. "Mr. Miller," he said, "may I congratulate you on your choice of ladies?"

"But am I," John asked, "her choice of men?"

"Three shots," said Quality.

"The last two were mine," the Gargoyle said. "I missed."

"Luncheon?" asked Quality. Her voice was almost cordial. She seemed to approve of the man, and John was surprised.

"Even Gargoyles," said the man, "must eat." He bowed graciously, and grinned again. "I despise breaking up a day of mirth and gaiety," he went on, "but after we have eaten, will you be so awfully good as to get the hell out of here?"

"As a favor to you," Quality said, and smiled.

chapter NINETEEN

On Monday morning the cast of the Famous Names Group was assembled in that section of the huge studio building which had been allotted to them. They clustered while technicians arranged lights, put finishing touches upon scenery, wheeled cameras into position. Quality's shooting schedule was on her knees. It indicated the sequences, indicated what time of day it was, special music, sounds, props. Time was of the essence. The story must be told by the actors in twenty-six and a half minutes, leaving three minutes for commercials and station identifications. The scene was, in effect, a duplication of Dolly Dove's living room in which rehearsals had been going on. An hour was consumed in preliminaries while the actors stood around anxiously. There were consultations with Quality in her capacity as director, with Agnew. And then, after what seemed an interminable time the production people, the camera crew, the sound men and the grips were ready.

The first scene was between Ben Franklin and Kent Farraday. The set was a small oasis surrounded by a welter of equipment. Rising above were suspended platforms from which lights poured down upon the set; wires sprawled; cameras were in position; the boom carrying the microphone reached out its long arm; twenty people clustered in a semicircle around the set—most of them essential, but some drawn by curiosity. Quality, board on lap, sat just under the camera.

Kent Farraday sat at ease in a chair at his desk, waiting with the outward calm of a veteran.

"Ready?" asked Rolf Agnew.

Quality nodded. Farraday assumed his character; the door opened and young Ben Franklin entered and spoke his first line. From then to the break for luncheon it was drudgery. For hours it was repeat, repeat, repeat! Sharp commands were heard. "Kill the junior. . . . The midget's too hot. . . . Lift the full flood and keep it soft." The juicers were speaking. "Feed that broad through the window. . . . Gobo the baby spot."

The position of each actor in which he stands or sits for any appreciable time must be lighted for position, actually for a portrait, and a scene in which three actors appear, each with, say four movements, means to the electricians and camera crew the meticulous lighting for twelve portraits such as would be taken in a photographer's studio. And all this must be done so adroitly that the audience will be unaware of it. It must seem natural. No lighting effect should distract attention from the actors.

No matter how thoroughly a company may have rehearsed in someone's parlor there will be essential changes in position, in gesture, in intonation when the people come before the cameras and speak to the ear of the sound box. When Quality spoke it was softly, but tersely. Before long the crew accepted her as one who knew what she was about.

As the day passed the pleasant certainty emerged that young Ben Franklin was better than good; that Martha Scruggs, whose name now was Jenny Lind, was appealingly adequate. Dolly Dove, once America's Darling playing saccharine parts, displayed a talent for comedy so subtle that even the grips chuckled from time to time. No one ever had doubted Kent Farraday's ability to enact the character assigned to him.

Late in the afternoon, with lights set, camera positions and angles determined, business decided upon, the entire play was run through almost without interruption. John Miller watched it with tired eyes. He suffered the doubts and apprehensions of an author who saw his words coming to life, but was so weary he could not tell whether it was good or bad.

"Save 'em," somebody commanded.

The lights were extinguished; the day's work was done. Tomorrow the thing would be recorded on film irrevocably. Throughout the rehearsal he had felt himself to be useless. He was merely present, contributing nothing. Yet he was curiously elated. There was a sense of accomplishment. His play was being produced. It might be bad, it might be moderately good, it might be a hit—but at least it was being done!

"What do you think?" he asked Dolly anxiously.

She grinned at him. "It'll probably be twins," she said. "How would I know how it went? I was in it, wasn't I? Personally I think I was terrific. . . . Who's the young squirt talking to Toots?"

"Never saw him before," John said.

"I wonder if he's who she's been running around with." She snorted. "He looks like the cat dragged him in."

John glanced at the young man. Certainly he was younger than Quality. He had a sort of unfinished look, but on the other hand there was something appealing about his face and awkward manner. There could be no doubt that Quality was interested in him. She was talking to him, not in monosyllables, and with earnestness. He looked down at her with what seemed to John a look of adoration.

"I've got other things to worry about," he said shortly.

"Yeah?" demanded Dolly. "Listen, chump—there'll be a billion other plays but there'll never be another Toots."

Kent Farraday walked to them, his handsome, dignified face a picture of worry. "What did you think, dear people? What did you think? Was I adequate? What about the play? In your opinion, has it a chance?"

Dolly placed a pudgy hand on his arm, and her smile was gentle. "Don't worry, old friend," she said. "It's in the bag."

"It means so much," he said almost inaudibly.

Zagic Quiros bustled from the background. "Colossal!" he exclaimed. "Super-colossal! It'll make *Lucy* look like spinach.

Since *The Birth of a Nation* there's been nothing like it. It's a pea-eyed, palm-eared pachyderm! Move over and make room for us—we're sitting in the driver's seat."

Instinctively the troupe turned to Quality. Her eyes were tired. The strain of the day had taken its toll. "Be as good tomorrow," she said. Then to John: "Hospital?" she asked.

At the hospital Danny Whitcomb could not be seen. "Possibly tomorrow," they were told. "He is out of danger, barring unforeseen complications."

"Is he," John asked, "being guarded?"

"A policeman," said the nurse, "sits outside his door twenty-four hours a day."

They went out into the evening. "Dinner?" John asked.

"Sleep," Quality replied wearily.

John insisted upon accompanying her to Dolly's apartment. He saw her to the door but did not go in. She turned before closing the door. "Rest," she said. "It will be all right."

For John the night passed in fitful, disturbed sleep. He awakened, hollow-eyed, nerves on edge and compelled himself to eat food that revolted him. Half an hour before the appointed time he arrived at Rolf Agnew's lot and paced up and down before the closed studio doors. Zagic was first to arrive, then Kent Farraday and Martha Scruggs. Dolly and Quality came five minutes later. John marveled at Quality. Upon her face was no sign of yesterday's strain. She was serene, immaculate. Even Dolly, old trouper that she was, showed wear and tear. "Where's young Ben Franklin?" she asked shrilly.

"Must have overslept," Zagic guessed.

They went into the studio and clustered before the set. It was zero hour. Everything was ready for the buzzer to sound, the huge doors to close and the red light to glow outside barring admission. Agnew came impatiently to John.

"All ready," he said. "What's holding us up?"

"Ben Franklin hasn't reported," John said.

"Well, where in hell is he? Hasn't he got an alarm clock? Time's money."

"I'll telephone," John said.

As he walked to the booth he saw, loitering in the background, the hobbledehoy with whom Quality had been talking so earnestly yesterday, and frowned. He dialed and the clerk of the cheap hotel where Ben Franklin lived answered. John asked for the boy.

"Franklin? Young Ben Franklin?" asked the clerk. "Not here. Checked out last night."

"Checked out?"

"Bag and baggage. Left for San Francisco."

"San Francisco! But that's impossible! Are you sure?"

"Sure I'm sure," said the clerk impatiently.

"Did he leave an address?"

"No. He paid his bill, checked out, and that's that."

John replaced the receiver. He walked with dragging steps back to the set where all eyes turned upon him expectantly. He spoke grimly. "I guess we can call it a day," he said in a brittle voice. "Franklin has walked out on us. He's gone to San Francisco."

"Impossible!" Farraday exclaimed.

"But true," John answered. "So," he said hopelessly, "I guess we can all go home."

"No," Quality said.

"But—but what can we do without him?" John's despair was past profanity. "We've been done in," he said savagely. The desertion, he realized, had been deliberate. Ben Franklin had been planted on them for this very purpose. There was an unhappy silence which Zagic Quiros broke with choice epithets. John glanced at Kent Farraday. The face of the old actor was a tragic picture of hopelessness. Agnew was swearing.

"What the hell kind of management is this?" he roared. "Look at this crew! . . . Look at this set! It costs money. . . ."

"Quiet," Quality said.

"Eh?"

"We are ready," she told them.

"Ready? With an actor missing!"

"Edwin," Quality said.

The hobbledehoy stepped forward.

"Yes, Miss Piper," he said in an adolescent voice, quivering with eagerness.

"This," said Quality, "is Edwin Booth. He will take Franklin's place."

"Without rehearsal?" Farraday gasped.

"I have been rehearsing him," Quality said. "He was present yesterday." She looked at the boy steadily. "Ready, Edwin?" she asked.

"Yes, Miss Piper."

"But—but—" John found difficulty in speaking. "How—why—"

"Wasting time," she said sharply. "Ready, everybody. On set, Mr. Farraday."

The old actor, almost tottering, took his appointed place at his desk. The slate numbering the scene clacked.

"Ready!" Quality snapped. "Camera."

The new, the astounding member of the cast made his entrance. He was letter perfect in business and dialogue. At the boy's first word Kent Farraday gained assurance, drew upon the experience of a lifetime. It was smooth; there was no roughness but a finished performance. As scene after scene followed the performers gained confidence in the new member, forgot, indeed, that he was a new member. Quality held the strings in her tapering fingers, alert, self-confident. She inspired confidence not only in the actors but in the crew. She knew what she wanted, demanded it tersely and got it. The noon hour arrived. "Save them," said a voice.

The company surrounded Quality. They slapped the hobbledehoy on the back. They loved him because he had saved them.

"But, Miss Quality," Farraday asked in his orotund way, "how did you work this miracle? How did you foresee the need? Where did you discover this young man?"

Quality was not flattered. She was businesslike, brisk, curt. "Didn't like Franklin," she said. "Something wrong. Snooped."

"And found?" Farraday asked.

"Humphrey Salmon was his agent," she answered.

"And then."

"Insurance," she said. She smiled at Edwin Booth.

"Name and all," Zagic exclaimed. "Genius. Sheer genius."

Dolly Dove kissed Quality on the cheek, "And I, bloody old cackling hen that I am, thought you'd blown your top over a teen-ager!"

They were back at work again. Scene followed scene, and when each was completed that was that. It was final. As in a motion picture there would be no daily rushes to appraise and revise. What here was recorded on film must stand. Perfection, or at least an acceptable facsimile of perfection, must be attained on the first taking. The afternoon wore on. At last came the end. Each of them had done all he could do, and now it was in the hands of the technicians, the experts, the magicians of the sound mixer and of the cutting room. The dubbing process would go forward tomorrow. The assorted varied sounds, dialogue, music, doors closing, dogs barking would be recorded on a single track, recording each where it should occur; and the track would be printed along the side of the principal film, and all would be in readiness to unveil to an audience.

"Son," said Kent Farraday to young Edwin Booth, "you astounded me."

The boy grinned shyly. "Miss Piper worked me like the very devil," he said ruefully. "She's a slave-driver."

The old actor gazed at Quality with something very like to reverence in his eyes. "Thank God for Miss Piper," he said solemnly.

"Hey," said Agnew. "I called up the commissary. They're knocking together a spread. We'll celebrate."

"We'll eat and run," Dolly said firmly. "I'm going to put Toots to bed."

Rolf Agnew fell into step with John Miller as they walked down the street to the commissary. "Well, son," Rolf said, "you've pulled it off. A couple of days and it'll be in the can. Then what are you going to do with it?"

The question brought John to a sudden stop. His mind had been occupied with writing and production to the exclusion of everything else. "Why," he said, "I suppose we'll peddle it. . . . That's in Zagic's department."

"You can deal with the networks; you can dicker with advertising agencies; or you can syndicate."

"Let's talk about it tomorrow," John said wearily. "I'm in an advanced state of brain fag."

It was not an animated meal and it was soon over. The troupe dispersed to their several homes. John insisted upon driving Dolly Dove and Quality to their apartment, but left them at the door. They said tired good nights and John turned away, but halted, moved by some subconscious warning.

"Go to bed," he said. "Lock the door. Dolly, don't let anyone in until morning."

"What hit you all of a sudden?" she asked.

"I've got a feeling." Suddenly the matter became urgent. "Can you fix me up on the davenport. . . . I'll stay all night."

"You'll scamper home," Dolly said, "and crawl into bed."

"But," said Quality, raising her eyes to his, "thank you."

He did not drowse in the taxicab that took him to his apartment. He was not sleepy. He felt he would not be able to sleep; that he was to be tortured by one of those white nights, which came seldom but which he dreaded. On those nights his mind seemed to live in a sort of incandescence. It could not concentrate. It was as if he were being bombarded by ideas and images and pictures like a succession of tracer bullets. Or as if some camera shutter in his brain flicked open and shut relentlessly, never stopping, never resting. It was impossible to concentrate and the disconnected, haphazard series of thoughts became physical pain.

He undressed but did not get into bed. He reached for a book, but the lines of print were meaningless and incoherent. Hurling the book on the floor he paced up and down and smoked and smoked and smoked. It seemed to him that hours had passed, but when he glanced at his watch it was not yet eleven. It was insomnia in its most poisonous form. He turned off the lights and threw himself on his bed, but it was in vain. Nerves, tautened by a day of concentration and anxiety, would not relax.

The telephone rang. It was a crashing sound. He reached for

the instrument and spoke. A voice that was not twittering now but shrill came over the wire.

"Johnnie, I'm scairt," said Dolly Dove.

"What is it?" he snapped.

"She's gone out—Toots. The hospital telephoned. They said Danny Whitcomb wanted to see her. . . . She rushed out before I could stop her."

"How long ago?"

"Twenty minutes. . . . I didn't start to worry . . . and then I got scairt."

"Hang up," John said viciously. "Get off the wire."

Swiftly, with tense fingers, he dialed the hospital. The answer was slow in coming.

"This," he said, "is an emergency. Has Miss Quality Piper arrived to see Danny Whitcomb?"

"No."

"Did you or anyone telephone her to come to see him?"

"No."

John slammed down the instrument and sat rigid. He picked up the telephone again and dialed Dolly Dove. She answered promptly.

"Was it," he asked, "a man or woman who called Quality?"

"I answered the phone. It was a woman."

"What kind of a voice?" he demanded.

"What do you mean—what kind of voice?"

"Describe it," John said tersely.

There was an instant's silence, then Dolly said in a puzzled way, "It was kind of low, like contralto."

"With a sort of lilt to it?"

"Yes—sort of like that. It was a pretty voice—"

"Good-by," John said.

He put on his clothes deliberately in order not to waste time in fumbling. He pulled on his coat over unbuttoned shirt and tied no necktie. Grim-faced he opened the door and ran down the stairs to the street.

chapter TWENTY

Jabez Winkleman's great bronze gates were closed. The small stone house from which they were operated was dark. John groped for the bell but could not find it and battered on the door. It was opened grudgingly by a scowling servant.

"What the hell?" he rasped.

"Open the gates. I want in," John said.

"At this hour! Who are you? What do you want?"

"It's an emergency," John said. "Get Mr. Winkleman on the phone."

"What I'll do is call the cops."

John put his shoulder against the partly opened door. He shoved the man aside. "Where's the house phone?" he demanded. "I tell you this is an emergency. Man, it's life or death."

The dismayed guardian, an elderly man, was not without courage. His hand reached out and pulled a lever. Instantly lights went on illuminating the grounds, alarm bells sounded. There was the crunch of the running feet of a watchman on the driveway.

"Get Winkleman," John repeated as the armed watchman burst into the hallway.

"Not a move, you," he commanded. "What goes on here?"

"Drunk or crazy," said the gate keeper.

"I'm not drunk and I'm not crazy," John said. "I must see Mr. Winkleman. I'm John Miller. Get my name to him. Quickly."

The watchman hesitated. A telephone bell rang. The gate-keeper answered. In reply to a question, evidently from the house, he answered, "A man broke in here. Says he's got to see Mr. Winkleman. Says it's an emergency. . . . He says his name is John Miller."

There was an instant's pause. The gatekeeper scowled at John and spoke to the watchman. "Orders are to take him to the house," he said.

"Mosey," ordered the watchman, motioning with his pistol. "No funny moves."

John climbed the driveway, now brilliantly lighted. A butler in slippers, pajamas covered by a robe, stood outside the door. Jabez Winkleman in an old-fashioned nightshirt and bare feet stood just inside. He peered at John, recognized him.

"Come in, young man. Come in," he said. "What's all the rumpus?" He seemed neither alarmed nor irritated. His New England deacon's face was grave. "Come into the office," he said, and led the way, nightgown flapping around his bony ankles. He closed the door after them and walked to his chair behind the desk, and waited.

"Where's Loretta?" John demanded.

"In bed, I presume."

"Find out," John said peremptorily.

Jabez did not seem to resent the tone or manner. He pressed a button and the butler appeared.

"See if Miss Loretta is in her room," he directed. The man hastened away. "Now," Jabez said crisply, "what is it, John?"

"Miss Piper," John said, "has been snatched."

Jabez lifted his thin brows. "What," he asked, still patiently, "has Loretta to do with that?"

"It was she," John said, "who telephoned Miss Piper to go to the hospital."

"How do you know?" Jabez asked.

"Her voice," John answered.

"Certainly a recognizable voice. I infer that Miss Piper did not reach this hospital. Why should she have been willing to go there?"

"An old friend. An attempt was made to kill him. Danny Whitcomb, as you must know."

"I know," Jabez replied.

The butler re-entered the office. "Miss Loretta," he said, "is not in her room. The bed has not been slept in."

"Thank you," Jabez said. "Go back to bed—all of you." He turned to face John and his leathery face was grave, concerned.

"You have more to tell me about Loretta," he said in his dry, nasal voice.

"I'm afraid so, sir."

"I'm listening," Jabez said.

"On the night," John said, "when I was knocked unconscious, Loretta telephoned a warning to me."

"Her voice again?"

"Yes. You don't mistake her voice, sir. I heard it again in the Beverly Hills Hotel. At luncheon. I did not know her, but I followed her home."

"There can be no mistake?"

"I'm sure there is no mistake," John said.

"I did not think it was so bad," the old man said, and closed his eyes for an instant. "Folly—yes. Immorality—possibly. But not this." He sighed. "I hoped she was attracted to you, John."

"Humphrey Salmon?" asked John.

"Yes," answered Jabez.

"He passed her a note at Santa Anita," John said.

"I saw it," Jabez nodded.

"It ordered her to meet Salmon at the same place at the same time."

"The same place," Jabez said. "It is not good, young man, to be compelled to spy upon a member of one's household. A member entitled to affection and protection. I consider it necessary. To her welfare. . . . She is beautiful, John, and winsome. But wayward. Worse than wayward, I fear."

"Did you," John asked, "employ the Gargoyle?"

"Gargoyle?" Jabez raised his brows in inquiry.

"A strange man who has come into the picture."

"I do not know such a man."

179

"But," John asked, "do you know this meeting place?"

"I do," Jabez answered. "First check on the hospital. Make certain Miss Piper has not arrived."

John dialed. The hospital answered. "Has Miss Piper arrived yet?" he asked. "To see Danny Whitcomb?"

"No one has come to see that patient," was the answer.

"You know the road to Dimity Farms—where I first met you, sir? Where I keep my horses?"

"Where," John asked, "Salmon's stallion broke his neck?"

"That is the place. Three miles beyond, on the same road, is a house that Humphrey Salmon uses. In the hills. The name on the mailbox is Sligo McNulty. It is there," Jabez said in his nasal voice, "that Loretta has kept assignations with the man."

"I can find it," John said.

"You will need a car." Jabez summoned the butler again, who had not had time to get into his bed. "An automobile at the front door at once," he said curtly. When the butler scurried away Jabez opened a drawer of his desk and picked up a dully gleaming automatic.

"Can you shoot a gun?" the old man asked.

"Yes," John answered.

"Take it," Jabez said. "A pistol in the pocket is good for morale."

"Thank you, sir," John said, getting to his feet.

Jabez' voice was a bit shriller. It was the only sign of emotion. "If it's possible," he said, "have a thought for Loretta." He rounded the desk and his clawlike hand patted John's back. "This may," he said, "be a wild goose chase. . . . I will not be idle this end."

He accompanied John to the door, stood outlined in his absurd nightshirt against the light from within and flapped a bony hand in farewell as John started the engine and swerved down the driveway to the boulevard.

He drove steadily at such speed as would not attract the unwelcome attentions of a traffic policeman. The automatic was heavy in the pocket of his jacket and the power that purred under the hood of the car was somehow a comfort. It was a chance, this errand upon which he was embarked, but it was the only thing he could see to do that might bring help to Quality. Certain it was that she would be taken somewhere and possibility, if not probability, was that the destination might be this remote house which Humphrey Salmon used for secret purposes.

But there was always the dreadful thought that she might be driven to no destination at which she would arrive alive. At this moment Quality might be no longer living. It was an agonizing thought that her beautiful body might, even now, be lying in some ditch where it had been tossed from a rapidly fleeing car. That she had, in the argot of the underworld, been taken for a ride.

Face to face with that black possibility he realized what Quality Piper meant to him; what it would do to his life if she never could be a part of it. He was possessed by cold rage, steadied by it. If death had overtaken Quality he knew what he would do. There would be no waiting for law to take its course. He would seek out Humphrey Salmon and kill him with his hands. He never had known that he was capable of such hatred as he felt tonight.

He increased speed, careless of consequences. There was, fortunately, little traffic. At last he turned off the boulevard into a country road and pressed the accelerator to the floor. Sixty—seventy miles showed on the speedometer. It did not occur to him that he might be followed, that it might be as necessary for Salmon to dispose of him as it was to eliminate Quality. Almost by instinct he found his way. He hesitated at no crossroad but drove surely, thundering through the night.

He flashed by the gates and the white buildings of Dimity Farms, and his destination was but a few short miles away. The road commenced to mount and to twist. There were acute angles and hairpin turns that compelled a slower pace. Three miles beyond Dimity Farms, Jabez had said. Then caution would be necessary. It would be reckless folly to roar up to the door of Salmon's hideaway and march up to its door demanding Quality. He must approach silently, reconnoiter, discover the lay of the land, make certain that Quality was indeed a prisoner there.

He slowed the car, drove cautiously around a sharp curve. Before him was a straight stretch of narrow road, and then he saw that the road was blocked. A couple of hundred feet ahead an automobile stood across the road, broadside on. His headlights illuminated it and two men who stood at its head and tail.

There was a warning shout. A man leaped into the road waving his arms. It was a trap and John had driven into it recklessly. What happened then was not the result of thought or of plan. A silly thought flashed through his mind. "What the hell!" he exclaimed aloud. "Winkleman's got lots of cars."

With his left hand he flung open the door of the car. His right gripped the wheel for an instant, steadying it. He thrust his foot down upon the accelerator and leaped. His feet struck the soft side of the road and he rolled head over heels, but even as he rolled he heard a scream and a crash as Jabez' car catapulted into the vehicle that blocked the way. For an instant he lay stunned. Half conscious he struggled to his feet and lunged into the thick cover of undergrowth that grew upon the hillside.

John looked backward and downward, a burst of flame roared up from the wreckage of the cars. He did not pause to watch but scrambled on, circling to his right. What had happened to the two men he did not know or care. But there was no pursuit.

He scrambled on. There was, he calculated, half a mile to go and the going was rough. There was no moon. The night was black. He struggled on, guided by the slope of the hill. After a time there was a steep descent down which he slid until, on the floor of a little valley, he saw the gleaming of a light. This must be the house—Humphrey Salmon's house.

As he neared it there was no sign of life. It was apparent there had been no alarm. The noise of the collision had not reached the ears of those within the house. John crouched in the shelter of the trees and strained his eyes toward the lights. There was a house, a farm house. Behind it loomed the black outlines of a barn, a shed, a garage. Two windows in the upper story, curtained, glowed faintly. There was illumination in what he took to be the living room on the ground floor. John crept nearer hoping there was no dog to give warning of his approach. But there was only silence. He reached the fence that surrounded the farmyard and paused there listening. It must have been that the intervening mountainside had prevented the crash of Jabez' car into the one that blocked the road from reaching this spot. Nor had either of the two men arrived before him.

He wriggled through the fence, and, treading cautiously, feeling with each foot before he set it down, he approached the front of the house, the lighted windows. He crept close to the wall. The window under which he crouched was raised a couple of inches to permit air to enter through the screen. The shade was only half drawn. John straightened and peered into the room.

It was not such a parlor as one would expect to find in a lonely farm house. The furnishings were luxurious, expensive. A handsome antique break-front bookcase stood against the wall. There was a mahogany drop-leaf table, a pair of Chippendale chairs, a carven mantelpiece, a huge davenport. Paintings adorned the walls and John noted with surprise a square-cut vase of K'ang Hsi black hawthorns. Salmon had spared no expense in furnishing his nest.

Upon the davenport, book in hand, lovely as a peri, serene and comfortably at home sat Loretta Kimball. On a graceful side table was a half-filled glass which, now and then, she lifted to her lips without removing her eyes from the page. The door was thrust open and Sligo McNulty entered. Loretta lifted her eyes in annoyance.

"Now what is it?" she asked, but even in impatience her voice was beautiful to the ear.

"He should of been here before this," Sligo said.

Loretta shrugged. "Something has delayed him," she replied.

"I don't like things to delay on a night like this." It was apparent that Sligo was worried.

"Go make yourself a cup of coffee," Loretta said.

"What," demanded Sligo, "if he's left us holdin' the bag?"

"No danger," Loretta assured him.

"I don't like snatches," Sligo said. "Look! You bump somebody and you got to deal with local cops only. But a snatch! Them G-men!"

"Nonsense," Loretta said. And then, brightly, "Any complaints from our guest?"

"She ain't said a word," Sligo answered. "Not a blasted word. I never seen such a woman. Can't she talk?"

Loretta smiled and for the first time John became aware of something unnatural, unwomanly, hard and inhuman about the girl. "She'll talk," she said crisply. "That I'm going to enjoy. Making her talk."

John shuddered as if a cold hand had been laid between his naked shoulder blades. He sensed something abnormal, a cruelty, a delight in cruelty that was not sane. Loretta licked her lips.

But one point was settled. He had been right, Jabez Winkleman had been right. Quality Piper was here, and Quality Piper was alive.

"But where's the other one?" Sligo demanded. "I got a thing to settle with him. He made me look bad. He got me in wrong with Salmon."

Loretta frowned. "Maybe John Miller wasn't so easy to bring," she said and made an odd little *moue.* "Bringing him in could be a man's-size job." She was pensive. "If it weren't for this and that," she said, "I'd be quite a friend of John Miller's."

"Better not let Salmon hear you say that," Sligo warned.

She flashed a hot look at the man. "There never," she said, and her lovely voice lost its cadence and was harsh, "there never was a time or a place where I couldn't take care of Humphrey Salmon," she said.

"Cripes!" Sligo exclaimed.

John had heard enough. There were things to do besides listen through a window. Quality was here. She was a prisoner in an upstairs room—probably the room in which a light was visible. His objective here was not to eavesdrop but to reach Quality Piper and to extricate her. How many people were in the house he did not know. Probably at least one other on guard over the girl. But his best chance for success was immediately, before Humphrey Salmon arrived. Before matters reached their climax. He turned away from the window and crept around to the side of the house and stood beneath the lighted window of the room in which Quality was a prisoner—undoubtedly bound with ropes. Would there be a ladder by means of which he could mount to her window—or would it be possible to enter the house and climb the stairs?

There might be a ladder in the barn. Stealthily he made his way through the darkness to search. As he reached the cluster of outbuildings he became aware of a glow of light. A car was approaching. It turned into the drive and the rays from the lamps almost caught him where he crouched. The door of the car was thrust open and a man stepped to the ground.

"Turn the car around," the man said. "Head it for the road. We may want to get out of here in a hurry."

Humphrey Salmon had arrived!

chapter TWENTY-ONE

Sligo McNulty would be on guard either inside or at the door of the bedroom in which Quality Piper was confined. Other men on the premises were Humphrey Salmon and his chauffeur. Doubtless there would be one or more others whom John Miller had not seen. The most hopeful odds were three to one; they might be four or five to one. Nor could he consider Loretta Kimball as negligible. In the few minutes during which he had observed her through the window he had altered his opinion of the girl. She was not a sweet, yielding, perhaps wayward young woman who, through indiscretion, had allowed herself to become Humphrey Salmon's dupe. There was steel in her character. Whatever she did was done deliberately in obedience to her own will. She was not negatively bad; the evil in her was positive. It was shocking to him—well-nigh incredible. It was altogether possible that it was she who dominated Salmon; not Salmon who imposed his will upon her.

Another element to be considered was that Salmon had passed the wreckage of the two cars on the road. John could not guess what had happened to the two men who had formed the human part of that roadblock. It was certain that Salmon had brought neither of them with him to the farm. This argued either that the men had been injured and left on duty, or that they were dead or injured and had been callously left where they lay. In the first case they would have alerted Salmon to the presence of someone inimical in the hills.

There was no ladder to reach Quality's window. The only way to come to her was through the house and up the stairs. He was possessed by an urgency to come to her, to be with her, to stand between her and whatever threatened her, and time was passing. The weight of the gun in his pocket was indeed a comfort, but a gun is a noisy weapon. Against the side of the garage wood for the fireplace was stacked and John fumbled for a suitable cudgel. His hand closed about a billet that fitted his fingers, and as he sensed that primitive weapon he himself became primitive. Culture sloughed from him, and the teachings of a gentle heredity. As he stood there in the darkness he reverted, became a lurking, furtive, prehistoric savage prowling in the murk of some jungle in search of prey.

Softly he trod the grass to the back door of the house; stood crouching beside the square, small stoop, listening with straining ears. As he stood there in the blacker shadow making ready to risk an entrance, the door opened and dim light glowed. A man who loomed large in the night stood there making a sort of whistling sound through his lips. Slowly he descended the steps, unaware of John crouching in the blackness. A feeling of ferocious elation accompanied the lift and fall of John's arm. The cudgel descended. The only sound was the dull thump of wood against skull.

John bent to loosen and kick off his shoes. Then with silent stockinged feet he mounted the three steps and drew open the door. He was looking into a kitchen, dimly lighted from a fixture in the hall beyond. He guessed there would be but one stairway in that small house. Pushing the swinging door he listened. Voices came mumblingly from the parlor. Four paces away a narrow, railed staircase hugged the wall to the second floor.

Keeping to the inside edge where the steps were less likely to creak, John mounted, holding his breath. He expected to find Sligo McNulty on guard at Quality's door, and crouched as he neared the top of the stairs. There was a chair against the wall, but McNulty was not there. He must have stayed down in the living room when Humphrey Salmon arrived. Good fortune was on his side. He glided along the hallway. The key was in the door and John turned it, exerting careful pressure to make sure it would not click. The door opened soundlessly and he saw a square bedroom, furnished with the luxury the embellishments of the living room below had taught him to expect. At the left was a low, wide bed and upon it was huddled the body of a girl. Quality was there.

He pushed the door shut and slithered to her side. Her hands and ankles were secured by tape and a strip of adhesive closed her lips. But her eyes were alert as she peered up at him. As gently as he could he stripped the tape from her mouth; then with pocket knife freed ankles and wrists. She sat erect, rubbing numb lips with a hand that was all but paralyzed.

"Hello," she said.

"Hello," John answered.

Somehow this did not seem to be inadequate. Quality swung her legs over the side of the bed and sat erect.

"Now?" she asked.

He walked to the window and looked down. Twenty feet away was Salmon's car, the driver in the front seat smoking. It would not, then, be possible to raise the window, lower Quality at arms' length and drop her to the ground. That way was forbidden to them.

"Shoes," he said, and pointed. Quality looked at his unshod feet and understood. She kicked off her tiny footgear.

"Can you walk?" he asked.

"Rub," she directed.

He chafed ankles and slender calves while she wriggled her wrists to restore circulation. In a moment she was able to stand.

"Out through the kitchen," he whispered. Quality nodded. Color had returned to her cheeks; her eyes were very bright; John could not tell whether or not she was frightened, but frightened or not she was resolute, in command of herself. His eyes admired her. Even after the rough usage to which she had been subjected she was not rumpled. Even her hair was in order. It seemed to John as he gazed at her that it must be a sort of law of nature that she always would be trim, untousled, neat and self-possessed. He spoke without intention. The words came involuntarily.

"You're wonderful," he said. "I love you."

She looked at him quickly but her expression did not change. "Later," she said.

That was characteristic, too. It promised nothing. It dismissed the subject. Everything should come at the right time and in the right place. He frowned as he turned to the door troubled by a doubt. Could it be that her defect was a lack of emotion? That would be tragic—so much beauty without passion to animate and perfect it.

With deliberation and caution he opened the door the merest crack and applied his eye to the opening. The stairway was clear. But nevertheless he hesitated an instant before stepping out into the hall. It was fortunate that he did so. A hand appeared on the newel post at the bottom and Sligo McNulty swung around and put his foot on the lowest step. He did not look upward. John closed the door silently and backed away.

"McNulty," he whispered.

"He'll look in," she said.

"On the bed," he directed.

She flung herself on the bed in the position she had occupied before John had freed her hands and feet.

"Will he come in?" John asked.

She nodded in the affirmative.

John stepped to the side of the doorframe. The door would open away from him. Sligo when he entered would be turned slightly away as his right arm pushed the door. John poised, billet of wood upraised. There must be no glancing blow, no opportunity for McNulty to cry out the alarm. The man's feet mounted the stairs, his hand turned the knob of the door. He thrust it open and stepped over the threshold. John's bludgeon descended with accuracy. He caught McNulty as he slumped forward and dragged him fully inside the bedroom.

"Neat," said Quality, arising from the bed.

John stooped over the man, slid his hand inside the coat and removed a gun from its shoulder-holster. He balanced it in his palm and looked up at Quality.

"Any good to you?" he asked.

"Yes," she answered.

"You can shoot?"

"Yes."

"What," he demanded, "can't you do?"

She made no reply but accepted the automatic in efficient fingers.

"How many more?" she asked.

"Don't know," John answered. "Come along."

"Tie him first," she said.

John peered down at Sligo's prone body. "Unnecessary," he said, imitating Quality's terseness.

"Safer," she said and jerked a sheet from the bed. Her strong hands tore it. They bound Sligo's hands behind him and tied his ankles and stuffed his mouth full of fine linen.

"Now," she said.

But it was too late. Humphrey Salmon was on the stairs. Loretta Kimball was at his heels and a man John had not seen before occupied the rear—a big stooping man with gorilla arms that seemed to dangle below his knees.

"Hold it, Salmon," John said sharply.

The man's reflexes were quick. He shouted. "Munger! Mike! . . . Here!" and with an agility one would not expect he turned, brushed Loretta and the gorilla before him and was around the corner and hidden—out of range of the gun John held in his hand. John heard the slam of the door of the automobile as the chauffeur responded to the summons. There was the sound of running feet in the hall below. Then silence.

In a moment Salmon's voice called. "Miller," he said, "throw down that gun."

"Not likely," John responded.

"You're cornered," Salmon said.

"Then," John taunted, "come and dig us out."

"We will," Salmon said ominously. "Munger! Call the stables! Tell Sands and Ginger to get here quick."

There was the crash of a shot and a bullet tore upward through the floor not a yard from where John stood. He moved backward. It was blind shooting and nothing but chance could score a hit. The gun thundered again harmlessly. John missed Quality from his side and, turning, saw her dragging the mattress from the bed. He leaped to aid her. They spread it on the hall floor beneath their feet.

"You think of things," John said.

"So will they," answered Quality.

John took stock of their position. "We can hold these stairs till Michaelmas," he said. "And the bedroom window."

"Other windows," Quality said.

There was the danger. There were three other bedrooms on the floor, each with doors giving upon the hall in which they stood. When reinforcements arrived; when a ladder or other means of mounting to the second story was found, it would be possible to take them in the rear. Two people could not defend so many possible entrances. John flung open the three other bedroom doors so that any sounds of attempts to climb and enter would be audible.

"Why," demanded John, "didn't you stay put at home?"

Quality accepted the rebuke. "I should have checked the hospital by telephone," she answered.

"Spilt milk," John said. "No crying over it."

Quality had expressed no surprise at his coming nor asked how he had found her so quickly. She merely accepted the fact. John explained. The silence of the house tore at his tense nerves, and talking was a relief.

"Dolly telephoned," he said.

"Yes," Quality said.

"She described the voice that called you," he went on. "It had to be Loretta Kimball. I went to Winkleman's. She was not there. Winkleman knew about this house. He had had Loretta watched. He loaned me a car. It was the only thing I could think to try, coming here."

"Loretta!" she said. Her manner of speaking that name expressed more than a hundred words could have done.

"Winkleman," he said, "begged me spare her if I could."

"Would she spare you?" Quality asked.

"I don't know," John answered. "I don't know what she would do."

"I know," Quality said.

"What?" John asked.

"Kill," she said. "For the thrill of it."

"No," he protested.

"Men!" she said. There was irony in the word.

They saw through the window the glare of headlights as a car drove into the yard. The men summoned from the stables had arrived. The front door opened and slammed shut, and, leaning over the stair well, John could hear the murmur of voices. Heavy feet hurried along the hall below and the back door opened and closed. Some plan of attack was being put into action.

Salmon, standing invisible at the foot of the stairs, called up to them. "Miller?"

"Listening," John said.

"Give it up," Salmon said. "You want to live."

"What," John asked, "is the proposition?"

"Throw down your guns," Salmon said. "We don't want killing. You won't be harmed. We had no intention of harming Miss Piper. Only to hold her a few days until things could be taken care of."

"If that's all you want," John answered, "you've got us. We can't get away. And we have a hostage. We have Sligo McNulty."

Salmon sneered. "Sligo," he said, "is expendable."

"Your boys," John said, "will be glad to hear that. Good for their morale. How many more of them are expendable?"

"Stop blathering," John heard Loretta's voice say. It was not beautiful now. The rich cadences were no longer present. It was harsh, rasping. "A gallon of gasoline on the stairs and a match." She giggled. It was an unpleasant, inhuman sound.

"My god, no!" said Salmon. The man, bad as he might be, was appalled.

"You're soft, Humhprey," Loretta sneered.

"And you're crazy," he retorted.

Her voice rose shrilly. In it might have been a note of terror. "Don't say that! Don't dare to say that, damn you!" she cried.

Quality spoke quietly over John's shoulder. "Maybe not mad," she said. "But evil. Is there a difference, Loretta?"

At this taunt an eldritch scream tore from the girl's throat. She tore herself away from restraining hands and crouched at the foot of the stairway, spitting like some infuriated cat. John's arm threw Quality to the mattress and he flung himself beside her as Loretta's finger, pressing the trigger, sent a stream of bullets upward. A hand snatched her back. There was the sound of a tussle, hysterical cries and then silence.

"My god!" John exclaimed in Quality's ear.

"Didn't you know!" Quality said.

They lay still and listened. In a moment they heard Loretta's voice again, not shrill, not hysterical now. "I'm all right, Humphrey," she said. "It's passed. I'm all right now."

John's hand sought Quality's and held it—not so much to reassure her as to steady himself. So this explained Jabez Winkleman's manner, the grief in the old man's eyes. It explained why he had had Loretta watched and followed, and why he had pleaded with John to save her if salvation were possible!

John sensed rather than saw movement in the hallway behind him. He rolled quickly, reaching for his weapon.

"Now! Now!" said a quietly agreeable voice. "Mr. Miller, you do get yourself into predicaments. "Good evening, Miss Piper."

"Good evening, Wilmot," Quality said.

"Gargoyle!" The word was an exclamation. He stared upward at the man, not knowing if he were friend or enemy. "You do bob up."

"I've been around quite a while," said the Gargoyle, smiling—or John took it to be a smile. "In a crude way, Mr. Miller, you're quite efficient. Not the professional touch, of course, but for an amateur very effective."

"Whose side," asked John, getting to his knees, "are you on?"

"Always," the man answered, "on the side of the angels. Am I not, Miss Piper?"

"Is it over, Wilmot?" she asked.

"Not exactly over, Miss Piper," the Gargoyle answered gravely. "There are a few unsavory citizens still intervening. We haven't leaped the final hurdle. . . . Mr. Miller," he went on courteously, "I haven't quite decided if you have brains, or animal intuition, or just blind luck."

"It can't be brains," John said ruefully, getting to his feet and helping Quality to arise. "Quality seems to know you, Gargoyle."

"John!" Quality said reprovingly.

The man grimaced. Probably it was his version of a charming smile. "I don't mind in the least, Miss Piper. Gargoyles have been much admired by critics of art. . . . I'm taking over, Mr. Miller. Will you permit discipline to restrain your boyish impulses?"

"If Quality says so," John answered.

"I say so," Quality said.

" 'All in the valley of Death,' " John quoted, " 'rode the six hundred.' "

chapter TWENTY-TWO

The windows no longer were black. They were gray with approaching dawn, but a dawn obscured by heavy fog. It was a fog so heavy that it dripped. John, peering through the pane, could not see the ground. The cold was penetrating. He turned to Quality and the Gargoyle.

"Anything could be happening out there," he said uncomfortably. And then, still puzzled, "Gargoyle, how did you get here?"

"I was here," the man said. He made no other explanation, but stood beside John frowning and listening.

Sligo McNulty, on the floor, was wriggling with returning consciousness. His eyes were open and rolling. Muffled, gurgling sounds came from his throat. Quality stood over him. John peered at her as she stooped and removed the cloth from Sligo's mouth. Her face was set, implacable.

"Talk," she said sharply.

McNulty rolled his head and fear was in his eyes, but he did not speak.

"Still in a haze," said the Gargoyle.

"He must talk," Quality said.

"First things first," the Gargoyle said, and then, "Damn the fog."

He walked to the stairs and stood listening. Then he went to the window and cocked his ear. The only sound was a dripping from the eaves. There came the murmur of voices from the yard below. The Gargoyle stepped aside from the window. The silence was shattered by the blast of a gun. It was the roar of a shotgun and the glass fell in a thousand fragments. There came a second roar and the noise of running feet. Something thumped against the side of the house.

"Ladder," said the Gargoyle. "Watch the stairs."

The strategy was apparent. While men scaled the ladder the defenders were to be covered by the shotgun marksman.

"Flat on the floor," the Gargoyle ordered.

John lay on the mattress at the head of the stairway. There was the trampling of feet below. Something appeared around the newel post. It was a heavy metal table from the kitchen held as a shield. It commenced to move up the stairs, the men who carried it invisible. John fired and fired again without effect. The table top lurched upward step by step. There was nothing at which to shoot but that expanse of metal, not even an exposed hand. It was a quarter of the way up the stairs. John sensed that Quality was no longer at his side. Within the bedroom he heard noises, a movement as of something heavy.

"Get back," Quality said. "Pull away the mattress."

In the doorway stood a massive, carven highboy. Quality and the Gargoyle were pushing it out of the room. Now the table-top was halfway to the top. With a surge the highboy reached the brink of the stairway and three sets of arms pushed with all their might. The heavy piece of furniture catapulted downward, crashed against the metal tabletop with a tremendous crash, hurling it backward, sweeping it downward with those who manned it until it crashed against the wall at the bottom. There sounded agonized cries from the debris.

Invisible hands dragged two groaning men from the wreckage. Salmon's voice could be heard cursing.

"You're a warrior," the Gargoyle said to Quality. He spoke over his shoulder as he crept toward the window. Suddenly the fog glowed as a powerful light strove to penetrate. There was a shrill whistle from the blankness. The Gargoyle thrust his fingers into his mouth and answered it.

"Took their good time," he said.

There were alarmed shouts outside. The front door opened and slammed shut. A voice shouted for Salmon.

"People in the fog," called the man's voice. "They got a searchlight. Searchlights! . . . Make a break for it!"

Salmon cursed again.

"There's a chance in the fog," urged the man who had given warning.

"No! . . . No! . . ." cried Loretta's frantic voice.

"Scatter!" yelled a voice. "Everybody for himself."

"No! . . . No! . . ." Loretta screamed again.

"The car," Salmon ordered. "Make for the car."

There was a struggle, a pistol shot, running feet. Loretta Kimball stood at the foot of the stairs, a bucket in her hands. She drenched the carpet with its contents. Fumes of gasoline lifted. She hurled a match and flames roared with awful suddenness.

"Fire!" John shouted. "Out of the window."

"No," said Quality. She was kneeling beside Sligo McNulty. "Talk!" she commanded.

"Drop him out of the window," John urged. "Make him talk later."

"Now!" Quality. "The house is on fire, McNulty," she said. "Talk and we get you out." Her voice was cold as steel. "Talk," she said, "or roast."

"Get me out! Get me out!" Sligo screamed.

"Did you kill Shiner?" Quality demanded.

"Untie me! . . . Get me out. For God's sake, get me out," McNulty pleaded.

"Quick, Quality. . . . Quick," John commanded.

"Did you kill Shiner?" Quality asked, her voice grimly steady.

"Yes! Yes!" the man mouthed the confession. "I shot him. Let me out."

"My father," she went on, not glancing toward the door through which smoke came rolling ominously. "It was a shotgun. Did you kill my father?"

"I—It was Salmon. . . . He hired me. He paid me. . . . Get me out of here. . . . Please. . . . Don't let me cook."

"Did you hear?" Quality asked.

"We heard," said John and the Gargoyle.

They lifted McNulty. Hung him at arm's length through the window and let him drop. "You next, Quality," ordered John. They helped her over the sill and she scrambled down the rungs followed by John and the Gargoyle. The fog enclosed them, imprisoned them. Behind them flames roared. Voices shouted in the obscuring moisture. The motor of a car roared to life. Gears ground. Blindly the car leaped forward. The fog enveloped it as it lunged toward the road. There was a crash as it missed the gate and tore through the fence. Tires screamed as hands wrenched at the wheel in desperation. Then came a splintering crash—and silence.

Men converged on the burning house, stumbling, colliding. Flashlights gleamed dully.

"Drag McNulty away from the house," John said, groping for the man, finding the collar of his coat and tugging until the man was at a safe distance. Flames roared upward, sparks swirled. A voice cried for help. Utter confusion reigned in the clinging blindness. The cries for help continued and John groped toward them, blundered into steps. It was the front porch of the house. A voice, at his very feet, called weakly for help, and John bent over the body of a man who seemed helpless to move. He grasped an arm, dragged the inert body down the two steps and into safety. John's hands were wet as he bent over the man he had saved, face close to face. It was Humphrey Salmon.

"Salmon!" John exclaimed. It was a nightmare. There was no reality. He felt himself a disembodied shade groping in limbo.

"Miller. . . . Is it Miller?" Salmon asked in a voice so faint as to be almost inaudible.

"It's Miller," John said. "What's the matter, man? What's the matter?"

"She shot me. . . . Crazy bitch. . . . She shot . . ." Salmon gurgled, became silent, unconscious or dead.

It was lighter. Each moment it grew lighter as the morning sun climbed over the hills and shone down upon the low-lying fog. Behind him flames roared and surged and billowed. The roof collapsed with a sound like an explosion. Heat seared his face as he staggered to his feet and dragged Salmon further from the conflagration. A sudden chill breeze fanned his cheek. Around him invisible men called.

"Quality!" he called. "Quality!" It was shouting into a nightmare. "Where are you, Quality?"

"Here, John," she said. Her voice seemed but a few feet away, though he could not see her.

"Quality," he called again.

"Coming, John," she answered. And then she was there, bending over him, touching him. He staggered to his feet and his arms encircled her and held her. She was real. She was not a part of the phantasmagoria. She was material, living, an assurance of reality.

"Hold me, John," she said very quietly.

She did not cling to him frantically, or in surrender, but rested in his arms quietly as if she needed for a moment to rest and to be in safe haven. She did not tremble. She freed herself gently, stood listening intently to the confused sounds in the concealing mist.

The fog took on a luminous quality; it was less solid; gray streamers were wafted by the rising clean breeze. Objects became faintly, formlessly visible.

She moved her foot as if to assure herself of solid earth. "There is a world," she said.

"A solid world," John answered. "Is the nightmare ended?"

"Almost, I think," she said.

The fog was thinner. Sunshine penetrated; there was blue sky above. A voice called. "Miller! . . . Miss Piper!"

"Here," John answered.

The Gargoyle stood beside them. "All right?" he asked.

"Quite," Quality answered.

He bent over the body at their feet. "Salmon?" he asked.

"Yes."

"Dead?" he asked.

"I think not," John replied. "He spoke. Loretta shot him."

The man nodded. "He tried to stop her," he said.

"Did she get away?" John asked.

"There was a crash," said the Gargoyle. "My men are look-ing." His face was distorted by an expression of concern. "The fog!" he said. "I wanted them alive. We couldn't foresee the fog."

"Better this way," Quality said.

"Not neat," the man said. "Not workmanlike."

The world was real again, solid, visible. Wind was driving away the fog. One could see for fifty yards. A man stood near the demolished fence, calling. "Wilmot," he said.

"Yes, Dickens," the Gargoyle answered.

"We found it. The car bounced off a tree. Went down the gully. Wheels in the air."

"The girl?" asked the Gargoyle.

"Inside. Dead."

John exclaimed. Loretta dead! It was not believable that so much had ceased to be—so much physical beauty. Though tainted in spirit. It would have been less tragic had Loretta been old and unsightly. John bit his lips. Quality touched his arm.

"Does it hurt?" she asked.

"Not that way," he said. "Old Jabez wanted me to save her."

"He'll be content," Quality said softly.

"He must never know—everything," John told her.

"No," Quality agreed.

"I don't know your name," John said. He felt it was not right to call the man Gargoyle again.

"Wilmot," said Quality.

"Special agent," Wilmot said. "Federal Bureau of Investiga-tion."

"Not a faun!" John exclaimed.

"Quite human," Wilmot said. He raised his voice. "Dickens," he called, "radio for ambulances. . . . Salmon seems to be alive."

"How do you Federal men come into this?" John asked.

"Miss Piper," Wilmot said. "She knew her father had been murdered."

"But," John objected, "you have no jurisdiction over murder. That's local police."

"In this case," Wilmot said, "we had jurisdiction over the motive for the murder. Miss Piper hunted for that motive, and came to us. Her father had been disturbed. Had hinted at a shocking discovery—shocking to a man of his integrity. The night before he was killed he told her it was his duty to report and to expose. He loved horses and racing. He was reluctant to disclose a scandal harmful to the reputation of that sport."

"The last words I heard him say," Quality said, "were, 'I've got to do it. Men like Humphrey Salmon must be destroyed.'"

"A network of crooked horse parlors," Wilmot said. "Under a dozen aliases. Tapped wires. Fraud that crossed state lines. The jockey Shiner—who was murdered to shut his mouth. The boy rode a dozen straight races and then threw one upon which Salmon made a killing. Miss Piper unearthed facts; we discovered more. Salmon was versatile. Narcotics. Hot securities." Wilmot nodded. "Plenty of jurisdiction," he said. He frowned down at Salmon's unconscious body. "I want this man to stand trial," he said grimly.

"You have Sligo McNulty," John said.

"Just a gorilla," Wilmot answered. "But he'll sing."

"And," Quality said tersely, "sit in the chair."

"I think," John said, "Miss Piper has had enough. I wrecked Winkleman's car. How am I to take her home?"

"We," Wilmot said, "can spare a car and driver." He peered a moment at John and grimaced horribly. "For a writing bloke," he said, "you're quite a fellow."

John smiled wanly. "For a Federal dick," he retorted, "you're no cluck yourself. . . . When do we start?"

Wilmot called a man, gave instructions to drive Quality and John back to the city. As John held the door open for Quality he turned to Wilmot. "Can Loretta's name be kept out of this?" he asked.

"For Winkleman's sake," Wilmot said, "I wish we could."

The car door slammed shut and John and Quality were driven away. "Heading back," John said, "into a normal world."

"There is," Quality said, "no normal world."

She turned sidewise and laid her head against the rear cushion. Her eyes closed. Presently she drooped and John put his arm around her. Her hair was against his cheek. She was asleep.

She did not awaken until they were near the city again, when she sat erect, did not rub her eyes, seemed instantly alert. John stared at her. It was incredible. Neither in face nor in dress did she show traces of the tragic night through which they had passed. She was unrumpled. Every hair was in its correct place. She might just have arisen and dressed with care.

"You," he said, "are amazing."

"Is that good?" she asked, looking at him with steady eyes.

"First class," he told her, and she smiled. "We have a tough duty," he said gravely.

"Mr. Winkleman?"

"Yes," he replied, and she nodded. "I think we should tell him at once."

"Of course," she answered.

John gave directions to the driver. In minutes the car turned into Jabez Winkleman's driveway and stopped before the imposing bronze gates. The old gatekeeper appeared. "Mr. Miller?" he asked.

"I am John Miller."

"Mr. Winkleman expects you," said the man. He disappeared in the lodge house and the gates swung open as if by magic. The car climbed to the front entrance and Quality and John alighted. Before they could ring the bell the door opened, and the butler greeted them. "Mr. Winkleman is in the library," he said, and led the way.

Jabez Winkleman, still in old-fashioned nightshirt and slippers, sat behind his desk, his deacon's face expressionless.

"Well?" he asked in his dry, crackling voice.

"I could not save her, sir," John said directly.

"Loretta is dead?" asked the old man.

"She is dead," John answered.

Quality walked to the old man's side and her soft fingers touched his cheek. "It was best," she said softly.

He looked up at her. His claw of a hand touched her fingers. His eyes did not waver nor his voice tremble. There was iron in his old soul. "It is best," he said, and then hesitated. "I wish, my child, she could have been like you."

"They will bring her here?" he asked.

"Yes," Quality answered.

The old man's eyes turned to John. "Thank you, young sir, for trying," he said. He was as composed as if this were some social call. "Have you slept?" he asked.

"No," Quality said.

"Will you sleep here?"

"I must go home," she answered.

"A cup of coffee, perhaps?" he asked. "It is ready."

It was as though he wore invisible armor which no arrow could penetrate.

"Thank you—no," Quality said.

He nodded and stood up, spare, bony, but not ridiculous in his flannel nightshirt.

"Perhaps," he said, and there was an almost detectable note of wistfulness in his parchment crackling old voice, "perhaps you will come to see me sometimes."

"Yes," Quality said simply.

"You and the young man?"

"Yes," she replied.

"The butler," he said formally, "will show you to the door."

"Good morning, sir," John said. He knew he must offer no word of sympathy; show no emotion.

"Good morning, Mr. Miller. . . . Miss Piper."

He remained standing as they went out of the room. When they had disappeared he returned to his desk and seated himself. He rang the bell. When the butler appeared he spoke two words. "Coffee, please," he said.

Quality and John re-entered the car. Quality spoke softly, quietly. "That fine old man!" she said.

In fifteen minutes the car stopped before Dolly Dove's apartment. They thanked the driver and climbed the stairs. Quality opened the door. Dolly had not gone to bed. She sat at the table on which were remnants of bacon and eggs and toast and a half-filled coffeepot. She filled the chair; in her fluttering robe she seemed to fill the room. Her comical, treble voice squeaked with pretended outrage.

"Nice hour to be getting in," she snapped. And then great tears rolled down her dumpling cheeks. "Toots! . . . Toots! . . . I was like to go out of my mind." She gathered Quality to her monstrous bosom. "Ducky! Ducky!" she whispered. Then she was herself again. As if she were asking about the ending of some exciting book she inquired, "And how did it all come out?"

"Don't ask questions now, Dolly," John said. "Put her to bed." He looked about him with eyes that refused to stay open. "Me," he said, "I'm going to sleep on the davenport. And sleep. And sleep."

chapter TWENTY-THREE

It was midafternoon when John Miller awakened to a pleasant aroma of coffee wafting in from the kitchen. He threw off the blanket, pulled on trousers and shoes and shirt and sat on the edge of the davenport listening and orienting himself. Dolly Dove peeked in from the dining room.

"Bathroom's empty. Help yourself," she said and disappeared.

Someone had laid out a razor and shaving cream and new toothbrush. He used them mechanically. His mental state was peculiar. A normal, placid world of toothpaste and coffee seemed abnormal. Every nerve, every impulse had been keyed high in the scale of violence, tragedy, dynamic action. Those matters had consumed but a few short hours, but blanked out everything else and seemed to constitute his whole life's history. Those hours of high emotion, dynamic action, circumscribed in time though they were, dwarfed the rest of his life and its activities into negligibility. That episode was ended, and he was drained, possessed by a sense of futility. Somehow it seemed to him as he stood lethargic that nothing ever would be worth while doing in the future. After the experiences of the night just passed he could only envision a future so drab as to be appalling; a future with no appeal, no challenges—meaningless and futile. It was the inevitable letdown; reaction from shock.

Dolly greeted him as he re-entered the dining room. "Nice morning," she said in her shrill treble. "Sleep well?"

"Quality?" he asked. "Is Quality all right?"

"Sure," Dolly piped. "Had breakfast an hour ago." She eyed him askance. "According to her tell, you're quite a citizen."

"She's quite a citizen," John said dully.

"Snap out of it," Dolly commanded. "You act like you got a hangover."

"Worse than a hangover. Where's Quality?"

"Gone to the studio," Dolly said. "Agnew's."

"What?"

Dolly shrugged so that a ripple agitated her whole body. "Did you think the world had come to an end? They're dubbing today."

"You mean that after last night she could bother with that—now!"

"Why not?" Dolly asked placidly. "Got to be done, hasn't it?"

It had to be done, so Quality did it! Her fiber was tougher than his. She could take up normal life and pursuits again as if nothing had interrupted. With no intervening period of readjustment. There were things to be done, so, without fuss and feathers, she proceeded to do them.

"She said," Dolly told him, "for you to come out when you woke up. The Character's with her."

"The show must go on," John said.

When they arrived in Culver City the re-recording process was in operation in a sort of projection room. This technical labor is called dubbing, and its function is to assemble all sounds such as incidental noises, dialogue and music which are scattered on several tracks so that they synchronize with action. They are recorded on a single sound track to be printed down the side of the film so that when shown in a theater there results a coherent performance.

John and Dolly entered the tiny projection room where a number of technical men were seated in comfortable chairs. A small spotlight sent its beam upon a desk where mixers sat at the dials, hands on the pots, eyes strained upon the screen. Sounds were emitted by the loudspeaker. An illuminated footage counter clicked. It was bedlam to John as the experts strove for lifelike balance. Discussion of volume, of the importance of this or that sound went on steadily. "Catch the racket in the kitchen. Ride it up when the door opens. . . . High with the rain but don't blow the tubes. Start it two beats after the boy comes in." It was jargon, but intelligent jargon.

As John's eyes became accustomed to the light he saw Quality intent upon papers held on her knees. She was concentrating as if nothing in the world mattered except what she was doing—as indeed was the case. Her little hat was pushed to the back of her head. Her face, in profile, was eager, intent, lips slightly parted. She was an appealing picture. Zagic sat beside her, skinny legs crossed, an expression of boredom on his face.

Rolf Agnew sat down beside John. "Confusing, eh?" he asked.

"Yes," John replied.

"Expected you out earlier," said Agnew turning to eye John curiously.

"Slept late," John said.

"Hard night?" persisted Agnew.

"Tough," John answered.

"Papers say the FBI made a raid."

"Haven't seen the papers," John said.

"Salmon got himself shot."

"Indeed," John said without turning his head.

"Man named Sligo McNulty confessed to a murder," Agnew said.

"So?"

"Of a man named Piper. Horse trainer. Any relation to Quality?"

"Ask her," John said shortly.

"The underground is spitting sparks," Agnew ventured. "Why so cagey?"

"I'm not cagey, Mr. Agnew. I merely want to close the book."

"Have it your own way," Agnew said, not huffily. He listened a moment. "Things are straightening out," he said. "We're getting close."

"How close?"

"Day after tomorrow we'll have a pilot film."

"Fine," John said. He found, to his surprise, that his interest was quickening. "How does it look?"

Agnew shrugged. "Wait till it's in the bag," he said. He got up and seated himself beside Dolly Dove a dozen feet away. John's eyes followed him. He saw that Dolly was not being reticent; indeed, she was voluble. Agnew's eyes kept flicking to John and then to Quality. Fifteen minutes later he returned to John's side.

"Dolly," he said, "recited the epic."

"She would," John said.

"So you were there—belting people with a hunk of timber."

"I was there," John admitted.

Agnew grinned at him. "You don't look it," he said, and then, "That Piper gal is a trouper. After last night she's here on the job, and not a hair out of place."

"She's iron," John said, somewhat disconsolately.

"Wrong, young fellow," Agnew said. "Not iron—gold." Then he said, with characteristic Hollywood attitude, "What publicity!"

"Over my dead body," John said, and Agnew did not doubt that the young man meant it.

The day's work came to an end. John waited for Dolly and Quality, and Zagic.

"Listen," Zagic said, "tonight I labor. I turn loose a ponderous, pea-eyed, palm-eared blurb. Famous names! It won't be a publicity handout. It'll be news. They'll eat it without pepper. . . . Got it fixed with Agnew for a sneak showing. In his projection room. Invitations to the networks, advertising agencies, the newspaper gang. After I get through with the fancy words, they'll be jostling to get in."

Quality smiled at him; then frowned. "No mention of last night," she said.

"Am I crazy? Like a red-headed fox I'm crazy! Leave that to the rumor factory. Me, I'd rather have a whisper in Hollywood than a column on the front page. What you two, Quality and John, will be surrounded by is craning necks. More people will be craving a peak at you than would turn out to see Dorothy

Lamour doing Lady Godiva down Sunset Boulevard in short hair."

They bundled into Dolly's car, John in the driver's seat and Quality beside him. They drove out of the lot, Dolly and Zagic chattering like magpies, Quality and John in rather strained silence. After several blocks Quality, without turning her head, said, "Hello, John."

"Hello, Quality," he replied.

"No talk," Quality said.

"Right," John agreed.

They did not speak again until they reached Dolly's door. Quality alighted quickly before John could get down to open the door.

"Not tomorrow," Quality said.

"What ails you folks?" Dolly complained.

"John knows," Quality said.

"I don't," Dolly said crossly.

"Springs would be too tight," Quality said.

"Will they relax?" John asked.

Quality only smiled and walked with clicking little steps straight back into the house.

"Some people," snorted Dolly.

There was no communication between John and Quality the next day. He knew there were arrangements to be made, but he was confident she would make them. The members of the Famous Names Group must be notified to be present at the private showing of the pilot film. Quality would take care of that.

The night and day and the following night seemed interminable to John. His play had assumed proper proportions in his thoughts. He quivered with anticipation and anxiety. It was impossible to work. He walked for hours avoiding even Zagic Quiros. Repeatedly he sallied out for editions of all the papers and read each fresh development of the raid on the hideaway of Humphrey Salmon. The man, it seemed, hovered between life and death. In a late edition was reproduced a formal release.

At five-nineteen in his closely guarded hospital room,

Humphrey Salmon died. Before his death Salmon, in contemplation of his end, uttered a dying statement which constituted a full confession of guilt on numerous counts of the charges brought against him. The full text of the confession will be made public tomorrow after study by the authorities.

That confession, John was confident, would include the procuring of the murders of Quality Piper's father and of Shiner, the jockey. For Quality it ended the long road upon which she had toiled. . . . John sat musing. What effect would it have upon the girl? How would it alter her? Would the tension of the too tightly coiled spring be relaxed? And if it were relaxed what sort of woman would be revealed? It came to him as he sat wrapped in thought, that he would regret it if there came revolutionary change. He was sure he would regret it. He loved her as she was.

In the morning John went alone to Culver City for the ten-o'clock showing of the film. When he arrived the small theater was already well filled with those who had performed a part in its making. He stood in the door a moment. Seated he could see Agnew and Dolly and Quality Piper. Grouped around them were Kent Farraday, dignified but grim; Martha Scruggs about to see her initial appearance as Jenny Lind and the boy who had taken the place of the deserting Benjamin Franklin. John slunk in and seated himself in a far corner.

"All ready," Agnew called presently.

The monitor came to life, disclosing Farraday at his desk. There was soft background music as his son entered and the first words of dialogue were spoken. John, tense, sat forward in his seat as he watched the thing upon which he had worked, the child of his creation, come to life upon the screen. Avidly he followed each word, every action, and gradually tension relaxed as the story unfolded itself. He became not author but spectator. He forgot that this thing was his, for his part had been the writing down of words. It was strange to him as if he had had no hand in its creation. It gripped him. He heard himself laugh, felt his eyes become moist as situation after situation developed, moving toward a climax. Twenty-six minutes and a half seemed all too short. At the curtain line he sat back limp, elated, almost surrendering to an impulse to applaud. His ears were elated at the sound of spontaneous applause from electricians, technicians, the hard-boiled of the studio. He did not thrust himself forward but waited.

Agnew charged down upon him, banging enthusiastic fists against his chest. The troupe surrounded him. He looked up into Kent Farraday's aging, aristocratic face and saw that tears were brimming from his eyes and rolling down his cheeks. Farraday fought to control his voice, to speak as a cultured gentleman should speak. But it was a failure.

"Thank you. . . . Thank you," he said brokenly. "Thank you for bringing me back to life."

Dolly pounced upon him, enfolding him in billows of tulle and crushing him to her more than ample bosom. "Johnnie! . . . Johnnie!" she piped. "It'll slay 'em. It'll roll them in the aisles." She drew back and grinned. "America's Two-ton Darling!" she cried.

All were elated, excited, jubilant—all but Quality. She did not even smile, but stood there self-contained, unmoved. "Adequate," she said, and that was all she said.

"Thanks to you," John told her.

"Thanks to all of us," she corrected, and turned to Agnew with efficiently businesslike manner.

"All ready for tomorrow?" she asked.

"To the last button," Agnew answered.

"You people," John said with emotion to the troupe, "have stood by through thick and thin. You haven't grouched at delays. You've been patient and pretty swell. Tomorrow tells the story."

"Today told the story," Farraday said. "I know theater when I see it. Tonight I sleep."

"Tonight I eat," Dolly Dove trebled. "Come on, all you hams. I'll cook a dinner that'll make you bulge."

"No," said Quality.

"Why not, I'd like to know?" Dolly demanded.

211

"Not," Quality said firmly, "till we're sure."

Dolly bridled. "If," she said, "I can make a blasted electrician laugh—I'm good."

"Electricians," Quality said firmly, "don't sign contracts."

They got into Dolly's car again—the four of them. Dolly bubbled with enthusiasm. Zagic practiced words and phrases. Quality sat relaxed and composed. John was inclined to boyish elation, but Quality's silence quelled him.

"Mainspring still too tight?" he asked.

"Yes," she said.

"What happens when it unlaxes?"

"Ask me that," she said demurely, "tomorrow night."

So there was another night of unease and anxiety to endure, and a long morning. The official preview was set for three o'clock. Then they would know. Cold, wise, perhaps unfriendly eyes would view from the standpoint of the cash register. There would be no sentiment. It would be a cynically practical audience who would pass judgment. Each viewer would be asking questions of himself. Would the show they were seeing achieve a worth-while rating? Agency men would be asking if it would attract a sponsor, if the manufacturer of some product would believe it would sell his article. Network men would be considering the cost of time, what would be the competition, with always the thought of sponsorship and audience appeal in mind. There would be those who would demand to lay violent hands on the show and demand revisions or rewriting. There would be sponsors who would demand to stick in their noses and meddle. The road to acceptance and success was cluttered by a hundred obstacles. It would be a trying audience to face and John dreaded it.

At the door of Dolly's apartment Quality paused a moment and issued a curt order. "You," she said to John, "will welcome the audience and introduce the film."

"Must I?"

"Yes," she said firmly.

John went alone to a motion picture that night, but he scarcely saw what took place on the screen. He ate a snack, bathed and went to bed. He was physically and mentally weary and dropped off almost instantly to sleep.

In the morning he labored over what he was to say when he introduced the picture, and was dissatisfied. It was an ordeal he dreaded. He threw away what he had written and determined to rely upon the inspiration of the moment. At half past two he was again at the office of Rolf Agnew and in a state of jitters that was a torture. He sat alone and smoked before trudging to the projection room. Cars were arriving and parking, and a score or more of men important in the industry and in advertising were strolling toward the building. . . . The hour arrived.

"Now," said Quality.

John advanced to the front of the little theater and silence greeted him. Suddenly he was confident; fluttering butterflies abandoned his stomach, and he spoke briefly without hesitation, describing the Famous Names Group, its organization, its membership.

"We," he said, "are pleased with what we have accomplished. On behalf of the troupe I hope it will find favor in your eyes."

There was a ripple of restrained applause as he took his seat and the room was darkened. Figures became visible on the screen of the monitor and sound filled the room. John sat with eyes closed but ears acute to hear any reaction. As the film progressed he detected no shuffling of feet, no rustling, no signs of disinterest. He opened his eyes. The men and women in the tiny theater sat motionless, some even bent forward, sitting on the edges of their seats. There was no whispering—only engrossed silence. Minute followed minute until the end. John braced himself as there ensued a moment of silence. And then came applause, sincere, enthusiastic. That blasé, professional, cynical audience had been moved, had been stirred. The audience stood up, gathering in little knots, discussing. The first man to speak to John was from one of the networks.

"Mr. Miller," he said, "we are interested. A nice little piece," he said cautiously. "When can I make an appointment to discuss it with you?"

"Miss Piper," John said, "is in charge of business affairs."

213

"Don't," said a genial voice, "sign on the dotted line with this vulture." It was a man from MCA. "I'll be in my office in the morning."

An advertising executive shouldered his way. "Definitely a possibility, Mr. Miller," he said. "When can I bring a sponsor to see this film?"

"Arrange with Miss Piper," John said.

And so it went. It was a success. They wanted it. Each and every one of them wanted it. Rolf Agnew made himself heard. "Gentlemen," he said so that all could hear. "I'm delighted that you show interest. Temporarily my office will be occupied by Miss Quality Piper. If any of you have propositions she can be reached there tomorrow. Thank you all for coming."

The audience dispersed. John and Quality, with Dolly and Zagic, went to Agnew's pleasant office. Agnew was bouncing.

"Folks," he bounced, "you're in. If ever I saw a smash, this is it. You can pick and choose. . . . Everybody happy?" He grinned with delight. "Which network do you pick?"

"None," Quality said.

"What!"

"We syndicate," Quality said. "Tomorrow Zagic goes on the road. We'll be our own bosses. The Famous Names Group will run its own affairs."

"It's a gamble," said Agnew.

"No," Quality said. "That's how it is."

She smiled from one to another, and her face was transfigured. "Everybody," she said, "please go out. I want a private word with John."

"Whoops!" said Dolly.

Presently they faced each other before the fireplace. Quality smiled into John's eyes.

"Mainspring unlaxed," she said softly.

"Is there much to say?" he asked.

"Not in words," Quality said, and slowly she raised her arms and held them out in invitation. Her lips might be taciturn, but they were not cold. She was not taut but yielding, wonderful in surrender. Presently she released herself.

214

"Plenty," she said, ". . . for now."

"It's true?" he asked, amazed.

"Since," she said, and her smile was impish, "the first time I set eyes on you. . . . Call them in."

John opened the door. "Come in, friends," he said. "Quality has a thing to say to you."

They grouped just inside the threshold, and Quality, beautiful, all woman, all desirable, made the briefest announcement of a betrothal in all recorded history. She pointed to John and her face was alight.

"Mine!" she said.

"Whoops, Toots," squealed Dolly and folded the girl to her ample breast.

Set in Linotype Caledonia
Format by John Rynerson
Manufactured by The Haddon Craftsmen, Inc.
Published by HARPER & BROTHERS, *New York*